SHADOW OF FEAR: A CHRISTIAN ROMANTIC SUSPENSE

SHADOW LAKE SURVIVAL
BOOK 6

SUSAN SLEEMAN

Published by Edge of Your Seat Books, Inc.

Contact the publisher at contact@edgeofyourseatbooks.com

Copyright © 2024 by Susan Sleeman

Cover design by Kelly A. Martin of KAM Design

This book is a work of fiction. Characters, names, places, and incidents in this novel are either products of the imagination or are used fictitiously. Any resemblance to real people, either living or dead, to events, businesses, or locales is entirely coincidental.

1

Kinsley dove to the concrete, her heart pounding in her chest. She had to dodge the bullets and get to her car. Her dirty laundry in the backseat was her last chance. It had to save her life.

Seriously. Dirty laundry stopping a bullet from taking her life. Laughable if her life wasn't on the line. She was grasping at straws, sure, but she'd try anything to stay alive.

Another gunshot rang out. A bullet struck the sidewalk by her legs, shards of cement biting into her ankles.

She wanted to dig her phone from her pocket and call 911, but she had to get out of his line of fire first.

She rolled. Once. Twice.

The rough surface razored against her skin. Rocks bit her knees.

Don't stop.

She tumbled behind her car.

A bullet whisked through the air, sounding like a missile to Kinsley and splintering the tree behind her.

If she hadn't moved...

No, don't think about that. Just keep going.

She army crawled forward, sliding behind the front end of her small Honda. Additional bullets pinged into the side.

Keep going. Now!

Inch by inch. Skinned arms getting worse. So what. She was still alive.

She reached the backseat door. Her target. The location where she'd haphazardly thrown her dirty laundry on the floor to take to the laundromat.

She rolled to her back and clicked the remote to unlock the doors. They beeped in unison with another bullet.

Who in the world was shooting? Was it some random shooter firing at her because she was in the wrong place at the wrong time, or was someone out to kill her?

No. Someone wouldn't really be trying to kill her. Not *her,* of all people. She was just an average person. A nobody. Nothing special.

Shivers raced down her arms, and her muscles wanted to collapse.

Didn't matter. Someone fired bullets from across the parking lot. Bullets that could kill her, and she had to act. Fast. Smart. *If* she was going to survive. And she planned to survive.

She belly crawled onto the seat and swept her hand over the floor. Feeling for. Searching for. Needing her Kevlar vest that lay tangled in the heap of laundry.

A bullet shattered the windshield above. Glass sprayed through the backseat. She ducked and covered. Prayed.

Even if her vest was at her fingertips and would provide protection for her body, it only worked if she could put it on without first taking a bullet.

∼

"No, LT. Stop. Just listen." Devan Graham—Dev to everyone who knew him—counted the barrage of bullets discharged in the far parking lot.

One. Two. Three. Four. Five.

"We have an active shooter situation at the morgue. In the overflow parking lot."

"Why there?" his former lieutenant asked. "It should be empty at this time of day unless they have an event going on."

"No event, but that doesn't mean someone didn't park back there." The overflow lot for the medical examiner's office and Oregon State Police Forensics Lab was just beyond the tree line that Dev was heading for.

"You think someone is just taking pot shots?" LT asked.

"Could be. If so, they chose a crazy location. Officers and deputies are in and out of here all the time."

Like all the time. Going to the morgue. Picking up or delivering forensics. Dev being one of them. Okay fine. He was a retired deputy and didn't come here as often anymore, but he was still carrying and wasn't going to walk away from an active shooter scenario.

"Regardless, I'll have units there in a minute," LT said. "Stay put and don't try to be a hero. You stand down."

No way. "You know I can't do that. There could be someone injured back there. Bleeding out and needing my help."

"It's not like you can help them if you're injured yourself. If we have a concealed shooter, that could happen."

"I'll just have to take the chance." Dev rounded the corner. Took cover behind a soaring maple tree. Assessed the situation.

One car. A small white Honda Civic. The back door open. Glass shattered. No movement.

A bullet sliced through the cool October air and struck

the front tire. Another one followed, blasting into the back door, the concussive force sounding like a sharp ping.

Dev turned his attention to the call with his former lieutenant. "There's one car. Shooter is aiming at it and not just taking random shots."

He itched to go after the shooter on the far side of the lot and stop him. No, as a former law enforcement officer, his duty was to protect innocent lives at all costs. That meant anyone in the car. Check to see if they needed his help.

"I'll relay that to the responding officers," LT said.

"You'll find me at the car. Be sure the deputies know I'm not the shooter." Dev ended his call and shoved his phone into his pocket.

He slipped behind the trees. Moving from one to another. His footfalls silent on the grass. Trying to travel with speed so he wasn't spotted. He came parallel to the car. A body lay on the backseat, unmoving.

He opened his mouth to call out. *Stop.* Don't alert the shooter to his presence. Better to be a surprise. He dropped to his knees. Crawled across the grass to the concrete, the change in ground sharp and irritating. He reached the door. A woman, at least according to the spiky heeled shoes and tight jeans fitting slender legs.

He reached in and tapped her leg. "Are you okay?"

She whipped over, gun in hand. "Get away from me or I will shoot. I mean—oh—Dev. Is that you? What are you doing here?"

He blinked at her. Blinked again. Couldn't be. "Kinsley?"

She lowered her weapon. "Yeah. I'm trying to get my vest on, then I was going to call 911. There hasn't been a shot in a while. Is he still out there?"

As if the shooter heard her question, another bullet pierced the front door of the vehicle. Kinsley cringed and rolled into a ball. Dev wasn't going to stand by while a bullet pierced that door and killed her.

He dove into the car and pulled her out, curling her into his body and putting his back to the shooter. Any bullet would have to pass through him before finding her.

"What are you doing?" She looked up at him.

"Taking you out of the line of fire," he said and checked their surroundings to make sure she wasn't vulnerable. "Was there anyone with you or are you alone?"

"Alone."

"Then we wait here for deputies to arrive. I called my old lieutenant. Should be here any time. I can already hear the sirens in the distance."

He expected her to struggle, but she remained curled in his arms. Soft. Warm. Smelling of peaches as she had for years.

Stop. Someone is shooting at you, and you're thinking about how wonderful it feels to hold her. Priorities, man!

Even if keeping her safe wasn't at the top of his mind, nothing had changed in the many years he'd known her. She was still his little sister's best friend. His vow still held true. He'd promised his sister, Jada, never to get romantically involved with Kinsley. Others might not understand why he kept such a promise, but their dad died unexpectedly when she was only six years old. Years passed after that when she refused to do much or make friends. Until Kinsley came along, and they somehow connected. He would never risk Jada losing the friend that helped her get over such a loss.

He searched for something to say to keep him on task. "Since when did you start wearing a Kevlar vest? I didn't think it was standard operating procedure for a forensic engineer."

"It's not." She focused those big, luminous eyes on him, a

grayish blue that almost looked green at times. "But you remember a couple of years ago when there was a shooter on a construction site and they never found him?"

"Yeah, he wounded like five people, right?"

"That's the guy, and that's when I had to start wearing a vest whenever I was investigating a site if I wanted to keep my liability insurance at a reasonable rate. At first I didn't like it, but honestly, I've come to appreciate the protection. And today if you hadn't shown up, it might've saved my life." She shivered in his arms.

He would do anything to protect her and erase her fear, but all he could do was tighten his hold. "Well, I *am* here and sounds like the deputies are almost here too."

She cocked her head and squirmed to try to get free. "I need you to let me go. I don't want them to see me like this."

He held fast. "It's no big deal."

"It is to me." She pushed free and tugged down her shirt. "I have to work with them all the time, and being a cowering damsel in distress isn't the professional appearance I want to portray."

He held up his hands. "Fine, I'm good with that. But we'll wait here until they arrive."

She settled on the ground next to him, her thigh touching his. He liked the contact and didn't move. Thankfully, after the deputies took her statement, she would part ways with Dev, and those eyes that got to him every time would no longer be tempting him to do something his sister wouldn't like.

That is, if the deputy offered to provide protection for her. If not, Dev wouldn't let her out of his sight until the authorities caught the shooter and locked him away.

2

Kinsley glanced at Dev from her seat on the back of the ambulance. He stood by her car as a soft breeze blew the savory scent from a nearby bread factory over them in the early evening. He talked to the deputy who she had given her statement to about an hour ago.

She blinked a few times at Dev and pinched her arm below the blood pressure cuff to prove she wasn't dreaming. She could hardly believe it. Of all the people to come to her rescue, it had to be him. The guy she'd been crushing on for years but wouldn't get involved with due to her friendship with his sister.

Oh how Kinsley wished she hadn't made a promise to Jada not to get involved with her brother. She considered breaking it every time she'd seen Dev since then, but she would never do anything to jeopardize a long-term friendship. A connection that spanned so many years and was too priceless to even consider risking over a relationship that could go wrong.

Besides, did he even return her feelings? He'd teased her when they were young, but once they'd graduated from high school, she got the feeling that a romantic tension sizzled between them. She had to be wrong. He'd gotten engaged and would be married today if his fiancée hadn't left him at the altar. If that was any indication of his interest in her, she'd been way off base about the sizzle.

He'd invited her to the wedding. She didn't want to go, but Jada pressured her to attend. The pain on Dev's face when it became clear that Hailey had taken off nearly broke Kinsley's heart. But at the same time, she was thankful he wasn't getting married. Why? She didn't know. Not when there wasn't any hope of Jada ever changing her mind.

Dev shifted and planted his hands on his hips, gaining her attention. Streetlights in the parking lot shone harshly down on him and highlighted the rigid set of his jaw.

Oh no. She recognized that look. He was getting angry about something. But what could it be?

"Fine." His voice carried on the breeze, and he spun toward her, marching across the distance between them, kicking up dust with his boots. "Come on. Let's go."

"What? Where?"

"You're coming to Shadow Lake with me." He jutted out his jaw, discouraging any argument she might have as he marched toward her car.

Jada had told Kinsley about Shadow Lake Survival, where Dev worked. Located just outside the town of Shadow Lake in the next county east of the campground. Reid Maddox and his brothers, Russ and Ryan, owned the business. Their family's old resort had closed, and they converted the place for weeklong survival training camps, using the resort cabins to house their clients.

"Your car will be towed for evidence," he said, still moving at a crisp pace. "But the deputy said we can take any belongings you need with us. Let's get what you need and get out of here."

8

Why did he think he could boss her around like this? He'd never done it before, and she didn't like it. Not at all.

"I can't go to Shadow Lake with you," she called out after him.

He shoved his fists into his pockets and looked over his shoulder at her. "Yeah, well, the department can't offer you any protection, and you'll need help if the shooter comes back for you."

She wanted to jerk him to a stop and tell him she didn't agree with him, but he'd taken off so fast she had to run to try to catch up. "You're assuming I was the target. I could've just been in the wrong place at the wrong time."

"True, and that's why I said *if* he comes back for you. But I'm not taking any chances." He looked ahead again. "If he was indeed aiming at you, hoping to kill you, he'll try again. Shadow Lake Survival has a secure compound, and our team can protect you."

She didn't like the sound of being under their watchful eye when she planned to have a relaxing vacation. Wouldn't getting out of Portland be enough to keep her safe? After all, why would anyone have reason to look for her at the campground she hung out in as a child?

She caught up to him and stared at him. "I was going to your family's campground at Boulder Lake from here. I doubt he's going to find me there."

"The campground?" He spun. Watched her. His eyes searching. "Why in the world would you want to go there?"

She didn't like being told what to do or being questioned like a criminal, but she also didn't like his judgmental attitude right now. "Jada and I planned a week-long reunion vacation. We're celebrating twenty years of being friends."

"But why there?" Dev came to a stop at her battered car.

The many bullet holes dotting her vehicle reminded her of the barrage of bullets coming so close to striking her. A harsh wind blew over her, and she tightened her sweater around her body to fend it off and maybe her fear with it.

"At this time of year," he said. "Those poorly insulated cabins will be cold and damp. Why not celebrate somewhere warm and comfortable instead?"

"You know Jada and I hung out at the Bluebird Cabin all the time and had like a million sleepovers there. Revisiting the place will give us a break from life and bring back memories."

He watched her, and she could almost see his thoughts parading through his brain like a runaway train. "Sounds like something the two of you might want to do. Could be fun, I guess."

"Don't sound so convinced." She laughed.

"Sorry." He frowned. "When I think about the campground, I don't especially think about fun times. Mom and Dad always had Colin and me doing so much work around the place, in some respects, it seemed like we never really had a childhood."

He was only remembering the hard times he and his brother had, not the good ones, and she felt the need to remind him. "What about all those sunny days at the lake? Swimming out to the raft and laying in the sun. Doing nothing but watching the dragonflies humming across the lake. And the barbecues? The horseshoes? And just hanging around and goofing off?"

He stared into the distance, his gaze vacant. "I guess we did have some good times."

"I know I did, and I always appreciated your mother letting me hang out at the campground when my mom and dad worked all the time. I can't wait to get back there." She glanced at her watch. Late. Just as she thought. She couldn't waste any more time. "After all of this mess, I'm late, and

Jada's waiting for me. I suppose it would speed things up if you gave me a ride."

"Now who doesn't sound convinced?" He eyed her.

"Sorry, this has all thrown me for a loop." The shooting, yeah, but seeing him was almost as unsettling. "I can call Jada on the way to tell her you'll be with me."

"She's not going to like me horning in on your time together, but it can't be helped." He frowned. "I'll help you with your things."

"If you'll grab my box of memories, I'll get my suitcase." She spun for her car trunk and popped it open.

Over the years, she'd saved memories from their past, the box growing larger and larger. If she added much more, she would need multiple boxes to make things manageable. All thanks to growing up around the Graham family. Summers especially were such fun that she couldn't wait to get to the campground.

Kinsley stared into her trunk. She could just see their week now. They would take out each item in one of her favorite places on earth, and they would walk down memory lane together.

"Earth to Kinsley." Dev bumped her out of the way and grabbed the box.

She returned to the present. "Careful with that. It's got breakable things inside."

"Feels heavy to be a bunch of memories."

If he only knew what the box contained, he would definitely razz her about the things she'd saved. She retrieved her suitcase and caught up to him. They crossed the crumbling parking lot, walking past the forensic staff, who'd placed markers by every bullet strike. The sight of so many tiny plastic tents dotting the concrete evaporated any joy Kinsley's memories had just provided.

She moved closer to Dev and averted her eyes from the

white-suited workers until she reached his black SUV, caked with Oregon mud. The vehicle could definitely use a wash. He'd never been the neatest guy and maybe that hadn't changed.

They stored her things in the back and got into the SUV. Empty protein bar wrappers, energy drinks, and Hershey bar wrappers—something he'd always had a fondness for—littered the interior of the vehicle. Yep, he hadn't changed. Her cleanliness and desire for order begged her to clean it out. That would be rude, so she sat on her hands.

"Sorry about the mess." He got the vehicle running, gunning the gas and sending a trio of crows pecking at something in the parking lot into the air. "I was on a stakeout all last week and haven't had a chance to clean it up."

"Stakeout?" She swiveled to look at him, kicking a few energy drink cans on the floor and sending them rattling. "I thought at Shadow Lake Survival you taught people how to live off grid, but that sounds like police work."

"Sort of." He clenched the steering wheel. "We had a break-in at the campground. We think it was a bunch of kids, but I was trying to figure it out so I could teach them a lesson and keep them away in the future."

"Break-in at the campground as in Boulder Lake Campground where we're headed?"

"Yes."

Another crime. This one less serious, but it was unnerving. Was it safe for her and Jada to be staying there? "And did you figure it out?"

"No." He let the one word hang in the air, then glanced at her. "Gave it a week before I had to get back to work. I probably devoted too much time to it anyway. It's not like anything was taken. Someone just broke a few of the locks on the cabin doors. Seems like they were scared off before doing any damage or stealing anything."

He exited the parking lot, his gaze constantly searching around them. "I've already replaced the doors and locks, and despite my mom's disappointment, I put up security cameras on the property."

"She was always the trusting type who loved to make sure her guests had privacy." And she afforded her children the same privacy but wasn't at all hesitant to step in when they needed a parent butting in and taking over.

Kinsley loved that about her. "How is she doing, by the way? Jada said she was living with you and Colin for a while due to a big lupus flareup."

"Actually, things are better right now. Her flareup has subsided, and we're hoping her current medicine will keep it that way so she can move back home. But we'll see. No point in pushing it. Not when we don't mind having her around."

She had always liked his mother, who, even when she was a teenager, had put up with her moods. His mother had encouraged Kinsley to call her by her given name, Sandra— Sandy. At the time, Kinsley had thought that was so grown up and embraced it fully.

"I'm glad to hear she's doing better. She's one of the kindest people I know. She's always considerate of everyone and knows when to approach and when to stay away. She deserves nothing but the best."

"Agreed," he said. "Though I remember her pushing me at times instead of staying away."

"She was probably a little more laid-back with me since I wasn't one of her children." But how Kinsley wished she had been. Her mother basically ignored her in favor of her career. And when she didn't, she steamrolled over any of Kinsley's hopes and dreams and insisted Kinsley do what she asked. And her father? He was intimidated by her, stood back, and watched it all happen.

But when Kinsley was in first grade, she met Jada at a day camp, and they hit it off right away. At their first play-date at the Graham's big family cabin at the campground, Sandy welcomed Kinsley with open arms. Kinsley's mother had been more than willing to drop her off at the campground most every day on her way to work. Kinsley spent many nights sleeping over with Jada in their favorite cabin. When they got older, they climbed up on the roof late at night when no one knew they did it. Watching the stars. Dreaming of the life she always wanted to have. Later dreaming of a life with Dev that she never would have.

She peeked at him. He still gripped the wheel and was checking the surroundings as he drove. After the break-ins and the shooting, was he going to allow her to stay at the campground with Jada or would he make such a big deal of her safety that he ruined the week?

If he got it in his mind that it wasn't safe, she doubted he would let either of them stay. But she wasn't the wide-eyed, naïve teenager he used to know and who followed him around whenever possible. She was an adult now and could make her own decisions. October meant off-season at the campground, and she and Jada would be the only ones staying there. She was sure it would make it easier to spot anything out of the ordinary.

"You're taking me to the campground, right?" She held his gaze. "Jada will be there waiting for me."

"We'll stop by there and let her know you'll be staying with me at our compound instead."

"Even if I agreed to go to the compound with you— which I'm not saying I will—I won't leave Jada at the campground by herself."

"Too bad one of our guest cabins isn't available this

week. You and Jada could have your reunion there and pretend it's the Bluebird."

"I appreciate your concern, but we'll be fine at the campground. Besides, you just said there wasn't an available cabin, so where would we stay? Before you suggest your cabin, you don't have room. Jada told me that you only have three bedrooms."

"No worries. I can bunk with Colin, and you two can share my room."

She'd forgotten how persistent—stubborn—he could be when he wanted to get his way. "There's no need to put yourself out like that. I'm fine at the campground, and that's where I want to stay."

He fired a testy look her way. "Even if someone wasn't shooting at you, it might not be safe for you and Jada to stay there right now. Not with the recent break-ins."

"We don't even know that the shooter was shooting at me per se. He could've been firing at me because I was the only person in the parking lot. And you said you think kids broke into the cabins. They're not going to hurt me."

His fingers tightened on the wheel. "That could be true, but if the shooter wanted to fire at random people, he would've chosen a parking lot that wasn't usually empty unless a special event was going on."

"Maybe he thought a special event was being held today."

He coasted to a stop at a four-way stop sign and took a hard look at her. "We can speculate all we want. All I know for sure is that the Shadow Lake compound is well secured. A while back someone tried to steal weapons, so Reid built a perimeter fence and a solid gate with a keypad lock. That would be the safest place for you right now."

She didn't want to talk about this anymore, but she also

didn't want to agree to it at this time. "Jada and I can discuss it, and we'll make a decision together."

"I love my sister, but she doesn't always make the best decisions. You know as well as I do that she can be kind of flighty."

At the thought of her impetuous friend, Kinsley smiled. Jada was usually up for an adventure that she hadn't quite thought through before acting on. Kinsley was more a straightlaced, by-the-book kind of person and appreciated her friend's imaginative personality.

She looked out the window to avoid his piercing intensity. "We'll see. You can drop me off at the campground, and I'll let you know."

"No!" He revved the engine and peeled away from the stop sign. "I'll take you to the campground, but I'm not going anywhere. I'll stay there until you make a decision. And if you decide to stay at the campground, I'll be staying in the cabin next door. So if you really don't want to put anyone out, then you should join us at the compound."

Grr. He was making things extremely difficult. He clearly thought she was in danger, but she still wasn't certain she was the target of those bullets, and if teenagers broke into the cabin, they wouldn't come back when someone was staying there.

"I really don't think anyone would be firing at me."

He sucked in a short breath.

She glanced at him. "I can't think of a single person who would want to kill me."

"What about your job? You examine crucial failures to find criminal wrongdoing. I'm sure you've shut down projects where the person under investigation wanted to seek revenge for your part in sending them to prison. Surely, someone has threatened you."

She didn't want to admit to being threatened or even

think about it, but he was right. A particularly nasty situation five years ago came to mind. Nico Huff, a building contractor, cut costs on concrete footings and other structural materials for a high-rise apartment building. He paid off the inspector and would've gotten away with it if his foreman hadn't blown the whistle. If he'd completed the project, the building's foundation most certainly would've failed and hundreds of people could've been injured or killed.

"Well?" His demanding tone set her teeth on edge. "Has anyone threatened you?"

Despite his insistent behavior, to which she didn't want to answer, he wasn't going to let it go until she did. "I'd be lying if I said it hasn't happened."

He pressed on the accelerator and turned south at the Boulder Lake turnoff. "Anything that sticks out in your mind?"

She told him about the situation with Huff. "But he couldn't be shooting at me. He's in prison."

"Doesn't mean he doesn't have a person on the outside doing his job for him. He could easily have paid someone to take you out."

"I suppose, but that would be pretty far-fetched, right?"

"It would be less likely than if he was out and shooting at you, but people hire hitmen all the time these days. People you wouldn't expect. If Huff's willing to pay off an inspector for substandard footings that he knew would fail and potentially kill a lot of people, that says a lot about his character. I wouldn't put it past him to hire someone to take you out."

She swiveled to face him. "But what would he stand to gain by killing me? Someone else would just take over the case, and he would still be prosecuted."

"Revenge." He fired the word at her just like the bullets

that had nearly struck earlier. "Pure and simple, he would feel better about it."

"I suppose that could happen." She sighed. "But I would think if he wanted to hire someone to kill me while he sat in prison, he would've taken revenge before now."

"Just think about it on the drive." His tone had softened. "And think about anyone else who might have it out for you. If you can honestly say that they're not out to get you, then maybe staying at the campground isn't so risky. But if you can't say that, then the compound is the safest place for you."

She turned back to the window and watched the wooded areas pass by. Familiar areas filled with soaring pines, large maple trees, and tangled understory plants that grew only in shade. Then a break in the trees displayed unkempt acre after acre of wild grasses undulating in the breeze in a rhythmic wave that only God could orchestrate.

She hadn't returned here in at least five years, but something was different. Very different. The sky was a hazy gray, darkening the night and obliterating the setting sun's rays. In the distance, a sickly yellowy-red color stained the sky.

She shot a look at Dev. "You didn't tell me there were forest fires in the area."

"Two of them, actually." He grimaced. "Experts are afraid they might merge into one large blaze, and we're all keeping an eye on it."

She sat stunned for a moment. This was not something she expected at all. "It's kind of late in the year for a fire isn't it?"

"Things are changing. Fire season used to end in September, but due to drier weather in the fall, fires have occurred more often in early October."

She shook her head, worrying for her friends and the

property in the area. "Is it supposed to come close enough to threaten us?"

He didn't answer right away, upping her anxiety.

"Dev?" she asked.

"They're saying it could, if the firefighters don't get it under control."

"Then let's pray that they get it under control." She looked out the window again at what could be the real danger to her life. "What about evacuations in the area? Do we need to worry about that?"

"No alerts for us yet, so no. You just have fun with Jada, and I'll let you know if an evacuation order is issued for our area."

Kinsley tried not to add this to her worries, and instead, changed her thoughts to her friend. Jada was deployed in the Navy on giant ships, and Kinsley traveled a lot for her job, so it had been too long since they'd seen each other. She was away from home more often than not. They kept up with emails, texts, and video chats, but it wasn't the same thing as face-to-face interaction. Despite the shooting, excitement over seeing her very best friend found a way to the surface.

What would Jada say about where they should stay?

Only time would tell what she would choose, but Kinsley fully intended to plead her case for holding their reunion at the campground. If Dev insisted on staying in the cabin next door, so be it. At least he hadn't gone completely nuts and demanded to stay in the same place as Kinsley.

Jada had arrived. Dev had no doubt. The campground gate had been flung wide open, the chain and padlock hanging from the crossbeam. That was Jada. Not a care in the world.

In a hurry. Exuberance for life moving her faster than she could possibly go if she took the time to think. She was the opposite of Kinsley. He often wondered why they were friends, but maybe it proved the theory of opposites attracting.

Did that mean he was more like Jada than he wanted to consider? Impulsive. Quick to react and not think first. One look at his behavior at the parking lot, demanding that Kinsley stay with him instead of talking to her about it, and he could say he'd behaved just like that. Maybe if he took the time to call up some of his other actions, he would see the same thing.

Like maybe he hadn't thought through getting engaged when he did, and look how that turned out. His fiancée Hailey leaving him at the altar. Not only had he been hurt but he hurt someone else. His behavior wasn't as extreme as Jada's, but he had to admit he did have the same tendencies. Which meant he had to stop and think before he alienated Kinsley.

He pulled up inside the gate and glanced at her. "Hang tight while I close the gate."

He hopped out into the cool night, smoky air instantly irritating his breathing. Even if there weren't fires in the area, it wasn't unusual for easterly winds to blow smoke from other fires across the state, so he should be used to it. But he never got used to it. Man wasn't meant to inhale this kind of smoke.

He swung the massive gate closed and fixed the padlock to the chain, double-checking the lock to be sure it was latched. The lock wouldn't stop a person from climbing over the gate, but no way a vehicle could access the campground without crashing through the wood. Gave Dev some peace of mind.

Back in the vehicle, he shifted into gear and pulled

forward on the barely lit road that led past the check-in station and owner's cabin. The sun had fully set about thirty minutes ago, and with the smoky air, the four-bedroom cabin he'd grown up in looked dark and shadowy. Since his mom's health prohibited her from running the campground, the property was run by a live-in manager, but Warren was out of town while the campground was closed.

Further down the road sat all twelve cabins and the lake, a large playground with several swings, and a climbing apparatus across a narrow road on the property. The road behind it held twenty-four campsites for tents and trailers, some with water and sewer connections, and others had zero amenities.

"Ooh." Kinsley leaned forward to stare out the window. "I'm so glad to be back here. I missed this place like crazy."

Her wistful tone caught Dev by surprise. He rarely thought about the campground these days, short of reading the annual report from the manager and trying to find the person who broke into the cabins.

He surveyed each of the small cabins lit by two street lights near the end of the road. Normally a soft wash of light from the moon hanging over the lake helped illuminate the area, but smoky air prevented that tonight. The whole space was eerily shadowed, and he wished they were arriving in daylight instead of the evening. If someone wanted to shoot at Kinsley here, he could certainly find areas to take cover.

"It's just like I remember it. At least on the days when we had wildfire smoke in the area." Kinsley sighed. "But most of the time it was the perfect place for families to enjoy their vacation and get closer together. Too bad my parents never thought to do something like that. I don't remember going on a single vacation trip with them. They never took off work, as far as I remember."

Unfortunately, her parents were pretty lame. Thankfully,

Dev's mom unofficially adopted her, and she was able to spend a lot of time with them to see what a committed family was like. Even if they did have to work hard to keep the campground in tiptop shape, they worked together, so Dev should be thankful for his parents working alongside him. He certainly learned his work ethic from them. Well, mostly from his mom, because his dad passed away when he was seven. Still, years of interacting with his father helped him later in life to figure out what a real man was made of, and that didn't mean all He-Man sort of things, but included compassion and a strong desire to do the right thing by others.

He glanced at Kinsley and didn't like the sadness reflected back at him when she came here for happy memories. "I remember your mom and dad coming to our annual picnic a few times."

"Yeah, they did take a few hours off here and there. I don't remember any school events they attended or anything like that, but they did, for some reason, come to your mom's picnics. Your mom was pretty legendary around here for the different themes she had at each picnic, and everyone wanted to get an invite to see the theme she chose for the year."

"She was pretty cool like that. I hated when her lupus took over and she wasn't able to hold the picnics anymore. We tried to step in and help, but it hurt more for her to see it go on without her involvement than to not have it at all. I know she misses them still."

"Rotten lupus." Kinsley pounded a fist on her knee. "I hate that for her. For anyone. But she's the kindest, sweetest, most loving woman, and I hate to see her suffer."

"I hear you there," was all he could say because the agony his mother went through brought acid burning up his throat. He swallowed hard. "At least she's doing better right now."

Kinsley clasped her fingers in her lap. "Does she like living in town? I know it was hard for her to turn the campground over to a manager, but it would've been harder for her to sell it, right?"

"Right. The place hasn't been making much money for years now, but she still has dreams of coming back here to run it. They're pipe dreams if you ask me, but if they keep her going, then having a manager is the right decision for now."

"I expected to see him on duty, but I didn't see any lights on at the big cabin."

"He takes time off, but he'll be back at the first of November to start the off-season maintenance."

She looked out the window. "Your parents always took such good care of this place, I would imagine the manager is doing an equally terrific job."

"You know my mom well. He'd be long gone if he didn't live up to her standards." Dev laughed and swung into the parking area for the Bluebird Cabin, which was named after a cabin where his parents spent their honeymoon.

"I can't wait to see your mom," Kinsley said. "I wish it wasn't too late to go see her tonight, but she invited us to lunch tomorrow, so that'll have to be soon enough."

She opened her window and snapped pictures ahead. She was likely trying to capture the cabin where light flooded out the windows, but would more likely get smoke-filled photos. She sighed as she settled back in her seat and tapped the screen on her phone.

"What are you up to?" he asked.

"Posting a picture of the cabin on my social media."

He put his hand over her phone. "No. No social media."

She glanced at him. "So you're one of those people who hate social media?"

"I mean, as a former law enforcement officer, I don't recommend it for posting personal information. It can lead to all kinds of problems that could jeopardize someone's safety. But in this situation, you sure don't want anyone to have any inkling of where you are. Your safety depends on your anonymity."

"But I won't post my location. I know better than that. It's just a generic cabin in the woods."

"You'd be surprised at the information that can be gleaned from a single photograph. Then the information is extrapolated until the person discovers your location."

"But I—"

"Don't believe me?" He locked gazes with her. "Show me your last Facebook post when we get inside, and I'll show you how much I can learn about you."

"I doubt it," she said. "My post was simply a picture of my memory box, and I said I was going to review items inside with my bestie at our favorite place this weekend." She flashed up a hand. "Before you say anything, I didn't mention who my bestie was or even that we were coming here."

"How about you go ahead and promise me you won't post anything on social media until this shooter has been apprehended? Then, if I can't persuade you after looking at your latest post of what could be learned, we can talk about it."

"I want to promise, but I don't know if I can." She bit her lip. "I'm a self-professed social media junkie, and I post multiple times a day. Probably comes from leading such a solitary life with little time for social interaction outside of a few work colleagues."

"But that doesn't matter right now. Your life is more important than any interaction on social media." He continued to study her. "You can still go to the sites and see what your friends are up to. Just resist adding any information, including not commenting on anyone else's posts."

"Fine. I promise." She shoved her phone into her back pocket and didn't look too happy about her promise. Hopefully she would keep it.

The cabin door opened, illuminating the small porch with a swing. Jada bolted outside and down the steps before either one of them could get out of the vehicle. She whipped Kinsley's door open and nearly dragged her out of the SUV. His sister threw her arms around Kinsley and started swinging her in circles.

"I am so happy to see you," Jada said, her exuberance knowing no bounds. "I've missed you so much."

"But we've texted and FaceTimed," Kinsley said.

"It's not the same as seeing your face in person." Jada leaned back. "I mean, look how beautiful you've gotten. You were always a stunner, but come on, what are you doing for a beauty routine? I need to know. Stat."

Kinsley laughed. "You always did know how to make me feel good about myself."

"I'm right, aren't I, Dev?" Jada glanced at Dev. "Just look at her. She's even more beautiful than before, right?"

Dev shouldn't look at Kinsley, but he couldn't help himself. The outdoor lights cut through the smoke and shone on her face, highlighting her high cheekbones and large eyes.

"You don't have to say anything." Jada frowned. "Your look says it all. We should move on. Let's grab your things and get settled."

Kinsley turned toward the back of the vehicle, and Jada

grabbed Dev's arm. "I didn't like the way you were looking at Kinsley. Remember your promise."

Dev stopped and looked at his sister, her dark eyes reminiscent of his mother's intense gaze that she could pin on him at a moment's notice when he had messed up. "Maybe it's time to revisit that promise. After all, we're adults now."

"I need Kinsley in my life now just as much as I needed her growing up. I can't risk you ruining that because of a failed relationship."

He didn't like her assumption that it would fail. He didn't like it at all. "What makes you think any relationship we would have would fail?"

"I'm not sure that it would, but I can't risk it. So remember your promise." She spun on her heel and went to join Kinsley at the back of the vehicle.

Dev followed. "Before we unpack, we need to talk about whether or not it's safe for Kinsley to stay here."

Jada's dark eyes narrowed. "Why on earth wouldn't it be safe?"

Dev gave his sister a quick rundown of the shooting.

Jada spun toward Kinsley. "Did that really happen? Are you okay? Did he hurt you?"

"Calm down," Kinsley said. "I'm fine. He just shot up my car and the area around it. He didn't hit me. Dev arrived, so I think that made him take off."

"So Dev saved you?" Jada cast a suspicious look at him as if he had some sort of ulterior motive for making sure that Kinsley remained alive.

"I wouldn't exactly say saved." Dev couldn't look at Kinsley. The memory of her in his arms was too fresh not to give away everything he was feeling to his sister. "I didn't even know it was her at first. But I do believe that my presence did make the shooter take off. I also called my former lieutenant and probably got a faster law enforcement response. That's all I did."

Jada wrapped her arm around Kinsley. "Let's get you inside and out of this smoke so you can rest."

"I'm not fragile, Jada." Kinsley gave Dev a *thanks for bringing the subject up* look. "I'm fine and eager to get started on our reunion celebration."

"And then we'll talk about whether it's safe to stay here or not," Dev said, not caring that Kinsley was irritated with him.

She glared at him but then walked up the steps arm-in-arm with Jada. Inside, the feeling of going home hit him. Many times growing up, he and Colin had come down to the cabin when Kinsley was sleeping over, and the four of them would watch scary movies together on the ancient TV. Then Dev and Colin would leave for the night, but hang around outside the cabin to make scary noises and try to weird out the girls. Sometimes it worked, other times they saw right through them and came out to chase them off.

He remembered running away, laughing with Colin, and yet wishing he was still sitting inside the cabin with Kinsley. But now they were all grown up, and any scary noises outside could signal that the shooter had found her here.

Dev had no idea what the shooter knew about Kinsley. Did he know about her childhood? That she spent so much time at the campground, and she might come back here? Or was it as Kinsley said, just a random shooting and he wasn't even looking for her?

She could be right, but Dev wouldn't risk her life on it.

She settled on one end of the dark green sofa that his mom had bought when she remodeled the place. All of the cabins had undergone a renovation at that time, and the furnishings from the early sixties were cleared out to be replaced by furnishings from the early two-thousands, now outdated again. She didn't think he knew her reasoning for the renovation, but it was her effort to bring in more revenue and fill the place like in the early days.

Jada dropped onto the sofa next to Kinsley and took her hands. "Now tell me. Do you think that this man was shooting at you, or was it just some random act?"

She shrugged. "Dev made me think about it, and I suppose it could be someone I found guilty of criminal doings. A couple of builders threatened me in the past, but I didn't take them seriously. Maybe I should have."

"Exactly." Dev perched on the arm of an overstuffed chair. "You're no fool, sis. You can see it would be safer for Kinsley to stay at the compound than in an unsecure location like this one."

"First, thanks for the compliment. They're so rare, I should probably write it down." Jada laughed, but it quickly died away, and she focused on Kinsley again. "As much as it pains me to say this, he might be right. I could never forgive myself if something terrible happened to you here."

Kinsley freed her hands from Jada's. "But what about our big reunion party?"

"It's not worth remembering the old days if you were to lose your life."

"Dev said he could stay in the cabin next door. Don't you think that would be safe enough? After all, how could this person have found me here? And if there's any hint that the creep *is* nearby, we can move to the compound." Kinsley sat forward. "Please. It really would mean a lot to me to stay here."

Jada looked up at Dev. "That seems like a good compromise to me."

"Yeah, well," he said. "It's not a very good compromise for me. I'll agree to it if you let me stay here with the two of you."

Kinsley lifted her chin and eyed him. "You can stay here as long as you don't interfere with our time together. But don't think for a minute that you can decide what I do."

Yeah, her statement left no doubt she thought he was being bossy again. If he wanted her to run in the other direction, he was doing a really good job of it. "You're right. Your life is your life. I don't have any business interfering with it. Other than you're an important family friend. I care about you not getting hurt, and I have experience in law enforcement, so I know the safest route to take here."

"I get that," she said. "I appreciate your concern, and going forward, I promise to listen to you if there's any hint of danger."

"Then that's all I can ask for." Of her, but he could ask a whole lot more from his team and God. And he would be in prayer from now until when Kinsley went home safe and sound. "You two go ahead and start this reunion. I need to step outside for a minute."

"Running away from your past?" Jada laughed.

If he was running from anything, which he wasn't doing right now, he would be running away from the woman who captivated him.

Outside, where the air hadn't improved at all, he jogged down the steps. At least the smoke clouded the moon, or it would be hanging large and bright over the lake, creating a romantic atmosphere. Something he had no business thinking about right now. Because it also created light for any assailant to be able to find his way through the camp-ground to Kinsley.

He dug out his phone and dialed his brother, Colin. "Don't say anything. Just listen." Dev shared the afternoon events. "Jada and Kinsley are both at the Bluebird Cabin. I need you over here ASAP for an outside protection detail."

"You got it."

Dev knew he could count on his older brother. He never disappointed. "I also wouldn't turn down help from one of the other guys to man the gate if you'll arrange that. And I need you to pack a bag for me. I'm staying here tonight, and I'll need fresh clothes in the morning. I'm not leaving this property as long as Kinsley is staying here."

3

Kinsley lifted a charm bracelet from the memories box and set it on the table near her other mementos she'd unpacked so far. She'd imagined this trip down memory lane with Jada for months now, and she hoped it lived up to her anticipation. She put too much stock on her memories. Sure she did. She got that. But she was unable to change it. Each item was precious to her. They spoke to a particular time, telling her how much this family loved her. How they'd practically adopted her when her own parents were missing in action most of the time.

So the minute she and Jada hit the cabin, Kinsley started thinking about paging through the many diaries with colorful markers they'd used to document their summers together. Holding the fun shaped rocks they'd found by the lake. Looking at dry flowers. Reading the many notes they'd written to each other, and on and on.

But it wasn't turning out like she expected, and she couldn't say she was especially comfortable. Not with the way Dev kept watching her every move from his perch on a barstool near the kitchen peninsula. She and Jada had been choosing items from her memory box, and if he wasn't questioning the memory, he was just watching with tremendous interest.

She turned away to ignore him and lifted the sixties-inspired lamp from the box to place on the table.

"Oh no you didn't!" Jada's eyes flashed wide. "I had no idea you took one of the lamps when Mom redecorated."

"Well...she said we could have anything we wanted." Kinsley smiled. "I wanted something to remember the cabin the way it was when we were little."

"But a lamp?" Dev blinked his long, long lashes at her. "Isn't that a little extreme?"

"Extreme?" Kinsley met his gaze. "Not to me. I wanted the sofa, but it wouldn't fit in a box this small."

Kinsley changed her focus to Jada, and they fell into a laughing fit. When Kinsley could talk again, she looked at Dev. "If you insist on interfering in our trip down memory lane, remember the ages we were at the time this happened. That can help explain each item I kept."

He tapped a finger on his knee. "Yeah, you were pretty young."

Jada swiveled to face her brother. "I was only a year younger than you, and you never let me forget it."

"You're still a year younger than me." He grinned at his baby sister.

"But I'm three years younger than you." Kinsley continued to look at him. "And I don't recall you ever harassing me about that."

"Guess it's a blood relative thing." He rested his hands on the scarred Formica countertop. "You were the closest thing to a blood relative though. I'm sure you spent more time at our house than at yours."

Kinsley couldn't tell how he felt about that so she rushed on. "No question about it."

"I still think it's pretty sad your mom didn't want kids and took it out on you," Jada said.

Kinsley had long ago let go of the pain from that part of her past. "Trust me. It was no hardship for me. Your mom is the best, and I was the one who really benefited from my mom's disinterest."

She would've loved to have gotten to meet their father too. He died far too young.

"Why so serious all of a sudden?" Jada's eyes narrowed with concern.

"I was just thinking about your dad. From everything you all said about him, I wish I'd gotten to meet him. I know you all miss him a lot."

Jada slid down the couch and drew Kinsley into a hug. "He was great. If he lived, he would've been a second father to you."

Kinsley leaned back and glanced at Dev, his expression sullen.

Was it because she brought up his father, or was he still thinking about them staying at the campground?

She was glad Jada had agreed with her about staying here. She appreciated the support. But had she been too hasty declining Dev's offer to stay at his compound all because she didn't want him telling her what to do?

Whenever she made decisions, decisions that she'd prayed about and then had peace afterward, she knew it was the right decision. But without peace, she continued to look for the right thing to do.

She didn't have peace tonight and couldn't help thinking that God could be trying to tell her something. That it was time to devote herself to prayer, and time for her to listen and look for that peace with her decision.

Listen or she could die.

Dev sat at the table next to Kinsley and stared at her Facebook post on his laptop. Thankfully, he'd had his computer in his SUV, so he could prove his point.

Kinsley was right about one thing. The last image she posted was simply a picture of the box she'd brought along with her, sitting on a bed in an open room. Or at least it looked like a simple picture, but he knew looks could be deceiving. Once a photo was enlarged from the size you might see on a phone or iPad, it could display damaging information.

He peered at her. "I'll start with the least telling items and move to the most dangerous."

"Seriously?" she asked. "You really see something that could be a problem in this post?"

"Several things. The first is the desk in the background. Your mail is lying on it." He enlarged the photo on his screen.

She leaned forward and stared at the screen. "So? You can't read my address on it."

"I might only be able to make the photo this big while still in Facebook, but I can always save it to my hard drive and enlarge it even more."

"And your point is?"

"Before posting a photo, look at it in the largest size possible while still in focus to see if it reveals any information. For example, I can't make out the complete address on the envelope, but I can see a portion of it. With the way auto-complete works on our computers, I'd venture to say if I enter the portion I can read into an address form online, the app will complete the rest for me, and I'll know exactly where you live."

"Wow," Jada said from across the table. "I use auto-complete all the time and never really thought about how it could be used for something bad."

He switched his focus to his sister. "Most people don't. But once you've been in law enforcement, you have a tendency to look for those kinds of things. Even if you don't want to."

Kinsley shook her head. "So anyone who saw this post could enlarge my picture and see enough of my address to find me."

"Yes, if they thought of it. But as Jada said, most people don't think of it."

"So it's not as big of a deal as you're making it."

"Oh, it is." He locked gazes, because he didn't like her discounting this information. "Problem is, the people who *have* thought of it are the ones who are up to no good and will use it to their advantage. So when you post any pictures on your social media, you need to make sure you blur out anything that might lead to your location."

Kinsley tipped her head, like she wasn't fully convinced. "I don't hate the fact that my friends on Facebook might see something and figure out where I live. Not that I want them popping by unexpectedly, but it wouldn't be horrible. It's just the general public that I'd like to keep it from. I don't accept them as friends, and my friends are the only ones who can see my posts."

"Or so you think."

She jerked back.

Dev didn't like seeing her response, and he wished he had better news for her. "People can hack your friends' accounts. Happens all the time. If the friend isn't a close friend but more of an acquaintance, you probably won't notice anything odd about their posts, and you may not know they've been hacked until it's too late."

Kinsley frowned. "So what other red flags does the picture hold?"

"You received a package from Kohl's." He tapped the store's logo on the side of the box.

"How does that help you?"

"It tells me this box was likely shipped to you and to look for an address label." He shifted the photo on his screen until a prominent address label was displayed on the side. "I don't have to explain this one."

"I usually don't look at the pictures larger than my phone displays them. I guess that means I miss some things." She clutched her hands together. "But that changes now. I need to go back through my social media to delete any posts with items like this on it."

"You can and should do that so anyone who goes to your profile now doesn't see it. But once the photo is on the internet and other sites pick it up, it's pretty much there for life and remains discoverable." He rushed on to try to encourage her. "It's still worth the work, though. Once removed from your profile, it's less likely that anyone will see it."

"You've made your point." Kinsley set her jaw. "I'll take care of that tonight, and I promise in the future, I'll be more careful."

"And, you'll keep your promise that until our shooter is behind bars, you won't post anything at all." He kept his focus on her.

"Yes, I promise." She looked at Jada. "I'll need your help to hold me to that."

"Of course, sweetie. I'm always glad to stop you from doing things that are bad for you." Jada got a twinkle in her eye, and Kinsley laughed.

Dev appreciated his sister lightening things up. "We should also check your security settings. I know you said you have your posts set to just your friends, but do you have your friend list set to private?"

Kinsley's eyes narrowed. "I'm not sure on that one, but really what difference does that make?"

"Cybercriminals could open a fake account with your name and profile. Impersonating you, they then send messages to your friends list. They can ask for sensitive information or money, often claiming an emergency." He took a long breath. "And they could troll through your friends' pages until they find an unsecured account and hack it. Then use it to target you in the same way."

Kinsley blinked at him. "I didn't know."

"Now you do, so check out the setting and fix it if you need to." His phone rang, and he unearthed it from his pocket. "Got to take this. It's Colin, and he wouldn't be calling if there wasn't a problem."

"He's calling, but he's just outside the door," Kinsley said. "Can't you just go see him?"

"If he wanted me to step out there right now, he would have knocked. I'm guessing he's calling on a security issue." Dev knew it had to be bad news, so he moved to the corner of the small room to try to keep them from overhearing his conversation.

"What's up, bro?" He made sure to take on a laid-back approach to keep from alerting the women by his posture and tone of voice.

"We have a situation down at the lake," Colin said. "Guy in a boat near our dock. We need to check it out."

Dev forgot about the social media and came alert to their immediate threat. Colin must not have wanted the door open in case the man at the lake was their shooter and had a rifle. Dev wanted to go after this man, but his first priority was to make sure Kinsley stayed safe.

Their teammate, Micha Nichols, was manning the gate

to be sure no one tried to breach it, but having an armed guard close to Jada and Kinsley was far more important right now.

"Get Micha down here," Dev said. "Then we'll investigate."

"Roger that." It wasn't often that Dev's older brother easily took direction from him, which told him Colin was worried, and this situation could be a serious threat to Kinsley's safety if they didn't subdue the man in the boat.

He shoved his phone in his pocket and moved to the nearest window to close the narrow gap someone had left when closing the curtains. "Colin and I need to go check something out. Micha is coming down from the gate and will be standing watch outside your door. Stay inside. Door locked. Curtains closed. Until I get back."

Kinsley rushed up to him. "What is the something you're not telling us about?"

"I'll tell you everything when I get back. Just do as I say, and you'll be fine."

Jada crossed the room to put her arm around Kinsley's waist. "Don't worry. We'll do what you say."

"Lock the door right after me." Dev took a long look at the women and stepped outside. He waited to hear the lock click into place and then bounded down the steps to Colin.

His brother stood at the ready, his sidearm drawn. Dev drew his gun from the holster, but spun when movement to his right caught his attention. Micha pounded down the road, his booted footfalls hitting hard and kicking up dust until he planted his feet in front of Dev.

Dev looked at Micha. "Call us if anything—and I mean anything—out of the ordinary happens here."

"You got it." Micha handed him a pair of night vision goggles. "These might come in handy."

"Thanks, man." Dev strapped the goggles on his head

but didn't put them over his eyes yet as the streetlights could damage the goggles.

"Let's go," Colin said.

"Lead the way."

They started down the narrow blacktop road and reached the lake within minutes. Dev moved behind blueberry bushes, fiery red with fall color, and strapped on the goggles in the darker area. Colin joined him, stowed his gun, and lifted his night vision binoculars to his eyes. Dev peered over the lake and spotted movement. A small aluminum fishing boat had dropped anchor in the water near the end of the campground's dock. The boat held one man wearing a baseball cap and standing in the middle of the boat. His hand was clasped around a fishing pole, and his focus remained on the lake.

"Could be a false alarm," Dev whispered to his brother.

"Or not."

"Be prepared to fire. I'll call out to him to get his ID."

Colin pulled his weapon and aimed it at the man.

"Ahoy there," Dev shouted. "Identify yourself."

"It's me." He lifted his cap. "Chief Gibson."

"What in the world is he doing out here at this time of night?" Dev asked Colin.

"Got me." He stowed his gun.

Dev lifted his NVG's and led the way to the end of the dock. "Mind if I ask what you're doing out here so late, Chief?"

"Oh, hi, Dev," he said cheerfully, unaware of their anxiety. "Or is it Colin?"

Colin stepped up next to him. "You got us both. We didn't expect to find anyone out here fishing."

"I figure with the fires growing bigger, I won't have much time in the next week, so I'm getting in some night fishing." He cranked his rod. "I suppose you don't like it when people

39

fish this close to your property, but I can't help myself. Since your dad put those cribs in near your dock, it's the best fishing on the lake. Pretty much always guaranteed to catch something."

The open wooden structures filled with brush were magnets for fish to take shelter in, and they were always teaming with fish, so the area made for good-sized catches.

"No worries," Colin said. "It's a public lake and belongs to everyone. Even this little patch at the end of our dock."

"That's mighty neighborly of you. Fishing is my stress reliever."

"Kind of dangerous navigating all the boulders at the lake at this time of night, though, isn't it?" Dev asked.

"You guys haven't been hanging out around here much, so you wouldn't know that I come here often and have gotten to know the lake like the back of my hand. Your manager and I have gotten to know each other pretty well too. Standup guy."

"My mom was fortunate when she found Warren," Colin said.

"You haven't seen anyone else around here tonight, have you?" Dev looked around the lake, taking in the cabins, docks, and beachy shoreline. Such an idyllic setting that it would be hard to imagine a shooter in the area.

The chief shifted the rod in his hands. "Was one guy at the boat ramp when I put in."

"He fishing too?" Colin asked.

"Not exactly sure what he was up to, but he was pulling a boat out of the water. Not a simple one for fishing like mine, but a thirty-foot cruiser." He paused and shifted his weight, rocking the boat and sending ripples across the surface. "Probably just let the day get away from him and couldn't get to the ramp until after sundown."

"Anyone you recognize?" Dev asked.

The chief shook his head. "I didn't get close enough to see him, but he's not a local, that's for sure. No one around here has a boat like that."

"You get a look at his vehicle?" Dev asked.

"'Course I did. I'm a lawman, aren't I?" He chuckled but peered directly at Dev. "This isn't just some idle conversation, is it? You're concerned about something. Maybe as the chief, I need to know what that something is."

Did he need to know? Dev wasn't so sure about that. He glanced at Colin to get his reaction. His brother gave a brief nod. Okay. Dev trusted his opinion, so he shared their situation with the chief. "We'd appreciate it if you could keep your eyes out for anyone who seems out of the ordinary. And maybe give us the details on that vehicle towing the boat."

"I'll do you one better." The chief pushed his hat back and scratched his head. "I got the plates on the truck, and I'll go back to the office to run them. I'll let you know what I find."

Dev recognized this as the chief's way of inserting himself into the investigation, but Dev didn't have access to vehicle registrations. Even if the chief gave him a plate number, he would have to call in favors from one of his deputy buddies to get it run. And Dev couldn't be certain that he could get it done as the department was cracking down on such things. They couldn't ask Russ either. It was doubtful he would consider it even if they were in his jurisdiction. But out of it, like here? Nah, he wouldn't do that.

"We'd appreciate your help," Dev said. "And I'd appreciate it if you didn't mention to your officers that Kinsley is staying at the campground."

"You got it." He started cranking his fishing line into the reel, the whir of the reel taking Dev back to his fishing days. "I'll call you with the vehicle details."

Dev nodded and turned to march down the dock. The wooden structure held up by old barrel pontoons jarred beneath his feet and left him off balance, but didn't distract him from searching the area for any threat.

On shore, Colin caught up to him. "It'll be good to have him and his officers on the lookout too."

"Yeah," Dev said. "I just don't like the idea of this getting around town. Especially not Kinsley's location. We might be talking about sworn lawmen, but they like to gossip."

"The chief is pretty good at keeping his mouth closed."

"But I can't be sure of that, and I need to keep a lid on this." Dev shoved his hands into his pockets. If he didn't, he would punch shoreline pillars put in place to keep any wayward boats away from the play area. "I can't afford to screw up here."

Colin grabbed Dev's shirt sleeve and stopped him. "We all know how you feel about her, you know?"

Dev stared at his brother, his gaze unyielding. "What do you mean by 'we all'?"

"Jada, Mom, me. Actually anyone who's around the two of you for any amount of time can't miss it." Colin planted his hands on his hips. "And in case you don't know this, brother, she returns the feelings. So I don't know what you're waiting for. Make your moves."

Dev told him about the promise to Jada.

"Sounds to me like you need to have a heart-to-heart with Jada."

Dev resisted snapping at his brother when his frustration was directed at his sister. "I talked to her today. She hasn't changed her mind."

"Then change her mind for her. Loving someone the way you care for Kinsley doesn't come around very often, and you'd be a fool to miss out on it. Trust me. I almost did until I realized Brooklyn and I were meant to be together."

42

Dev knew his brother was right, and if it were just the promise to Jada, maybe he could overcome this and approach Kinsley. But what about Hailey leaving him at the altar? He'd jumped the gun with her. Sure, he'd known Kinsley for forever, but was the timing right, or was it just convenient right now? Could he ever trust his judgment in women again?

He didn't know.

He could be holding on to some schoolboy crush, or he could still have feelings for her. But were they strong enough to overcome his lack of confidence in a future with any woman?

He didn't know. God did, but He wasn't sharing the answer. Dev not only didn't trust his instincts when it came to his relationships, he had to admit his trust in God had fallen ever since Hailey walked out on him. What was it going to take for him to regain that trust?

Only time, and maybe an answer to his prayers, would tell.

4

Dev stood on the sidewalk outside the local candy company known for their homemade fudge in downtown Boulder Lake. He inhaled the sweet vanilla scent drifting from the building and cutting through the wildfire smoke that had increased overnight. Any other day he'd be in line to buy a piece of each flavor to go. Not today. He didn't approve of the trip into town, but Kinsley and Jada had insisted on it, and he'd given in.

After all, how would their shooter have tracked Kinsley to this location? The only suspects for the shooting that made any sense were disgruntled contractors she'd investigated. These contractors wouldn't possess the skills to find her at the campground.

The shooter could hire a private detective who could trace her back to her hometown, but her parents didn't live in the area anymore, so she really had no apparent connections now. The only way the detective could make that link to the campground would be to stop in town and talk to someone who lived here for years and knew everyone. Knew that Kinsley had spent most of her childhood at the campground.

And that's where the problem lay. And why Dev couldn't relax but continued to scan the sidewalk and street. Because, unfortunately, such people existed.

He prayed that Kinsley's whereabouts didn't reach the locals' ears.

Kinsley and his sister, arm-in-arm and mouths full, pushed out of the building.

Kinsley moaned and swallowed. "There is nothing better than Wilson's fudge. I hope they never go out of business and I can come back here more often."

Dev wished she could come back here permanently, but he wasn't about to say that. "For now let's get moving. Where do you want to stop next?"

"Don't be so pushy. Have a piece of fudge." Jada handed him a chocolate brown chunk with nuts. "I got your favorite even if you aren't being very nice."

He accepted the piece, but before putting it in his mouth, he gave her a pointed look. "You know I'm just concerned about you two. So can we please move on?"

She wrinkled her nose. "That was a nicer way to ask, so yes. Where do you want to go, Kinsley?"

Kinsley's eyes lit up. "Let's have T-shirts made with today's date. We can wear them all week like we did when we were kids."

Dev shoved the chocolate in his mouth to take his mind off the dire feelings that tightened his neck, threatening a headache.

Let it go. Focus, and she'll be fine.

He motioned for them to precede him down the walkway, devoid of tourists. Not typical for Saturday, not even in the off-season. Maybe the increase in smoke clogging the air was keeping most people inside.

At the door, he cracked it open, took a long look inside,

and gave a nod to the women while swallowing his bite of fudge.

Kinsley took out a maple piece and handed it to him. "To keep you sweeter."

He rolled his eyes, but she giggled and stepped past him to enter the store, where the odor of a hot press used to complete the T-shirt transfers drifted out.

He wouldn't turn down the fudge, and popped it into his mouth. He savored the maple sweetness as he searched through the yellow-tinged sky, seeing very few cars had parked on Main Street today. He could count them on one hand, and most of them were clumped near the grocery store. Likely locals getting their weekly supplies. Didn't mean he would take his eyes off them. No. Sweet sugar in his mouth or not, his attention remained focused on the street and any potential danger.

A patrol car turned the corner and headed in his direction. The large SUV pulled to the curb in front of him, and Chief Gibson got out. Wearing a khaki uniform, he strode over to Dev. "Glad I caught you. Saved me a trip out to the campground."

Dev stepped closer to keep a couple strolling down the sidewalk from overhearing their conversation. "Did you locate something on that truck at the boat ramp?"

"First things first." Gibson rested his hands on his duty belt. "I know who broke into your cabins at the campground."

News Dev had wanted to hear, but suddenly he wasn't sure if he did. "Who?"

"You know Jimmy Finchley?"

The name was familiar to pretty much everybody in town. "The guy who loves to race motorcycles through town?"

"One and the same." The chief frowned, drawing down

46

his already long face. "Guess he got tired of trying to evade my guys with his bikes. Anyway, he and a couple of teens went on a spree in the area, breaking into vacant homes. He said after they got into a few of your cabins and saw there was nothing of value, they took off. Thankfully, they didn't realize your manager has a home on the property. With him out of town, they could've raided his place."

"Well, I'm glad to have that case closed. I assume you put the fear of God in them, and I also don't have to worry about them coming back since they didn't find anything."

The chief frowned. "Not sure anyone can put the fear of God in Jimmy, but his friends' parents won't abide their sons' behavior and will take care of it."

"That's good then." Dev took a step closer. "Now, what about the boat? What did you learn there?"

"You're not gonna believe this." He lowered his voice. "It belongs to Louis Luongo."

"That guy!" Dev blinked at the chief until he could get his shock under control and think straight. "The guy who everyone thinks killed his wife but got away with it because he bribed a juror?"

"One and the same." The chief grimaced. "I don't like the fact that this guy is in my jurisdiction. I don't even like the fact that he'd be anywhere near my jurisdiction. But one of my men tells me he's buying the Addison property."

Dev knew that place. Everyone in town did. "The biggest house on the lake."

"Apparently not big enough for him. Rumor has it that he's planning to remodel the whole place and seriously enlarge it. Who knows, maybe he'll just tear it down and start over."

Dev thought back to everything he knew about this man. He made his money in numerous concrete driveways all over the Portland metro area. In fact, there was serious consideration at one point that he buried his wife in fresh concrete on one of his job sites. But X-rays proved that rumor wrong, and they never found her body.

"Did he retire after all the bad publicity from the trial or does he still run his company?" Dev asked.

"I think his son's in charge now, but Luongo's still the official head of the corporation. Probably making backdoor deals with some of the most unethical contractors out there."

Had Kinsley run into Luongo on one of her investigations and made him mad? He couldn't have known she would be here, could he, and this was likely just coincidental? But Dev didn't believe in coincidences. He would have to look into Luongo. First, by asking Kinsley if he'd ever been part of one of her investigations and had threatened her.

"Looks like you think this is important," Gibson said.

"Could be. Kinsley is a forensic engineer and could possibly have shut down one of his projects due to malfeasance. If so, he could be mad and seeking revenge. Even if he didn't know she was coming here, he could've easily figured it out while he was in town."

"Let's hope he's not coming back for the foreseeable future. I don't need a murderer in my town gunning for one of my guests."

"Is there any way you can determine how long he hung around yesterday? If he wasn't here during the shooting, he might not be our perpetrator. Or not. He could've hired someone else or has someone else on his payroll to do the shooting for him. Sounds like just the thing he might do."

"I'll ask around. See what I can find out." The chief eyed him. "Until we know something concrete—no pun unintended—I urge you to be extra careful and diligent with

48

Kinsley's safety. I hope she's at the campground now under the supervision of your brother or one of your teammates."

Dev's stomach churned. "Actually, she's in the T-shirt shop, but I fully intend to tell her about Luongo and encourage her to go back to the cabin. I can't say she'll go—she's pretty strong-willed—but she should take it seriously."

He tried to fill his words with confidence, but he wasn't at all sure she would comply. Especially if she didn't have any interaction with Luongo in the past. She might go about her business in town, putting herself at further risk. Maybe not for immediate attack, but anyone who saw her could find out where she was located. The grapevine was rampant in this town, and it wouldn't be long before the entire town knew she was staying at the cabin. Even if Luongo wasn't their guy, that bit of news spreading rapidly could very well get back to the shooter and end her life.

Kinsley stood with Jada next to the steaming T-shirt press where the store associate, whose nametag read Stella, was preparing vintage T-shirts. Kinsley requested a design very much like the ones she and Jada had worn as kids. The heat transfer for the logo emitted a hot smell as it melted the custom transfer onto the fabric, the familiar odor taking her back to the start of summer every year.

"Do you remember when we would come here?" Kinsley could barely contain her excitement as she fired off memories with Jada, who responded a bit less enthusiastically. Still, they giggled like schoolgirls, earning frequent eyerolls from the older sales associate who was new to the shop since Kinsley had last been there.

The door swung open and banged into a metal display

rack holding sample T-shirts. Kinsley startled and spun to face the door.

Dev raced into the room. He took one look at Kinsley and charged across the space.

"We have to go now!" His frantic tone erased her fun and sent her heart beating.

She took a deep breath to stop from falling victim to her emotions. "Our T-shirts aren't ready yet, and we want to go to three more stores."

He took her by the arm and led her to the back of the store, steps hurried and urgent. Jada rushed to keep up with them. When they stopped, he released Kinsley's arm, but Jada took hold of her.

Dev glanced around the room, then moved even closer to her. "I just talked to Chief Gibson. I don't want to get into details here, but trust me when I say we need to get out of here."

"I don't know." Kinsley looked at Jada to see if she wanted to leave.

Her cheerful expression had evaporated. "I know my brother, and he only gets this look on his face when he's seriously freaked out about something. We need to listen to him."

"Then let's go." Kinsley's worry ramped up even higher. She extricated her arm from Jada's hold and turned to leave.

Dev grabbed her shoulder. "Hold up. I don't want you on Main Street."

She didn't fight his touch but remained in place. "Then how do you propose I leave?"

"Through the back door." He faced Jada. "Since I was at the parking lot shooting, our shooter could associate me with Kinsley, but not likely with you. In case he's watching, can you get the vehicle and bring it around back while I wait here with Kinsley?"

"Of course." She held her hand. "Just give me the keys."

Dev dug them from his pocket, and the metal jingled as he dropped them on her palm.

"I'll be back in a jiff." She raced for the door.

"Hold up." Dev bolted past her. "Let me take a look outside first."

He opened the door and poked his head out, turning it right then left, then slowly standing back. "It's clear, but be careful. Keep your eyes open for anything unusual."

"No worries. Any action at all in this sleepy little town will stand out." She laughed and took off.

Dev closed the door behind her and marched up to Stella. "Can we use your back door?"

Stella took a step back, likely from the force he was projecting and opened her mouth to respond.

Gunshots rang out on the street, and she gasped.

Dev spun. "Down, Kinsley. On the floor. Now."

She dropped to the vinyl, her heart hammering.

He faced Stella, now lying on the floor, too. "Do you have a room without windows?"

"The office." She pointed to the open doorway.

"Kinsley, go in there with Stella. Lock the door. Move in as far away from the door as possible and lie on the floor."

A violent burst of bullets coming from the street sounded like staccato pops, one then another in rapid succession.

Kinsley didn't move. "But Jada—"

"I'll go to Jada," he said. "But not until you're safely in the office."

Her muscles were like solid brick, but she managed to get to her feet and run to the back with Stella. They stepped into a small, orderly office holding a desk and chair along with a credenza. Barely any room for two people to lie on the floor.

"Let's shove the desk against the door." Kinsley didn't wait for help but started pushing.

"Lock the door." Dev's raised voice came through the antique wood.

She turned the deadbolt and dropped to the dusty floor where Stella already lay curled in a ball. Wide and terrified eyes behind her thick-framed glasses peered at Kinsley. She swiped a trembling hand over her face. "Is this shooter trying to kill you? Does that mean he's going to break in here and kill us both?"

If Kinsley hadn't insisted on coming into town, Stella wouldn't have to be going through this terrifying experience. Likely life-changing experience. And not in a good way.

Why, oh why, had she been so stubborn and insisted on a trip to town today? Obviously she didn't really believe the parking-lot shooter had been gunning for her.

There'd been a reason for doubt until now. Zero proof existed that the shooter had intended her as the victim. That he wasn't randomly shooting at anyone, and she just happened to be in the wrong place at the wrong time. But today's situation confirmed his intentions, didn't it?

If a shooter was firing his rifle on Main Street in the tiny town where Kinsley had fled, she had to face facts. He was gunning for her, and anyone in her orbit was unsafe. That included Jada. Maybe Dev, too, and even this store associate. Kinsley was a pariah.

She gritted her teeth. From this moment on, she had to act accordingly.

She would follow each and every instruction Dev gave her. She would no longer argue. Not in the least little bit.

She got it now. Understood completely. Complying with his instructions could be the very thing that saved not only her life but the lives of those around her.

5

Before stepping onto the street, Dev completed a call with Chief Gibson, who'd already heard the shots and was on his way back. Dev stowed his phone and took cover behind the first car, an old station wagon with wood-grain paneling on the side. Not drawing any fire, he bolted for the next vehicle, then the next.

A bullet ripped into the concrete behind him, sending up razor-sharp shards that peppered his arms like a barrage of pins and needles. He ignored the piercing pain and moved on to a shiny red Ford pickup where he hunkered down for just a second to wait for another bullet.

Silence.

Taking a deep breath, he advanced, racing to a small sedan. Another bullet went high and shattered the store window behind him.

No! It was one thing to ruin some vehicles or break up the sidewalk. Both were easily fixed, but another thing to fire into a store where customers could be located near the window.

Please don't let anyone inside take a bullet. Please don't let anyone be injured. Period. Kinsley. Jada. Anyone!

He scooted closer to the edge of the sedan and made eye contact with Jada crouching in front of his SUV.

He signaled his intentions and dove for his own vehicle, taking a moment to scan his sister from head to toe. "You hit anywhere?"

She shook her head, her eyes wide, but they didn't hold the terror he expected to find there. Could be her military training on how to react to a siege.

She held his gaze. "I'm fine, but your vehicle has sustained some damage."

"Don't worry about it. All that matters is you're okay." He took another good look at her but didn't see any blood.

"I'm good." Her cool tone confirmed her ability to handle the situation. "Guess he figured out I'm with Kinsley, and now he's upped his game since yesterday—willing to take out her associates."

Exactly what Dev feared, too. Kinsley wasn't safe, and he needed to go to her. Despite the way his sister handled the situation, he still worried about her safety, too.

"Stay down while I get a better look at what we're dealing with here." He scooted to the edge of his vehicle.

He was certain the last two bullets had come from up high, telling him the shots had to originate either from a roof or an upper window across the street. He scrutinized the far side of the street, searching high and low for the shooter's stand.

Searching. Seeking. Nothing.

With the naked eye he couldn't find anything out of the ordinary. He needed binoculars or something to help him see more clearly at a distance. But what?

His phone. He could zoom in on the camera.

He dug it from his pocket and focused the lens across the street. He zoomed in. Scanned the area.

Two apartments sat above the drugstore. A third above a florist. Upper windows in both vintage buildings were closed tight. No rifle poking out. Zero weapons directed at them.

He shifted to the rooftops, then others nearby. All were clear of a sniper.

Nothing out of the ordinary. Nothing at all.

What was going on? Had their shooter fled? Did he relocate to the back alley to wait for Kinsley's escape? Or was he planning to breach the building from the rear to find her and kill her?

Dev's brain froze. What did he do now? The shooter could still be across the street, and Dev wasn't seeing him. So did he stay here and protect his sister, or did he go to Kinsley's aid? Maybe he could safely move his sister back to the T-shirt shop. Not down Main Street, that was for sure. Not unless he had proof the shooter had moved.

Oh, man! Which one did he help? He couldn't choose between them. He needed to protect both. But how?

Time ticked away, sounding like a clock clicking in his head. Every second important, and he couldn't make a decision. He glanced around. Sirens split the air in the distance. The chief and his men were close, perhaps available to help bring the shooting to an end.

Great, but Dev couldn't wait and do nothing. One quick bullet could end either Jada or Kinsley's life.

Jada had been taught how to respond under sniper attack and could better defend herself, but she wasn't likely carrying off-duty. The safest route would be to move her into a nearby shop, take her out the back if the alley was clear, and approach the T-shirt shop from the back door.

He eased back to Jada and shared his plan. "I need you to go ahead of me. Stay down, and I'll be right behind you."

She took a few deep breaths and nodded. "Let's do this."

He squeezed her shoulder and waited for her to take the lead. She started out confidently, and he didn't leave even a foot's length between them as they quickly duck-walked to the door and got it open. Inside the sweet shop, the mouth-watering smells he'd recently enjoyed now seemed cloying and sickening. He swallowed and stayed low with Jada.

He found the store associate on her knees behind the counter filled with trays of colorful treats. "Do you have a back door?"

"Y-y-yes." Tears clung to the older woman's eyes.

"Stay down," he said. "The police are on their way and everything will be fine."

"What do you want me to do?" Jada asked.

"Call Colin and tell him we need a ride from the alley and to get over here like yesterday. I'll take a look out back. Depending on what I see, I'll have you come with me or stay here." Dev crept down a dark hallway to the rear of the shop. He flung the door open and took cover behind the solid metal.

He glanced up and down the short alley. Thankfully, the throat-irritating haze didn't obscure his view.

The back wall of stores on the adjacent street faced him, and a small dumpster sat outside each building. No sign of a shooter, but he couldn't be too careful.

He stepped out on the blacktop and jerked back behind the door, trying to take fire if their shooter had moved to this location. He was greeted with silence, save a couple of birds he'd scared into flight. He did it again and again, gradually lengthening the time out in the alley.

No gunfire. If the shooter hadn't moved back here, Dev and Jada could take cover behind the metal dumpsters to make their way to the T-shirt shop. He called out for her to join him.

Her footsteps moved rapidly down the hallway. "What do we have?"

"Seems to be all clear," Dev said. "I can't be one hundred percent positive, but if you're willing to risk it, we can move one dumpster at a time and take cover. If not, you can stay here to wait for the chief, and I'll go check on Kinsley alone."

"I'm in." Her shoulders lifted in a hard line. "I need to make sure my best friend is okay too."

One thing was for certain. The Graham family members were a fiercely loyal bunch. "Then I'll go first to take any fire. If I *am* fired on, you stay put at the dumpster you're behind at the time. Got it?"

"Got it."

He drew his weapon. "Then let's move."

He took off for the first dumpster next to the Chinese restaurant. The rusty metal oozed liquid onto the ground and emitted a fermenting cabbage odor. Dev wanted to hurl, but he forced himself to slide behind it and wait for Jada to join him.

He held his breath. No bullets fired. The only sound was Jada gagging. He nodded at the alleyway and started for the next dumpster. The police sirens screamed closer now, sounding from Main Street and stilling.

Perfect. Chief Gibson would secure the scene out front, and if the shooter was still hunkered down in his stand, Gibson would hopefully arrest him.

Dev charged down the alleyway, picking up his pace now. One dumpster after the next. Jada matched his pace. No one fired on them.

He reached the T-shirt shop and burst through the door. He took a look around. Everything was as he'd left it. His heart said to race to the office to make sure Kinsley was okay, but he forced himself to wait for his sister just inside the building.

She entered and took a deep breath, then slowly eased it out and looked up at him. "We made it."

He gave her shoulder a squeeze. "Let's get to Kinsley and make sure she's all right."

He guided his sister down the hallway ahead of him and stopped at the office door. Keeping one eye on the hallway, he knocked. "Kinsley, it's me. Are you all right?"

"We're fine." A tremor in her voice spoke to her concern. "No trouble here at all."

He wanted to unlock the door and whip it open. Race in, grab her in a hug, and pull her into his arms until he felt certain she was unharmed. But he needed to employ a little more self-restraint. Hugging her wasn't the safest thing to do right now. He would have to control his urge to hold her in the same way he'd done for years.

He hissed out a breath between his teeth. "The police have arrived. It looks like the shooter's gone, but stay in there until I'm certain. Okay?"

"Anything you say." Her soft, almost timid voice was nearly his undoing.

If anything other than the anxious tone of her voice told him she was scared, her easy acquiescence and compliance with his instructions gave her away.

He hated this for her. Hated how the shooter had rendered the usually strong woman afraid.

He couldn't let this happen again. He had to do better and couldn't let the shooter come anywhere near her. Even if he hadn't succeeded in injuring her physically, he injured her emotionally, and that scar would live with her forever. Dev would do everything within his power to prevent that from happening again.

He would call on his team to assist even more. But he

wouldn't depend on them alone. With God's help, he would up his game. Failure wasn't a choice. If he didn't intensify his efforts, the consequences could be deadly. Not just for her, but his sister could lose her life as well.

No one was going to die on his watch. No one.

~

Police Chief Gibson stood across the office desk from Kinsley in the T-shirt shop. She would love to have Jada and Dev at her side, but the chief had banished them to the main store area. He'd separated them, so he could individually take their statements. He'd encouraged Kinsley to take a seat. A kind gesture, right? Wrong. She was sure he had ulterior motives. Standing tall over her left him seeming more in charge and reinforced the fact that he knew his job well and wasn't a person one should lie to or withhold the truth from.

He was nothing like many would expect a small-town police chief to be. When he arrived on scene, Dev told her that Gibson had previously served in the Portland Police Bureau, had risen to the level of lieutenant at a young age, and had a promising career there. But then his son had succumbed to serious allergies and needed to move out of a big city to an area with cleaner air. So when the chief's position had opened in Boulder Lake, the family moved for the job.

He rested his hands on the desk, casually, but the tightening of his eyes belied the relaxed posture. "I'll get to the Main Street shooting in a minute, but I'd like to discuss the one in Portland first. Why would someone be trying to kill you, Ms. Pearce?"

"Please call me Kinsley," she said for like the fourth time, but he'd ignored her requests and insisted on the formality.

He didn't respond verbally, but watched her, his eyes dark and probing, as if he thought he could push her along to answer.

Okay, fine.

She gave up and would make sure to keep things formal between them, too. "As I told you several times already, I don't know unless it's related to my work. Maybe someone I found negligent in their job has it out for me. My findings could even be the reason they went to prison. Or maybe they were just fined. Perhaps they lost their license. I suppose any of these things could've caused them to want to seek revenge."

He leaned forward. "Then, before I let you go today, you'll write down the names and contact information for these people."

Impossible. "I can give you a name or maybe two off the top of my head, but I need my computer to make a complete list. It holds all of my work files, and I can refresh my memory on older investigations."

His right eyebrow rose. "So you think this might not be a recent event?"

She shrugged. "I can only think of one person right now. Those findings would be from an older investigation, but he's still in prison."

The chief tilted his head and rested on the corner of the desk. "I would think you'd remember anyone who threatened you."

"You'd think so, but I get a lot of offhand comments. On the surface they sound like threats but aren't really meant as threats. Just a person spouting off. You probably get comments like that, too, but the person doesn't actually mean it."

He nodded. "Happens all the time when we arrest someone. Very few ever follow through. They're just speaking out in anger at the moment."

"Exactly." She punched a fist into her palm to emphasize her point. "But if I can review my files, I can provide a list of people who made those offhand comments."

He tapped a finger on the desk, starting slowly and ramping up speed. "Wouldn't you have reported those people to your supervisor?"

"No. I mean, I don't have a supervisor. I'm a contract worker. Even so, I've never had anyone actually act out against me. Guess I've never believed any of them." Memories of some of the more forceful comments raced through her brain. "Some were more strongly issued than others, and I can segregate those into a separate list."

He gave a sharp nod and stood. "When can you pick up the computer?"

She'd like to say she would drive back to Portland to get it right after she finished this interview, but she was fairly certain Dev wouldn't allow her to return to her apartment. He would insist on picking it up himself, or if he wasn't willing to leave her alone, he would send someone else from his team. She'd just promised herself that when it came to her safety, she wouldn't go against his wishes again, and she was at the mercy of his schedule.

Hoping the grilling was done, she eased to the edge of the chair. "I don't have a vehicle. Dev drove me here, and I'll have to check with him on his schedule."

"We can do that right now." The chief spun and went to the door. "Graham, in here. Now."

Solid footfalls crossed the floor and disturbed the quiet that had descended since the shooting ended. Dev soon appeared in the doorway, his gaze immediately racing to search her face. She smiled to waylay his concern. Concern perhaps mixed with caring for her that went deeper than she'd first thought.

Oh, man. Could he have similar feelings to her own but had been holding back for some reason?

Get a grip. Him having feelings for you is just a pipe dream.

Something she wanted to be true but wasn't.

The chief cleared his throat, bringing her thoughts crashing back to reality. He explained their situation, his focus riveted to Dev. "When will you be able to drive Ms. Pearce to her place to retrieve her computer?"

Dev scratched his head. "I don't think it's a good idea for Kinsley to go back to her apartment. I can arrange for the computer to be picked up."

He glanced at her, and she nodded her acceptance.

He let out a little breath. Right. He would expect her to argue with him, and why wouldn't he? She'd been arguing with him since the moment they'd laid eyes on each other again.

The chief planted his dangling foot on the floor, the loud thump reverberating in the small space. "One more thing before I let you go. How about Louis Luongo? Was he ever the subject of one of your investigations?"

"Yikes, that guy? The wife killer?" She glanced at Dev, who didn't seem at all surprised by this question. Had the chief told him something that he hadn't shared with her? If so, was Dev keeping other things from her? "Don't tell me you think he's connected to this."

"Right before the shooting, the chief told me that Luongo owns the boat he saw last night." The pitch of Dev's voice jumped up. "He's looking to buy a house on the lake, and I was going to ask you about him, but then shots were fired."

One of the last guys she wanted to talk about. "I investigated him a few times, but it's probably just a coincidence that he was in town."

"I don't believe in coincidences." Dev curled his fingers into fists.

"I don't either," the chief said. "Did you find anything that could be used to bring charges against him?"

"Nothing concrete, pardon my pun." She wrinkled her nose. "And let me tell you, one of the investigations was near the time of his arrest for killing his wife, and the DA pressured me to find anything to keep him behind bars. I did my very best, but besides a lot of hearsay and rumors, there just wasn't enough evidence to bring any charges."

"And knowing you," Dev said, "you did your very best to prove it."

"I did."

"Did he ever threaten you?" the chief asked.

"Trust me," she said, "if this guy had threatened me, I would've reported it. I would've done anything to help keep him behind bars until they could figure out if he killed his wife. I still think he got away with murder."

"As do most people." The chief frowned. "But it's not over. The detective is still working the case in his free time. I'll contact him to see if he has any thoughts on Luongo's relationship to the shooting, and see if I can chase down an alibi for the time of the shootings."

"The sooner the better, as far as I'm concerned," Dev said. "So take my statement, and you can get out of here to see if the creep has an alibi."

"If you'd like to use the office, I can go out front," Kinsley offered.

"Stay here," Dev said. "I mean, please, stay here. It's safer without windows."

A heavy feeling settled in her stomach. "You don't really expect the shooter to still be here, do you?"

63

"It's possible," the chief said, taking her attention from Dev. "Criminals often like to hang around to see the chaos they caused, even at the risk of being caught. Which is why my officers are canvassing out front and talking to anyone they don't recognize."

She clasped her fingers together on the top of the desk to stop the trembling that wouldn't seem to leave her body. She had to face facts now. Even with police presence, she wasn't safe. Anywhere.

Not anywhere at all.

6

_____

Kinsley exited through the back door of the T-shirt shop, Dev's hand on her elbow. Sharp winds carrying caustic smoke slapped her in the face, and she was greeted by several men she didn't recognize. Dev had told her his Shadow Lake Survival team had arrived to help escort her to the car. She didn't expect such rugged and forceful men, but why not? They taught people how to survive in the wilderness, and she would imagine that meant they would need to be in shape to survive on their own.

They formed an impenetrable line from the building exit to the back door of an SUV. A second SUV had parked behind this one, and Jada was in its back seat while another guy sat behind the wheel. The remaining men had their weapons drawn, and their gazes constantly roved around the area.

Looking for the shooter? Most likely.

She slowed to rub her sweaty palms against her thighs, but Dev urged her forward and into the back seat.

As soon as he closed the door behind her, the men broke their line. The first guy slid in beside her. Colin, Dev and Jada's brother, who looked very much like Dev minus some facial hair. The next two men, who she thought might be brothers, took the front seat.

"Get us on the road, Reid," Dev said.

The eldest of the group, a man with extremely dark hair, glanced back from the driver's seat. "On it."

Dev looked at her. "We're headed to the Shadow Lake Survival compound, but we'll take a roundabout route to be sure we're not followed." He bit down on his lip and sat back but kept searching the area.

His rigid body language told her to hold off on conversation. She took in the scenery as they whipped out of town and into the countryside. Reid soon had them on the highway at cruising speed, but all of the men continued to check out their windows and mirrors.

Dev glanced at her. "You and Jada will stay at our cabin, and I'll have someone go to the campground to pick up your things."

She still didn't like him making decisions for her, but she knew this was the right decision, so she gave him a reassuring smile. "Sounds good, if it's not inconvenient."

"Your safety comes first, and that could never be inconvenient." He nodded at the man behind the wheel. "That's Reid Maddox driving us, and his brother Ryan in the front seat. Along with their brother Russ, who's the local sheriff, they own Shadow Lake Survival and the property that it sits on."

"Good to meet you, Kinsley." Reid glanced in the mirror and gave her a quick smile before looking back at the road.

"Ditto." Ryan angled between the seats and gave her a beaming smile. "Even if it is under such difficult circumstances. Hopefully, we can improve that for you."

She returned his infectious smile. "I very much appreciate any help you're willing to give."

"Don't mention it," Reid said. "We're glad to help. And

on that subject, Dev, I rescheduled your and Colin's classes, so you're both free all week. I'll try to free up team members as you need them too. If this isn't resolved by the weekend, we can reconsider the schedule again."

A week? Or even more? No. Kinsley wanted it wrapped up in a few days. That would give her and Jada time to move back to the campground and still have that reunion they'd planned.

"Thanks, man," Dev said.

"No worries." Reid looked in the mirror. "If I were in your position, you'd do the same for me."

Dev gave a thumbs up, then leaned across Kinsley to give his brother a punch to the knee. "I live with Colin. You'll probably get sick of him when you stay with us."

She glanced at Colin to see if he was bothered by Dev's comment, but he just rolled his eyes. "I think what you'll soon remember is that I'm the older, wiser brother, and this bozo doesn't know what he's talking about."

Dev laughed. Oh, good. Some lighthearted banter in this very tense situation. Likely what they were going for.

"Besides," Colin said. "I think you'll find that our mother is the wisest of all, and she'll set us all straight if we're on the wrong path. Of course, Jada always tries. At least when she's around, which isn't often these days."

"It's nice of you to visit, Kinsley," Dev said. "That means we get to see Jada. Otherwise, she might not have arranged to take leave and come back here."

"I never saw that coming, did you?" Kinsley glanced between the two men. "I mean, Jada going into the Navy right out of high school. She never even talked about it when we were growing up, and then, boom. She comes to school one day and says she enlisted."

"It was a total surprise to our family too." Colin frowned. "But Mom finally got her to admit that she was worried about all of the uprisings and protests in our country and across the globe. She wanted to be part of the solution and not part of the problem."

Jada had shared last night about her love of being in the Navy. Her friend appeared to be very happy with her choice. "It seems to suit her."

"Like Dev said, she likes it so much she rarely comes home," Colin said. "But I think if she didn't have this trip planned to see you, she might've checked up on Mom."

Sandy? Just how badly was she really doing if it brought Jada home? Kinsley didn't know what to think. "I know Jada's worried about her."

"I'd like to say Mom's out of the woods," Colin said. "But time will tell if these meds keep working and she feels well enough to move back home."

They fell silent, and she offered a prayer for Sandy. Kinsley already prayed for her every day, but no one had told her that Sandy was doing as poorly as she had been. Kinsley couldn't wait to see her in person. Not only because she loved her like a second mother, but to make her own assessment of the very special woman's health.

Dev sat forward to peer intently at his brother. "I need you to put your computer genius to work and see what you can find out about Louis Luongo."

"Wait, what?" Wide-eyed, Colin asked, "What in the world do you want me to look into him for?"

Dev glanced at Kinsley. "As a former FBI agent, Colin's like most law enforcement officers and is very familiar with Luongo." He shifted to look at his brother again and explained Luongo's potential connection to Kinsley. "I don't think it's connected, but any time a killer moves into your neighborhood, you have to consider him for major crimes committed in the area."

"That's a name I hoped to never hear again." Colin

rubbed a hand over his face. "He's a slippery dude, and I don't like the thought of him anywhere near any of us."

"So look him up," Dev said. "See what you can find out. Maybe you can learn something that will at the very least stop him from buying property here."

"I'll write a few algorithms and see what I can find."

"Since Colin served in IT in the FBI, he has mad computer skills," Dev told Kinsley. "Hopefully he can give us information to go on. He can also help with your computer if we run into issues with it."

"Once we retrieve it," she said.

"Once *I* retrieve it." Dev gave her a pointed look. "You do understand why I can't have you go to your apartment to pick it up, don't you?"

She nodded. "What do you suggest I do now?"

"We get you settled at the cabin. My teammates, who all have law enforcement or military experience, will provide security for you, and Colin and I'll pick up your computer."

He was going to leave her behind? Really?

No. She didn't like that. Not at all. Not only for his safety, but she didn't like the idea that he would be leaving her. She felt safer with him nearby. But why? Sounded like his team had the capability to keep her safe, so what was her real reason behind wanting Dev at her side? Was she letting that teenage crush take over? Was it more than a crush? Did she have feelings for him? Real, legit, grown-up feelings?

All good questions, but an even bigger one was, if so, what was she going to do about it?

Dev had called his mother to tell her to expect Jada and Kinsley. He knew she would be waiting at the door for them, and she was. In fact, she hobbled down the steps with her cane, tossed it to the ground, and threw her arms out to draw Jada close. "Oh, sweetheart. I'm so glad to have you home."

"I'm glad to see you too, Mom, but you don't need to strangle me." Jada laughed and pushed back.

His mother turned her sights on Kinsley and dragged her into a hug as well. "And you, sweetheart. It's been far too long since I've seen you."

"I'm sorry about that," Kinsley said, but didn't withdraw from the hug as Jada had done.

In fact, she slid even closer. Maybe she needed reassuring after the shooting in town. Or maybe she just missed his mother, who he knew after all the time that Kinsley spent with their family, she thought of like a second mother.

They finally split apart.

His mother linked arms with both women and turned to the door. "Well, how about not making it such a long time before I see you again?"

They both muttered promises to make sure not as much time passed before they returned. Question was, could either one fulfill their promise?

Dev retrieved the cane and followed the trio up the stairs. Reid and Ryan remained outside as they'd agreed upon earlier, and Colin would go with Dev to the campground to pick up Jada's and Kinsley's belongings. Software on Reid's phone would alert him to any activity at the gate, and the Maddox brothers would form the first line of defense against any intruder.

Confident the cabin was secure for now, Dev stepped inside to a place in serious need of remodeling. A tangy scent oozed from the attached kitchen. The lunch they were late for. He was thankful his mom could prepare the meal, but he needed to keep an eye on her so she didn't wear herself out during Jada and Kinsley's visit.

This large, three-bedroom cabin belonged to the Maddox brothers and their business. The rooms were over-loaded with fishing décor from a time when the cabin was rented out as part of the family resort. After the resort closed, Russ moved in but only updated the mattresses and living room furniture. Then he got married and moved into Sydney's newly built townhouse.

His mom sat on the sofa, with Jada and Kinsley flanking her. Brooklyn, Colin's fiancée, sat in an easy chair smiling at the other women. She'd once been paid to care for his mother, but had recently gone back to her job as a white hat hacker. Still, she'd really connected with their mom and spent a good part of her day tending to her needs, but then went home to a nearby rental house at night.

Colin closed the door and stepped into the room. Brooklyn shot to her feet and raced to join him behind the sofa. He gave a wide smile and opened his arms. She slipped into them, and he held her close, kissing the top of her head. It warmed Dev's heart to see his brother so happy. Maybe Dev should listen to Colin's earlier advice about Kinsley.

He leaned against the wall-to-wall stone fireplace, with its thick wooden mantle and big taxidermy salmon mounted above. The monstrosity took center stage in the family room. He watched the women chatter, one stepping on the other's words, falling into their old ways of easiness with each other.

He wanted to head to the campground to retrieve their things, then get on his way to Portland for the computer, but he hated to interrupt the fun they were having.

His mother clutched Kinsley's hands. "Now tell me, who would want to be shooting at you? I was shocked to hear what happened in town and in that parking lot in Portland."

Kinsley's smile evaporated. "I don't exactly know who it

could be, but I think it's someone I investigated and found something illegal in their work."

"We need to get started on figuring out who it is," Dev said, as this was the perfect opportunity to interrupt. "First, I'm going to run over to the campground to pick up their possessions, then a trip to Portland to get Kinsley's computer. Maybe it'll contain information to give us something to go on."

"Well, let's hope there *is* something," his mother said. "And until you figure this out, promise me you'll be right by Kinsley's side, protecting her."

"I will be. Except this quick trip to the campground and to Portland."

His mother's eyebrows shot up. "Can't you send someone else to get the computer?"

"Trust me," he said. "I've considered that, and I'd rather be here. But if I get a look around Kinsley's place, I might see something else that could be helpful."

"Couldn't Reid or Ryan do the same thing?" Brooklyn asked.

"I take it you met Kinsley and know what's going on," Dev said.

"I did, while we were waiting for you to come inside."

Dev nodded. "I could send someone else, but I know her, and I think that makes me the best person for the job."

"I agree." Kinsley sat up straight. "I can't think of what he could find that would help, but I think I'm still in shock from another shooting, and you never know what I'm forgetting."

"Then we're all set, and I'll be going," Dev said, wanting to move on. "Now, what about your things at the campground? Is there anything I need to know before I grab them?"

Kinsley tilted her head. "Just don't forget to pack up the

box of memories I brought along. Don't forget a single thing."

"Especially not the lamp." Jada giggled and looked at her mother. "Did you know Kinsley kept one of those ugly lamps you got rid of when you redecorated the cabin?"

His mother swiveled toward Kinsley. "What on earth would you want one of those old things for?"

Kinsley blushed. "It's not that I specifically wanted a lamp, but when you remodeled the cabins, you were getting rid of everything that made the Bluebird our special place. The lamp was the smallest thing you were tossing out. So I took one for a memory of all the fun times Jada and I had in that cabin."

"Isn't that the sweetest thing?" His mother patted Kinsley's knee. "You always were one to cherish memories."

Kinsley covered her hand with her own. "I loved my time with your family. I don't know what I would've done growing up without you all. I learned so much from you about how a real family acted, and I'll forever be grateful for that."

"It's a joy to have you as part of our family, and I hope that will continue."

"I hope that never changes." Kinsley drew her into a hug, then released her to look at Dev. "Other than that, I never unpacked much, so please just throw whatever I have out into my suitcase."

"Same," Jada said.

He nodded. "Reid and Ryan will be outside. If they see any sign of danger, they'll let you know. Please do whatever they instruct you to do without question." Dev locked gazes with Kinsley. "Okay?"

"Sure."

He eyed his sister. "You too, Jada."

She waved her hand. "Don't worry about me, I can take care of myself."

"That kind of statement is exactly what I'm worried about." Dev fixed his sister in his sights. "I know you're better trained than Kinsley, but you're not an expert in personal protection. So please listen to the guys."

"Don't worry, I will." She turned to his mother. "Now, what's that wonderful smell coming from the kitchen?"

"Beef stew in the Crock-Pot. Brooklyn made it for dinner." She smiled up at Brooklyn, her love for Colin's fiancée evident in her expression. "I'd be glad to make lunch now."

"Now, Mom." Dev took a step closer to her. "I know you like to spoil all of us, but I won't leave until you promise not to wait on these two. They can help with the cooking and chores around here."

"I'm kind of out of practice on the cooking front," Jada said. "We have our own KP staff on the ships."

"I'm pretty sure you could still figure out how to make our favorite marshmallow fluff and bacon sandwich." Kinsley laughed and sat forward. "Just point me to the food, and I'll be glad to make lunch for all, and I promise not to make the marshmallow sandwich."

"I can show you around," Brooklyn said. "But then I have to get back home and get to work."

"You rest, Sandy, and I'll go raid the refrigerator with Brooklyn while you and Jada catch up." Kinsley crossed the room to slip her arm into Brooklyn's. "You'll have to tell me all about what you do for a living while you show me the ropes in the kitchen."

"I'm a white hat hacker." Brooklyn led Kinsley toward a small cut-out on the back wall that connected the kitchen to the living area.

"That sounds fascinating," Kinsley said. "I'd love to hear more, and you'll also have to tell me how you met Colin."

Dev loved how easily she fit with his family, even with Brooklyn, who'd only been with them a few months. With Kinsley settled, he should go, but he was reluctant to leave. A round trip to the campground with her things should only take an hour or so, and he'd be right back here with her.

Maybe he needed more assurances that she really would listen to the Maddox brothers if danger came to their doorstep. Because if their recent trip into town taught him anything, it reinforced that they could be surprised by a crazed shooter when they least expected him, and her life could be snuffed out at a moment's notice.

7

At Kinsley's studio apartment in an historical section of Portland, Dev shoved the front door wide open and took in the troubling scene inside. "Whoa!"

Colin pushed past him into the main living area. "What in the world do we have here?"

Dev remained rooted in place. Shocked. Surprised. He'd expected to find Kinsley's tiny place neat. She'd always been orderly. Came from her mother's demands, the one thing she hadn't even considered rebelling against back in the day. But this was more than messy. Her place had been trashed.

Colin turned to Dev, a grim look in his eyes. "What do you think happened here?"

Dev ran a hand over his face, hoping when he removed it the chaos in front of him would have disappeared. No such luck. "Someone trashed the place looking for something."

Someone had jerked out the drawers of Kinsley's desk in the corner and dumped the contents on the floor. Oddly, the laptop remained in place on the desktop. The matching bookshelf had been emptied, leaving three-ring binders and reference books lying on the wood floor.

The intruder had slit open her daybed's mattress covering and upended the mattress, leaving its pale gray comforter in a crumpled heap next to a nightstand holding cosmetics in a tray. The items in the nightstand's three drawers were discarded on the floor, too, and a small coffee table devoid of any decoration sat in front of it undisturbed.

Colin gripped the back of his neck with both hands. "How did they get in here?"

Dev looked at the deadbolt and the frame. "This is intact." He took a closer look at the lock. "Scratches on the deadbolt. Lock could've been picked."

Colin met his gaze. "If so, we could be looking at an experienced criminal. Not only a shooter, but someone who has the means to gain entry to places they shouldn't go."

Dev's mouth went dry, and he swallowed the cottony feeling away. "Makes him more dangerous than we thought."

Colin turned his attention to the apartment. "Not many things to look through here. Really just the desk and book-shelf in the corner."

"Agreed," Dev said, taking in the last of the studio apartment.

A simple kitchen with just the basics a single person would need to get by filled the back wall. All the cabinet doors had been flung open and the contents spilled on the floor. A door led off to the left. A quick glance inside confirmed it was the bathroom, and the small vanity's contents lay scattered over the black and white vintage tile floor.

Dev turned. "I have gloves in my SUV. Can you grab them?"

"Be right back." Colin took off out the door, and Dev stared across the room. They needed to look at items from the bookshelf. The desk too. They could be the reason for the break-in.

Colin returned and handed Dev a pair of disposable gloves on his way into the room.

Dev slipped on the gloves and joined Colin in the corner but didn't know which item to start with. "Kinsley didn't make this mess. That's for sure."

Colin put on his gloves. "I always liked that she was neat and once hoped, since you spent so much time with her, you would pick up on it. Sharing a room with you was a challenge."

Dev couldn't argue. He could be a real slob if he wasn't careful, where Colin liked things neater. "You're not the only one who had a challenge. The line of masking tape you rolled out along the middle of the floor was a real pain.

"But you still didn't keep your things on the other side of the line."

He held his brother's gaze. "This is more than someone letting their stuff fall over a ridiculous tape line."

Colin gave a disgusted snort. "The tape was necessary for my sanity."

"Hey, man. I tried and failed. What more can I say?" He couldn't stand around wasting time any longer. He had to accept that Kinsley's place had been defiled by someone and commit to a course of action to find that someone.

He picked up the closest three-inch binder. A large typed label stating the year was affixed to the front. Inside, labeled divider tabs held names of what he assumed were investigations.

"Kinsley said all of the investigative information is on her computer. If all of these binders contain investigation details we shouldn't need them." Dev moved to the next book, then the next, and the next, each one labeled with the year and holding investigation materials neatly ordered.

The plethora of photos on the pages were more interesting than he expected. She'd included not only pictures for construction sites or of the products, but of people involved in the investigation as well as their background information printed from the internet.

He looked at his brother. "If this break-in is related to the investigations Kinsley was involved in, and the intruder wanted the info, you'd think some of these files would be missing."

"Makes sense." Colin sorted through a fistful of materials from the floor. "We should bring the binders back to the cabin. We can cross-reference them to the computer files in case one or more of them are missing."

Dev liked where this was going. "Perhaps taken by our suspect and giving us his name."

"Or not." Colin narrowed his eyes. "There's another way to look at it. Whoever trashed this place was obviously looking for something smaller than these binders. If not, they wouldn't have emptied all the little drawers and cabinets."

What if Colin was right? He could be, but it was too early to tell. "Maybe trashing the whole apartment was to make us think they weren't looking for the binders and throwing us off their scent."

Colin tapped the laptop in front of him. "Then if they wanted their file, wouldn't they have taken this too?"

Dev hadn't thought of that, but Colin had a valid point. "You could be right. But we'll still take these binders."

"And we should have Kinsley go through the place to see if anything is missing."

Her. Here? No way. Dev's heartbeat picked up. "Good plan, but I don't want her coming here."

"I don't either, but she might have to. The whole team should be able to ensure her safety."

"That will be Plan B. First, I'll take detailed pictures of every inch of this place, and she can review them from the safety of our cabin." Dev reached into his pocket for his phone.

"And while you've got that out, maybe you should give Kinsley a call and tell her about this. Ask her what she might think someone would want to steal here."

"No!" Unease settled in Dev's heart. "It isn't the kind of information I'll give her over the phone. It'll be bad enough telling her in person."

Colin studied him, his eyes assessing in the exact older brother way as when Dev had done something wrong as a kid. "You've got it bad, man. Real bad."

Dev ignored him and finished taking pictures.

Colin stood. "We should call the police."

The right thing to do, but that didn't mean Dev would do it. Though, in his deputy days, he would've crucified someone who'd discovered a break-in and didn't report it right away. "You know the person closest to the victim is frequently the person who perpetrated the crime."

"And your point is?"

"The responding officer will point their attention at us, wasting valuable time. Besides, Kinsley might not want this reported at all, and as the leaseholder, it's her decision."

"You're right. But if she agrees, it would be good if the police took this seriously and didn't simply file a report and forget about it. The more people looking into it the better."

His brother had a point. "I can call the detective from the parking lot shooting and explain why we think this is related to our shooter."

Colin gave a vigorous nod. "That could help get them onboard."

"Then let's grab these binders and head back to the cabin so Kinsley can decide what she wants to do." He picked up the nearest stack to make his way through the mess to the door.

His thoughts went back to Colin's comment. Dev knew exactly what he'd been talking about when he said Dev had it bad. His feelings for Kinsley. Plain and simple. If his emotions were that obvious to his brother, was Dev coming across equally as obvious to her?

If so, he needed to concentrate on the drive home to find a way to mask them. No way he wanted to add to her unease. Not ever, but especially not when he broke the difficult news that her personal world and sanctuary had been violated by an unknown foe who could still be gunning for her.

Kinsley tried to concentrate on unpacking the box of memories and sharing and laughing with Jada and Sandy over each item. But she couldn't. She kept glancing at the clock on the fireplace mantle. Dev and Colin were taking much longer to get back than planned. He'd texted to say they were on their way, but gave no reason for the delay. Of course her mind went to all kinds of difficulties they might've run into.

Things like the shooter appearing and firing at them. Or maybe they'd gone in pursuit of the shooter. Or had something else life-threatening occurred?

She just couldn't seem to let go of her worry for him.

Sandy took her hand. "When Dev was a deputy and Colin in the FBI, I worried for their safety all the time. But you know what? My worry did no good. It just made things more difficult for me. I should've simply trusted God to watch over my sons."

She was picking up on Kinsley's worry. She supposed

she hadn't hidden it very well, but she didn't want to acknowledge it out loud, so she didn't say anything at all.

Sandy squeezed her hand. "Let's go ahead and pray for them now. Then let it go and enjoy looking at all of these memories. Well, maybe except for that hideous lamp." She laughed.

Kinsley glanced at the lamp with beige ceramic ribs and orange and black ceramic feathers circling the middle. It had an equally unattractive, large drum shade in a worn and fraying burlap-looking fabric. She had to agree that the lamp was gaudy by today's design standards, but she remembered flicking the light off at night and telling stories with Jada in the dark, each with a flashlight in their hands. She couldn't imagine going back to the cabin right now with the lights out.

She couldn't imagine going back there at all until the shooter targeting her was apprehended. Targeting her. Not just her. Her friends now, too.

Which brought her back to wondering if Dev and Colin had come under attack.

"Come on, child," Sandy said. "Focus now and let's pray."

Sandy gripped her hand tightly and led the three of them in a prayer for the men's safety. And for Kinsley's and Jada's safety, too. Kinsley added Sandy's name at the end for good measure.

Sandy clutched her shirt at the chest. "You can't think that I am in danger too."

She didn't want to tell the truth and worry Sandy, but she wouldn't sugarcoat it. "I think anyone who is near me is in danger. So that would include you and all the men who are trying to protect me."

"I agree with her, Mom," Jada said. "Which means you need to stay in the house unless someone else is with you."

"Well, of course if you think that's what I need to do, then that's what I'll do." She skimmed her hand over her hair as if to straighten it when every piece of the chin-length cut was already in perfect order.

This was her go-to move when she was extremely stressed, adding to Kinsley's worry.

No. Let it go. Let God take over. He'll protect everyone. He just has to.

"Look at this." Jada lifted out of the box a pair of cropped T-shirts displaying graphics of the Backstreet Boys. "The best boy band ever."

"We had such terrible crushes on them." Kinsley took her shirt and held it up against her chest. It featured Kevin Richardson, and Jada's shirt held a picture of Nick Carter.

Jada raised an eyebrow. "Among other people."

Kinsley wasn't sure who she was referring to, but maybe Jada had known about her secret crush on Dev.

"I don't know." Kinsley hugged her shirt against her chest. "There was no one like Kevin. He was so dreamy."

Kinsley laughed, and Jada joined in.

Sandy snickered. "All I know is if I had to hear any of their records one more time, I might've lost my sanity."

"Was it that bad?" Jada asked.

"Worse," Sandy said. "I thought when they played a concert in Portland, and we couldn't get tickets, the two of you might take off on your own and try to get backstage."

Kinsley glanced at Jada and then back at Sandy. "We talked about it."

"I knew it!" Sandy pumped her fist.

Kinsley got into the fun of things and slipped on her T-shirt over her blouse, then pointed at Kevin's picture. "Do you blame us? Just look at him. A dreamier teenage heart-throb never existed. I was so-o-o in love with him."

She started to twirl like a lovesick teenager and found

the front door had silently opened. Dev held the handle and stared at her, a question in his eyes.

She pointed at her shirt. "Kevin Richardson. The Backstreet Boys. My teenage crush."

He tightened his jaw. "Glad you're having fun."

He was upset about something. Did he really think they shouldn't be having fun while he was working on her behalf? Or did her teenage crush on Kevin bother him? Why would he care about that silly crush? He wouldn't. Short of reading his mind or asking him about it, she wouldn't get an answer. Best to just move on.

"Just trying to pass the time until you got back," she said, hoping to placate him. "You were gone for so long, I was worried. Did you run into trouble?"

He grimaced. "We should sit down and talk about that."

"That doesn't sound good." She quickly removed her T-shirt, taking care not to damage it. "Did someone get hurt?"

"No, we're both fine." He gestured at the sofa. "Go ahead and take a seat so we can talk."

His dire tone completely erased her good mood. Whatever Dev had to say wasn't going to be good news for sure. Part of her wished he would just rip the Band-Aid off and come out with it. The other part of her, the biggest part of her, didn't want to hear the news. Not at all.

8

Dev had destroyed Kinsley's fun. Jada's and his mother's, too, if the defeated looks on their faces told him anything. He didn't want to put an end to their joy, but he also foolishly didn't like how Kinsley was reacting to the guy on her T-shirt. Dev had hoped he'd been her teenage crush, but clearly not.

Stupid thoughts. Crazy crushes didn't matter. Not one bit. Especially right now, when he had difficult news to deliver to her. He should just come right out with it. But after everything that had recently happened, he couldn't bear to hurt her even more.

He leaned against the fireplace and looked at Colin, hoping he would take the hint and share the news of the break-in. But Colin simply shrugged and sat in an easy chair across from the others, looking expectantly up at him.

Dev pushed off the fireplace. Shoved his hands in his pockets. Made eye contact with Kinsley.

"Just say it," she blurted out. "Waiting is even more difficult."

"Someone broke into your apartment and trashed the

place." He wanted to look away but kept his focus on her face to gauge her reaction.

She gasped and blinked up at him, a vacant look clouding her eyes. "What exactly do you mean by trashed?"

He didn't want to share anything about the break-in, but no matter how much he wanted to spare her, she deserved to hear the details and would soon see the mess in his photos. "They emptied all of your kitchen cabinets and threw all of the items from your desk, bookshelf, and nightstand onto the floor. They also slit open your mattress."

Jada reached for Kinsley's hand, but she jumped to her feet and paced to the front window. She immediately spun and walked back, her eyes now glossy with tears. She opened her mouth to say something, but rushed back to the window. She rested her forehead on the glass, and her shoulders started to shake.

Jada hurried across the room to her and put her arm around her best friend's shoulder. Thankfully Dev's sister acted before he did the same thing and gave away his feelings.

"What do you think they were looking for?" his mother asked.

"We're not sure," Colin said. "At first we thought they wanted the records from the binders regarding their investigations, but then it dawned on us that they were looking in smaller places. Places where binders wouldn't fit. Makes me think they were looking for something else."

Kinsley spun, freeing herself from Jada's arm, and marched across the room. She planted her hands on her hips and her feet on the floor. Tears ran down her cheeks, but she looked angry now, not tearful. "Small, large, whatever. What could they have been looking for?"

"That's what we were hoping you could help us with," Dev said.

"I should go there to see if anything is missing."

Dev had expected her to say that, but he hadn't formulated a solid response. "I'd rather not take you there if we can avoid it. I took pictures of the entire place, and we brought the binders. You can cross-reference the tabs to your computer to see if an investigation is missing. If so, it could give us a lead to whoever is behind this."

"Then let's not waste any more time talking about it." She marched to the dining room table and sat. "Get my things from the car, and I'll get started."

Dev let out a long breath at her easy cooperation and looked at his brother. "You heard the lady. Let's get out there and grab what we need."

Dev followed his brother out the front door. Colin jogged down the steps to the vehicle, but Dev stopped on the porch to bring Reid and Ryan up to date. "Colin and I'll be inside tonight, but I'm hoping for a protective detail for the exterior. One man should be fine, if anyone is available."

"I'm sure the guys will help out." Reid planted his feet on the worn wood. "I'll arrange a twenty-four-hour duty schedule for the foreseeable future."

Dev couldn't help but be thankful for his boss's accommodating behavior. "Thanks, man. I'll owe you big time."

Reid waved a hand. "You were a big help when Megan was in trouble. I'm the one who owes you." His wife had been stalked by a man from her past, and it took the entire team to bring him to justice.

"Just doing my job as part of the team," Dev said.

"And we're doing the same thing for you," Ryan said. "One for all and all for one and all of that." He laughed. He was the team joker, and they could always count on him to lighten the mood when things got tense.

"Well, thanks anyway," Dev said. "If you could let me

know who's scheduled, that would be great. We'll grab the things we need from my SUV, and then I'll be inside."

Reid gave a sharp nod, and Ryan smiled. Brothers. Not just to each other, but brothers on a team. When Reid opened Shadow Lake Survival, it didn't take long before the business took off faster than he expected. With Russ, a full-time sheriff, and Ryan, a part-time wilderness counselor, he needed additional help and reached out to the guys.

Dev was blessed to be a part of the team. He knew Colin and Micha, the final team member, both felt the same way. They were all doing something they loved in the great outdoors and working for a terrific boss.

He ran down the steps. Colin met him at the bottom, his arms filled with binders. "Just like you to slack off and leave your big brother to do all the work."

"Yeah, that's my plan." He laughed, but the sight of the binders reminded him of the mess at Kinsley's apartment, and his laughter dried up like the desert under the scorching sun.

They had to find something in these binders or her computer to help. They just had to.

Kinsley opened her computer while Dev looked on from across the table. Colin sat at the end, a binder open in front of him, and Jada and Sandy remained in the living room. Kinsley navigated to her spreadsheet listing every investigation she'd participated in since she'd started freelancing as a forensic engineer. She investigated things like accidents, product failures, components, material or structural issues, or even environmental contamination, but her specialty was building failures.

In college, she'd hoped to find a company she could work for and not have to strike out on her own, but the assignments for a forensic engineer in a single city were too infrequent to provide a full-time job. As a result, zero companies employed them full-time in the Portland area or in any other major city in Oregon. She wasn't willing to move out of her home state to a more populus city where she might have a chance at employment with a company, so she had to go it alone and branch out to nearby states and travel frequently.

So even if Dev declared his love for her and asked her to marry him—a pipe dream for sure—she had to live close to an airport, and there wasn't a commercial airport nearby. Or he would have to give up his job and move to Portland, which she would never ask him to do.

Did it even matter? There was no proposal. Not even a hint of wanting a relationship with her, and she wouldn't break her promise to Jada.

Dev stood and cleared his throat. "Before we get started, you need to decide if you want to report the break-in to the police."

Did she? She didn't have a clue. "I guess I need to know what the benefits are to doing so."

"Normally I'd say they would send out a forensic team to process your apartment." Dev planted his hands on his hips. "But since nothing appears to be taken, at least nothing of great value, I don't think they would authorize those resources unless we can prove it's tied to the shooting. Otherwise, their resources are stretched far too thin to help."

Colin looked up. "But if there's any damage done, like the way they annihilated your mattress, and you want to file for insurance, you would need a police report."

"Another reason," Dev said. "Since we're former law enforcement officers, it's possible we could persuade them to do a more thorough investigation."

All good points, but did any of them actually help? She really didn't know what to do. She didn't want the hassle of having to meet a police officer at her place to review the break-in, but then these guys had good points about why she should do it.

But what about the opposite? "And reasons I shouldn't do it?"

Dev shoved his hands into his pockets. "The biggest downside is that our shooter could be keeping eyes on the property in case you return. Just showing up there could threaten your life."

She swallowed. Once. Twice. Three times. Got control. She wouldn't let this overwhelm her. "Wouldn't it be possible for you or Colin to meet the police instead?"

"No," Dev said, his tone lacking all emotion. "The officer would request to speak to the actual victim. No matter what the reporter of the crime—me or Colin or both—says, we'll either be a suspect or unable to answer completely and accurately as to any missing items. This wouldn't be negotiable."

His voice hardened as he spoke, leaving her even more uncertain. "Do you think it would be safe for me to go there?"

He didn't answer immediately but jerked his hands from his pockets and planted them on the table with a thud. "One hundred percent safe? No. I'm confident that our team can escort you there and provide the best protection possible, but there's always a risk to your safety."

She believed they would protect her, but one stray bullet they couldn't defend against was all it took to kill her. So, should she risk going?

Just the thought of it left her mentally numb, and she couldn't make a decision right now. "I guess the first thing I need to do is look at the pictures you took. Maybe I can identify something that was stolen. That could help make my decision."

Dev got out his phone and swiped the screen. "Viewing them on a bigger screen could help you not miss anything. I'll transfer them to your computer."

"Perfect." She sat back and watched thirty photos appear in her download folder. She didn't waste any time, but opened the first one.

"Oh, wow!" Her heart sank, and she clutched the external mouse with as much force as she could muster to keep from crying out in more distress.

Her small living area was in a complete state of disarray, exceeding Dev's description of the situation. Sure, he'd told her about the mess, but seeing it in a photo was a whole other thing. Seeing her possessions—even if a lot of them were simply work files—touched by a stranger in the privacy of her home violated every sense of safety and security that her apartment had previously brought.

Even if they apprehended the person stalking her, could she ever feel safe enough to live there again?

Jada came to stand behind Kinsley and drew in a sharp breath. "Oh wow! I'm so sorry, sweetie. I hate this for you."

"I...I." Kinsley shook her head. "I really didn't think it would hit me this hard."

"Your reaction is normal," Colin said. "It's a violation of your sanctuary."

Jada rested her hands on her shoulders. "So, bros, what are you gonna do about it? You can't let this guy get away with what he's getting away with. There's got to be something more you can do to help her."

Kinsley glanced up at Jada, whose face was

contorted with the kind of anger a best friend would have when her friend was threatened. Jada wasn't worried for her own life right now, which she should be, but she was focusing solely on Kinsley. Kinsley was forever grateful for her friend's deep sense of loyalty and protectiveness.

She rested her hand on Jada's. "They're doing everything they can do. We need to cut them some slack. They want to keep both of us safe and figure it out so we can find this creep."

"You know that's right." Dev clutched the back of the chair in front of him. "If I could stop this, I would in a heartbeat."

Jada sighed. "I know. I'm just getting frustrated."

"Investigations take time," Colin said. "You make forward progress and take a few steps back and make progress again until eventually you *do* find the bad guy, and hopefully he's brought to justice."

"He's right," Kinsley said, trying as much to encourage herself to face this battle as well as help Jada relax. "I can tell you that from experience in my investigations."

"Maybe we could call in forensics experts at the Veritas Center," Dev said. "It's a longshot, but they might be free to process the scene and possibly locate leads."

"Sierra Rice," Kinsley said, not even trying to hide her enthusiasm for the idea when so far they hadn't come up with anything good. "They're one of the premier labs in the country for DNA and criminal forensics. If there's anything to be found, Sierra and her team will find it."

"You're familiar with them, then," Dev said.

She gave a vigorous nod. "When I was getting my engineering degree, I had hoped to work for them and did a summer internship there. But, like most other companies that use forensic engineers, they don't need one full-time, and I've had to settle for working for them on a contract basis."

"So are you comfortable calling Sierra and asking her to process your apartment?" Colin asked.

"Of course," Kinsley said. "But I don't know if I can afford their fees."

"They do pro bono work," Dev said.

"No, I wouldn't feel good about using their budget set aside to help others. I'll just have to figure out a way to pay them." Though it could wipe out the savings she'd worked so hard to build up to buy a house.

Dev met her gaze. "I might be able to help, depending on the cost."

"No." Kinsley held up her hands. "This is my responsibility, and I'll find a way to handle it. I'll call Sierra first thing in the morning, but the best thing I can do right now is get over the shock of this and look through these pictures. Then decide on what to do about the police."

Jada pulled out the chair next to Kinsley. "I'll be right here to help you. I don't know what I'm looking for, but you never know what I might see."

Dev released his grip on the chair. "Do you have a list of investigations on your computer that we can compare to the binders?"

She tapped her screen. "I have a spreadsheet. I'll print a copy for you."

"Of course you do." He grinned.

"You may find my need for organization annoying, but it's going to be quite helpful right now." She sent the file to the networked printer.

"Not annoying." He smiled at her. "Cute."

Colin stuck a finger in his mouth and mocked gagging. "Enough of the flirting. Let's get on with the work."

Flirting? Was Dev flirting with her for real?

Kinsley couldn't tell. He didn't argue the point, so maybe he was. Everyone was looking at her, and heat raced over her face as it had when she was a child, drawing unwanted attention. She bent her head and forced her focus from Dev's potential flirting to her damaged apartment.

"I'll get the spreadsheet and be right back." Dev left the room.

She scrolled through the pictures, looking at every square inch of her floor for possessions that she would likely find in that area and made sure she didn't look up when Dev came back to sit at the table.

She spotted her jewelry box, dumped out, leaving a mound of tangled beads and earrings and a large pendant. "Thankfully, I don't have any expensive jewelry. Mostly just costume pieces. And, of course, I brought the things I value with me in my memory box."

Jada glanced at her. "Like our skeleton necklaces where they can hold hands when together?"

Kinsley clutched Jada's hand. "Tell me you still have yours."

"She does." Sandy stepped into the room with a tray holding a pitcher filled with red liquid and beside it, two Kool-Aid cups, one pink and the other white. "I remember packing it when I moved out of our house at the campground. If you want to reunite the skeletons—I can't imagine that you would, but then again, I never did understand your fascination with them—the boxes are in my storage locker."

Jada got a gleam in her eyes. "Oh, they'll be reunited before the week is out. You can count on that."

Kinsley laughed with her best friend and liked how being with her second family again could make even the horrible pictures in front of her seem not so dire. She could almost believe that God wanted her here with them. But that wasn't really possible for so many reasons.

Sandy poured the red liquid into the white cup and handed it to Kinsley. "Your favorite Kool-Aid flavor. You used to drink it nonstop. When I heard you were coming, I made sure I stocked up."

Kinsley gripped the little handle on the side of the Kool-Aid pitcher-shaped cup with the Kool-Aid man embossed on the front. "And you still have our favorite cups from when we were little."

"Figured I'd keep them for grandchildren. Not that anyone seems to be moving in that direction at this point." Sandy glanced between her children.

Colin looked up from his binder. "Hey, at least I'm engaged. That's more than I can say for these two."

"We should get back to work," Jada said. "And Mom, you should rest instead of waiting on us."

Sandy filled the pink cup and handed it to Jada. "Don't think I'm not onto your diversionary tactics. Just how is your love life lately?"

"Mom!" Jada groaned. "That's a topic for another day."

"Okay," Sandy said, humor in her tone. "Name the day and time, and I'll be there."

"Kinsley and I are going to be really busy. I'll have to get back to you on that." She lifted her small cup of Kool-Aid and drained it.

Sandy shook her head. "You boys want Kool-Aid?"

"Gross," Colin said.

"Ditto," Dev said.

"You don't know what you're missing." Kinsley laughed and looked at the last picture that held the contents of her kitchen cabinets strewn over the floor. With all the traveling her work required, she really didn't cook or entertain often and had few dishes and pots and pans. In fact, her cabinets were pretty empty. Just a few canned goods and some boxes of instant macaroni and cheese, along with her favorite morning granola and coffee pods.

Sandy tsked. "What a mess, but honey, is that really your entire kitchen's contents? What happened to your love of cooking? We spent so much time together in the kitchen."

"I travel a lot, and besides, cooking and baking seems like a lot of work to go through for one person."

"Then maybe we need to have a talk about your love life too." Sandy laughed.

Jada jumped up and took her mother's elbow. "Come on, Mom. I'll help you to the couch so you can rest."

Sandy's laughter deepened, and Kinsley reveled in the sound of it, remembering years of fun with this kind and generous woman. Even though Sandy's health had been suffering, she could still maintain such a cheerful disposition. Kinsley could learn from her second mother. Kinsley didn't have any health issues or day after day of pain and fatigue. She just had a messed up apartment that she had to reorganize. She didn't need to be so upset.

But it wasn't just the mess, was it? The person who ransacked her place also had likely shot at her and seemingly wanted her dead. That wasn't such a simple thing to get over and to maintain a cheerful disposition on.

Move on. Find a lead. So what if she had to think about what had occurred? To keep studying the pictures, or do anything that Dev asked of her? She would do it, and she would do her very best. And that included swallowing her fear until not even a shadow remained, looking at her apartment in person, and filing a police report.

She looked up to find him flipping through one of her large binders. "I didn't see anything missing in the pictures, but I really think I need to go there in person."

He cringed.

"I get it," she said. "Not what you wanted to hear, but I think it's the right thing to do."

"I do, too," he said, his voice strained. "After we do some careful planning."

She pointed at the binder in front of him. "How is your comparison to my list going?"

Colin closed his cover with a loud thump and set it aside. "One down for me, and so far, I haven't found anything out of the ordinary."

Dev opened his mouth to speak, but her phone rang, and she glanced at the name on the screen. "That's odd. It's Ozzy Butler. He's a detective out of Seattle who I worked with a few years ago. Wonder what he wants at this time of night."

Dev locked gazes with her. "One way to find out."

She tapped the answer button on her phone. "Ozzy?"

"Sorry to bother you so late." His unique, raspy voice came over the line. "But I wanted to give you a heads up in case you hadn't heard. Nico Huff was released from prison last week."

"Huff?" She couldn't believe she'd just been talking about him and now here he was, out of prison. Gave far more credence to him being the shooter. "I didn't know. How did you hear about it?"

"I was at the courthouse this morning and ran into one of the guards who oversaw his release. He heard Huff say that he was going to get back at everyone who put him behind bars. You remember his foul mouth, so you know he didn't say it quite that tamely, but you get the picture."

She got it, all right. She'd dealt with him not only through the investigation but through the trial, where he hurled too many expletives her way to count. She could just see the tall, beefy man with a shaved head and fierce-looking eyes glaring down on her, and her heart rate kicked up.

"So you think he's coming after me?" she asked Ozzy. "I mean, do you really think he would take revenge or was he just spouting off?"

Ozzy didn't answer right away, and the silence added to Kinsley's discomfort, but she waited it out by tapping her foot under the table where the others couldn't see her nervousness.

"Despite being a loudmouth," Ozzy finally said, "I honestly don't think the guy who went into prison would try to harm someone. He liked to shoot his mouth off, but I couldn't see him taking any real action."

She let out a relieved breath.

"That said," he continued, "the guard told me Huff had a rough incarceration and was coming out angry and with a giant chip on his shoulder. So I'm not really sure what he'll do. I just wanted to make sure you knew about his release and the threat."

So much for the moment of relief. She tried not to let panic take her voice as the others were watching her carefully. "Do you know where he's living?"

"I took a look at his prison discharge paperwork. He's back in Portland. Living with his mother. I can text you the address if you want it, but I wouldn't recommend you having any contact with him."

"Don't worry," she said. "I'll steer clear of him, but just want to know if a threat did originate, where it might be coming from."

"Then I'll text you the minute we get off the phone. I'll also call a detective buddy at PPB and ask if he can have patrol keep an eye out for him."

She appreciated him contacting the Portland Police

Bureau on her behalf, but that was just the kind of guy he was. Tough, but considerate.

"You should know, though," he said, "it's not unheard of for a felon to give one address to the authorities, then not really live there."

"Really? Do they think they can get away with that?"

"They're willing to take the risk. What guy Huff's age wants to live with his mother? But he needed the address for release."

"That makes sense," she said. "But I sure don't like hearing that he could be living at an undisclosed location."

"Yeah, and if his parole officer goes looking for him, his mother would cover for him, saying that he was staying with her but wasn't home at the time. So just be aware. And take care."

"Thanks, Ozzy, and thanks for calling to warn me." She disconnected and took her time laying her phone back on the table to gather her thoughts before explaining the situation to the others. She took a deep breath and forced herself to look up at them, then shared her conversation.

Dev's eyes narrowed. "The same guy you told me about earlier today, except he's not behind bars anymore."

"Could be nothing," she said to keep the others from getting worked up too. "Ozzy wasn't even sure if Huff would do anything."

Dev slammed his fist on the table. "We can't take any chances. We'll get eyes on him. Have a conversation with him. See where he was during the shooting. We can't be too careful with your life."

She didn't like the thought of Dev or any one of the guys going to see Huff. A tough guy, he was one of those men's men who steamrolled all over women and anyone who got in his way for that matter—not looking back, but taking advantage all along the way. By the time one of his foremen blew the whistle on him, he'd cut so many corners on the apartment building he was constructing that it had to be demolished. It couldn't be fixed and wasn't safe for habitation, yet he planned on finishing the complex and letting innocent renters move into a sure death if the right conditions came in to play.

So yeah, he could be dangerous. Just how dangerous was the question of the hour. And a question they needed to answer soon.

9

The direction the evening had taken left Dev jumpy and jittery. Kinsley's phone call caused him to clench his jaw. Hard. Tight. The muscles constricted, a headache forming, and he wanted to race out the door and get this Huff guy under surveillance.

Let it go. You have to handle this the right way.

He couldn't afford to fly off the handle and make a mistake. No way. Mistakes cost lives. Maybe the life of someone he cared about deeply. That meant not managing his search for Kinsley's suspects alone. Why would he go it alone when he had a highly skilled team on his side who would do everything within their power to come up with the best plan to keep her alive?

He'd immediately called his teammates together for a meeting with Kinsley and Jada around the dining table in his cabin. Dev had laid the binder, Huff's section face up, on the table in front of him. He ripped the pages out. It was either do that or punch a fist into something, letting his team know that he was overly distressed by the situation.

He'd reviewed Huff's file copious times while waiting for everyone to get there, but now he stared at the first page of his report. A picture of the menacing-looking man glared out from the paper. He was all muscle, strapping and tall, and his shaved head gleamed in the sunlight as he stood in front of a concrete block wall and scaffolding. His face held a grimace, and his expression said he was eager to take his frustrations out on the first person who slighted him, or at least whoever he felt slighted by.

Not the kind of guy Dev wanted threatening Kinsley. Not at all.

Dev forced himself to share Huff's details. "The guy was only forty-two years old when he went away. He'd risen up in the world of commercial construction. Surprisingly he had a solid reputation and was raking in the money."

Kinsley gripped the edge of the table, her fingers losing color. "Until the whistleblower brought all of that crashing down on him."

"What happened?" Reid asked.

"Huff's foreman had worked with him for years," Kinsley said. "But Huff got sloppier as time went on. The foreman couldn't let Huff get away with the egregious code violations anymore. He revealed dangerous construction shortcuts Huff had taken before the buildings were complete and tenants were hurt."

"But what about construction safeguards?" Russ asked. "Huff would've had to pass county building inspections, right?"

"Right." Kinsley's eyes darkened. "But he was black-mailing an inspector—guy named Arnold Wacker. Huff caught Wacker at a party forcing himself on an underage girl. At least Huff had enough decency to break it up and save the girl, but not before taking pictures."

"So let me guess." Ryan pinched his eyebrows together. "Wacker wanted to keep his secret from being revealed, so he rubberstamped all of Huff's work."

"Exactly," Kinsley said. "Lucky for him, he cut a deal to testify against Huff to avoid jail time."

"Didn't Huff threaten Wacker too?" Dev asked.

Kinsley nodded. "Huff tossed out threats at the trial to anyone who was within his hearing distance."

"So if he's our shooter, he could be going after Wacker too," Colin said. "We should contact the guy to see if he's heard from Huff or had anything unusual happen since he was released."

"We'll do that before questioning Huff." Dev tried hard not to sound angry.

"Are you sure you want to talk to him?" Reid asked. "If he's not our guy, you could set him off, and he might follow through on his threats. Then we'll have two people trying to harm Kinsley."

Dev had to admit when it came to Kinsley, he might not be thinking straight, and he should listen to his boss, whose years in the FBI had taught him how to run an investigation. "What do you suggest?"

"We get eyes on him and tail him to see what he's up to. If we find proof that he's trying to harm Kinsley, then we go in. If not, we remain hands off."

Micha tapped his sidearm. "And maybe while we have him under observation, we can see if he has any weapons. And before you tell me possessing a weapon is a violation of his parole or supervisory release, if he's out to exact vengeance, he won't care about that."

As the team's weapons expert and the guy who served with Russ in the military as a weapons tech before moving into military investigations, Dev wasn't surprised that this would be the area where Micha would offer to help.

"I agree with Micha," Dev said. "I think it's top priority that we find out if he has weapons and what kind so we can protect ourselves against them."

"Not me." Russ rested his elbows on the back of his chair and steepled his fingers. "I'm inclined to agree with Reid. We hang back for now. I'll look into the man. See if I can learn anything about him and his prison associates."

"Prison associates?" Dev asked. "His parole will prohibit him from hanging out with felons, too, so how will they help?"

"Just like living at their release address isn't always followed, neither is this." Russ wiggled his fingers. "Who knows? I might find someone else he's hanging around with who could be involved in trying to harm Kinsley."

"I don't know about any friends," she said. "Back in the day, he was a real loner except for Spencer Caldwell. He was Huff's right-hand man."

"Did he go to prison too?" Dev asked.

She shook her head. "We had no evidence of his involvement in criminal acts, so he managed to escape prosecution."

"And Huff's business acquaintances?" Russ asked.

"After his arrest and conviction, he alienated the true professionals in his universe."

Dev handed her a notepad and pen. "Jot down the guy's details. Caldwell's too, and give it to Russ." He looked at Russ. "Will you check into both of their records?"

"Can do." His nostrils flared. "But everyone needs to remember, without a legitimate investigation, whatever I do is off the record. Nothing official. So keep it to yourselves."

"You know we always have your back," Reid said. "We won't get you messed up in something that will hurt your career."

"You should know, Colin is already searching the internet for information on Luongo." Dev looked at his brother. "I'd like you to add these other guys to your algorithms, too. See what you can find."

Colin responded with an emphatic nod.

Reid was still looking at Kinsley. "Anyone else we should be looking at?"

"I don't know." She scratched her head. "His wife, maybe. She left him when his assets were frozen and had to seriously downsize her life. She was most vocal about that, but she never came across as the violent type."

"But she could be another person he might have it out for," Russ said. "At least in my experience, having the wife turn on a guy hurts the most because it's the greatest personal betrayal, and we should keep her on our radar."

"Plus, she took his kids." Kinsley leaned forward. "And even if he wasn't the greatest father, that was bound to make him angry. Hopefully you can find her contact information. I think she moved out of state after she split with him."

"Means Huff would have to leave Portland to find her," Micha said.

Russ released his fingers. "Add the wife's name to the list you're making for me, and I'll see if Huff traveled out of state to get to her." He held up a hand. "But before you get excited about it, it's not likely."

"How can you possibly know that?" Jada asked, surprising Dev that his little sister took this long to get into the discussion.

"If he's like most prisoners these days," Russ answered, "he didn't serve out his full sentence but got out on early release and is under supervision by a parole officer. They would have to approve any out-of-state visits."

Kinsley pressed her lips together, then released them with a breath of air. "He was brought up on state charges six years ago and sentenced to ten years."

"Which means he served sixty percent of his sentence and is out on early release." Russ let his hands fall to his side.

"Is that common?" Jada asked.

"Depends on the crime and the number of strikes the felon has. In this case, it's a nonviolent crime and he didn't have any prior convictions, so sixty to eighty-five percent is the norm for that."

Kinsley shook her head. "I've never understood why they don't have to serve their full sentence. Especially when Huff deserved even more than he got, in my opinion."

"Trust me," Russ said. "I agree with you, but there's nothing we can do about it."

Jada shot Russ a skeptical look. "Why would he follow this rule, when he's less likely to follow the other ones you mentioned?"

"It's the kind of violation that's more likely to get him sent back to prison. I'll get the name of his parole officer and give that person a call. We'll see if Huff's checked in since his release. If he hasn't, they're likely looking for him."

At the moment, Dev couldn't imagine a worse scenario in locating Huff.

Jada's eyebrows raised. "Looking for him, as in 'declaring a manhunt'?"

"Not likely anything so grand like you see on TV or in the movies." Russ smirked. "The effort to find him will be in direct proportion to how badly the authorities feel they need to address him. He hasn't been convicted of a violent crime, so I doubt they would be that urgently seeking him. I suspect they'll start out with a phone call and then a visit to his recorded address. In most cases, that solves the problem."

"And if they find him, will they send him back to prison?" Kinsley asked.

"Depends on the circumstances," Russ said. "But this early on in his release, it would be last resort to incarcerate him again. Especially with over a third of prison admissions being for parole violators. Still, if it's not just an innocent mistake and he's thumbing his nose at them and the rules, they'll do it if they have to. I can try to get a feel for all of this when I talk to his parole officer."

"Thanks, Russ." Kinsley smiled, a most unexpected response given the situation.

"Don't thank me yet." There was a grim note in his tone. "The officer will likely ask what my interest is in Huff. As I said, I don't have a legit investigation involving the guy, and I'll have to do some tap dancing."

Reid glanced around the table. "Might we be better off if we pass this information to the detective investigating the parking lot shooting. Huff could become a potential suspect, making him good for the shooting, and the detective would have a legit reason to follow up with his parole officer."

"I won't do that. Not now." Dev made sure his tone brooked no argument. Not even from his boss, who Dev had to make strong eye contact with to keep him from speaking. "I won't give up control over our first lead that easily."

"Then we should talk about how we get eyes on Huff and start watching his every move," Colin said. "If he *is* our shooter, we need to get a handle on it before he strikes again."

"So what's the plan?" Reid asked.

Dev stood, looking each one of his teammates in the eye for a moment. "As much as I want eyes on Huff, like *yesterday*, we first need to talk about escorting Kinsley to her apartment to file a police report." Dev explained his and Colin's logic at not calling law enforcement right away. "I thought we could leave before sunup so if our shooter has any intentions of watching her place, he probably wouldn't have rolled out of bed by then."

"Again, I ask, what's the plan?" Reid demanded.

Dev looked at him. "How many guys can you spare for the day tomorrow?"

"I need at least a skeleton crew here. We have to keep the business running." He glanced around the table. "Who's scheduled for training tomorrow?"

"I have the Basic Tools for Adventurers class at ten." Ryan mocked, yawning, and Dev knew it was because the beginner's class was often boring to teach. "After that I'm free."

"And I'm on right after him with my basic gun safety class," Micha said. "Then at one, I have three hours scheduled at the firing range with our guests."

Reid focused on Micha. "I hate to ask, but is there any way you can take Ryan's class too?"

"Two beginners' classes in one day?" Micha pretended to shudder. "All kidding aside, I can do it as long as Ryan gives me the props I need."

"Already in a bin in the storage area and marked with the class name," Ryan said. "I'll email you the class outline."

"Thanks, but I'll probably just wing it, so I'm not quite as boring as you." Micha laughed.

Ryan rolled his eyes. "Funny, man."

Reid glanced at Russ, but he flashed up a silencing hand. "Don't even bother asking me to take a class. You're giving me enough to do while I'm still trying to keep law and order in this county."

Reid turned to Dev. "So that leaves you with a four-man team."

Dev nodded. "That's enough to run a decoy SUV and confuse our shooter in case he's watching."

"What time do you want to leave?" Ryan asked.

"Sun comes up around seven. We should be on the road by three."

Ryan groaned. "Just when we can count on Austin sleeping through the night, I have to get up early."

"I'm so sorry," Kinsley said, sounding and looking as if she meant it.

Ryan waved his hand. "No worries. I'm just joking. Life is good and getting up is no problem."

"Thank you." She smiled, but her lips wavered. "And thank you to everyone. I'll never be able to repay you all for what you're doing for me."

"We appreciate your thanks, but we don't expect or need you to repay us," Reid said. "We're glad to help in any way we can. I'll also work on the schedule for the next few days to see how I can free guys up to put Huff under surveillance."

"Thanks, man," Dev said. "Once we get this visit to the apartment under our belt, I want to get eyes on Huff and start watching his every move. If he *is* our shooter, getting a handle on his movements could be the very thing that stops him from striking again."

After the team left, Kinsley remained at the table with Dev, who was comparing the binder against Kinsley's spreadsheet of investigations as Colin worked on writing algorithms for the other suspects. She'd expected them to want to go to bed since they all had to get up early, but Dev was like a dog with a bone and focused his attention on the binders.

She couldn't go to bed while they were still working. If only there was something she could do to help. Anything, really. She'd already looked up the latest contact information in her binder for their suspects, added it to her list of names, and passed it off to Russ before he departed. A starting point. One she wasn't so sure would pan out, but they needed to delve into it anyway.

They. This amazing and selfless team. She couldn't be more thankful for them. Reid reviewed his schedule, and Micha and Ryan would travel to Portland to keep an eye on Huff first thing on Sunday. There was no complaining. No questions asked. Just respect for the cause. For her needs.

Dev wanted to go with them. He couldn't hide it. His posture fairly vibrated from the desire. But he also didn't give in to his desires. He'd swallowed it away and chose to stay behind with her. To protect her.

Was he doing so because he had feelings for her or was he doing it because she was his sister's best friend? Kinsley honestly didn't know, but the intensity of his behavior led her to believe he had feelings for her. Or was that just wishful thinking?

Jada returned from tucking her mother into bed and linked her arm in Kinsley's to draw her into the family room. "I don't know about you, but I don't think I can talk about this anymore and still be able to sleep tonight. I need some downtime."

"Agreed. What do you suggest?" A good question, but could Jada come up with anything to take Kinsley's mind off Huff's glaring looks at his trial?

Jada pulled Kinsley closer. "Why don't we take your box to the bedroom and spend some time looking at more of the fun things you brought for our week together?"

The perfect solution. If she didn't mind goofing off while these men were working so hard on her behalf. But she had Jada to think of, too. Her friend was asking for help, and Kinsley could provide it. Especially if she wasn't needed out here.

She dredged up a smile. "Let me ask Dev if there's anything else he needs from me."

She started for him, but Jada held her back by the arm. "Do you like my brother?"

Kinsley worked hard to keep her mouth from falling open and came up with an appropriate answer. "Of course I like him. I like all of you. You're the family I never had."

"That's not what I mean, and you know it." Jada ran her gaze over Kinsley's face. "I'm asking if you like him. As in romantically."

"And if I did?" She extracted her arm from Jada's hold. "Would that be such a bad thing?"

Jada scowled. "Only if things went badly between you, and I ended up losing you as my best friend. I couldn't risk that happening. So promise me you won't go down that path with him."

"I don't even know if he wants to go down that path." Kinsley was fishing for any knowledge Jada might have, and she instantly regretted her behavior.

Jada's eyes darkened. "He'd go down that path with you in a heartbeat. He's only too ready to do it. He's had a crush on you since we were young, and it hasn't let up."

A crush? Really? Did Jada know what she was talking about?

Kinsley took a long look at her friend's face to see if she could gain any answers, but Jada was staring across the room at her brother.

"How do you know that?" Kinsley asked.

"He told me." Jada swung her gaze back to her. "Several times."

Interesting, but... "Then why hasn't he done anything about it? He hasn't even said a word to me."

Jada took a wide stance, planting her sneakers on the floor as if ready to do battle. "Because I made him promise not to."

"You did what?" Kinsley couldn't control her surprise and her voice shot up, drawing the brothers' attention. She lowered her voice and took a step closer to Jada. "When did you make him promise that?"

She rested a hand on one hip and jutted the other one out, her defensive posture that she'd had since a little girl. "Back in high school and again just yesterday."

Kinsley's heart sank. Yesterday's exacting of a promise from Dev truly meant Jada believed they shouldn't be together. "You shouldn't have done that. We're adults now."

"I'm sorry." Jada grabbed Kinsley's hands and held them tight. "Don't be mad at me. I know I was being selfish. If you want me to tell him it's okay to pursue you, I will, but promise me, you'll never let him come between us. Never."

Kinsley couldn't promise such a thing. She would like to, but she knew how romantic breakups could destroy all the relationships around the couple if they split up. If she dated Dev and they parted under difficult circumstances, Jada would have to support her brother. End of story. No matter how much she loved Kinsley, she had to side with her blood relatives, leaving Kinsley out in the cold.

And just like that, Kinsley remembered her tenuous hold to this family. She wouldn't do anything to jeopardize it. Even if this fine man had feelings for her for years, there was no way she would pursue them.

10

Gritty smoke greeted Dev as he made a final security check outside the cabin, looking past their two SUVs lined up like soldiers in front of the building, Reid and Ryan standing by. Dev would be lying if he said he didn't have a sense of imminent disaster. Even with four of them on duty, bad things could happen. Very bad if they weren't careful.

"We good?" Colin asked from behind him.

Dev swallowed away his worry for now and nodded. "We're good."

He turned to look at Kinsley. She'd dressed in tightly fitting jeans, short boots, and a pale blue sweater, over which he'd made her put on her Kevlar vest that he insisted she bring from her car. The guys also wore vests just to be sure, but it didn't seem to give her much comfort.

The opposite really. He supposed it emphasized the risk she was facing, and she was chewing on her lower lip, her gaze fluttering around the area. Dev's nervous energy probably didn't help. He was transmitting it, and he needed to let it go to help her take the edge off.

"Just a reminder of the plan," he said. "You'll be riding in the SUV with Colin and me. You'll lie down in the backseat until we get on the road and we're certain we weren't followed. I'm sorry if it's not comfortable, but no sitting up until I tell you."

"I understand, and don't worry about me being uncomfortable. I'll be fine. I'm just so grateful that you all know what to do to offer the best protection possible."

Dev only hoped they lived up to her expectations.

Colin tapped his foot on the floor. "Let's get going."

"Follow me, Kinsley. Colin will be right behind you. Straight into the vehicle and out of sight." Dev stepped out into the smoke-tinged air, moving at a rapid clip and glancing around to be sure no imminent threat lurked in the shadows and that Kinsley had followed him. Ryan and Reid stood between them, alert to any danger. The vehicle door stood open, and Dev stepped out of the way so Kinsley could slide inside.

She gave him a flash of a nervous smile as she passed by, but it went away as quickly as it appeared. He closed the door behind her, then looked each man in the face to be sure they were onboard with the plan. He got a sharp nod from each of them, so he climbed behind the wheel, and Colin took the passenger seat.

Reid and Ryan got into the decoy vehicle parked in front of Dev's SUV and pulled out. Dev glanced at the dashboard clock. Just a minute before three. They were right on time. He was eager to go, but he waited for Reid to get onto the road, heading in the opposite direction from the way Dev would take.

His phone rang, the call from Ryan. Dev answered.

"No tail," Ryan said. "I'll call again when we hit the switchback so you can take off."

"Roger that." Dev ended the call.

Reid was taking a back road that allowed him to circle around and meet up again with Dev in five minutes. Only if he wasn't followed. If they didn't pick up a tail, he and Ryan would serve as extra protection for Kinsley.

Dev tapped his foot, expending his nervous energy as the clock ticked down ten minutes. His phone rang, and he quickly accepted the call from Ryan, who gave them the all clear.

Dev glanced back at Kinsley in his rearview mirror. "So far so good with the other guys, and we're good to go. Colin and I'll be focused at the beginning to look for a tail, so if you could hold off asking anything that isn't urgent until I tell you, that would be great."

She mocked zipping her lips. "I'll be so quiet you'll forget I'm back here."

He was in charge of making sure she got to her apartment alive, and there was no way he'd forget she was in the vehicle. No way he would forget her no matter what.

He put the SUV in gear and passed through the gate to bump onto the road. They hit the pavement, and his pulse kicked up. Took him by surprise. But why? How could it not beat harder? Kinsley was completely exposed now.

They traveled twelve miles, the tires humming on the deserted rural highway. At the switchback he spotted a vehicle's headlights pointing to the road from the turnoff.

Dev glanced at Colin. "Be alert in case it's not Reid."

The vehicle's lights flashed.

"It's Reid," Colin said.

Dev's phone rang from the dashboard. He tapped the screen to accept the call from Ryan.

"Confirming that it was you who just passed us," Ryan said.

"Roger that," Dev said.

"Then we're falling into place behind you." Ryan ended the call.

Dev slowed to allow the vehicle to swing onto the road

behind him and catch up. Reid's headlights soon shone through the back window of Dev's SUV. The added protection should help Dev relax, but he remained on full alert, driving and checking his mirrors.

"She should be good to sit up now," Colin said.

"You think so?" Dev asked.

"We've gone what? Like twenty miles at this point with no tail? I can't imagine our shooter hanging out this far away from the property in the event that we might leave in this direction."

"Yeah, you're right." He looked in the rearview mirror. "You can sit up now, Kinsley."

He expected her to offer a sigh of relief or somehow indicate she was glad not to be lying down any longer, but when she got settled her expression was a dazed look of bewilderment.

Didn't she think this was a good idea?

"What's wrong?" he asked.

She rubbed her hands over her arms. "I just feel so vulnerable when I'm sitting up."

"Don't worry," Dev tried to sound convincing. "You're fine until we approach your apartment. Then you'll have to lie down again."

She started rubbing more vigorously. "I don't know how you guys can stay so calm during this. You're in as much danger as I am. If he shoots at me he could easily shoot you."

"We're used to suspects with guns, and we know how to handle it." Hah! Dev had only been fired on once in his days as a deputy, and he wasn't as experienced as he was trying to make her believe. But he did have extensive training, and his competence in that one shooting and the two times Kinsley had come under fire proved that his training kicked in when the gunfire started.

They all fell silent, Dev and Colin keeping a good look around them as the miles rolled under the tires. Kinsley wrapped her arms around her stomach and didn't seem to relax for even a moment, but she, too, kept looking out the windows as if she expected someone to attack them. There was nothing else he could say to comfort her, so he just did his job, making sure she stayed safe for the remaining drive.

As they approached the city, Colin's phone chimed. He picked it up from the console, the screen's glow lighting up his face and allowing Dev to catch his brother frowning.

He swiveled to face Dev. "My algorithm on Luongo has a hit. Looks like the DA who prosecuted him for his wife's murder and failed is trying to bring him up on any charges he can find to make the guy's life outside of prison a living hell."

"Charges like what?"

"Patrol officers are targeting him for any kind of moving violation and any other misdemeanor they can get him on."

Dev glanced in the mirror at Kinsley. "And you're sure he hasn't contacted you regarding your investigation into Luongo or to ask about any new investigation? Like maybe he called and left you a voicemail, but you forgot to call him back?"

She shook her head. "I would've dropped anything I was doing as soon as I saw a message from him and called him right back."

Colin leaned over the seat. "What if he simply threatened to bring Luongo up on charges related to his concrete business, and Luongo believed you would get involved again?"

She lifted her hands and shrugged. "I suppose that could've happened. I honestly doubt he would buy a house on Boulder Lake based on that though. And besides, I don't live there anymore. So wouldn't he want to get back at me in Portland?"

"That makes a lot more sense," Dev said, pinning his focus to the road now as they were coming closer to her apartment.

His phone rang through the vehicle infotainment system and the female voice announced a call from Russ. Dev tapped the button on his steering wheel to answer the call.

"Glad I caught you up so early," Russ said. "I talked to Chief Gibson, and he spoke to the Realtor who's working on the sale of the house Luongo is buying."

"What did he find out?" Dev asked.

"He tried to get an alibi for Luongo without raising any red flags. He wasn't so successful. The Realtor did confirm that Luongo was in town during the shooting. She wasn't with him at the time and didn't know what he was doing then."

Dev shared a pointed look with his brother. "So he could be our shooter."

"Could be," Russ said. "Gibson also asked about the parking lot shooting time, and she couldn't alibi him for that either. However, even though the chief didn't mention the reason for his questions, that one caught her off guard and left her suspicious. So you should be aware that she might blab to Luongo that Gibson inquired about him."

"So he'll be on guard now." Dev slammed his fist onto the steering wheel. "It'll likely make it harder to investigate him, but we'll just have to deal with it."

"I don't know," Russ said. "I think he's used to the police poking into his business and it's possible he might not think twice about it. Since his trial, he's been pulled in by PPB for various violations. Minimum things like speeding that they claim resulted in resisting arrest. But you and I both know he probably wasn't resisting. They're likely trying to punish him for killing his wife and getting away with it in the only way they know how."

Dev shared the discussion he'd just had with his brother, where officers from the Portland Police Bureau had done exactly what Russ suggested. "Someone needs to talk to the detective to see what he's recently communicated with Luongo."

"I'd call him, but he'd tell me it's none of my business," Russ said. "Since this is about Kinsley, and she worked closely with the detective, she's the most likely person to call."

Dev looked in the rearview mirror. "Are you willing to do it?"

"Of course. As soon as I get a chance."

"Maybe these recent questions will cause him not to buy property on the lake, and he won't be living nearby," Colin said. "That would be a positive result of asking for an alibi."

"I don't much like the idea of the guy residing in the area," Russ said. "So yeah, that would be a true blessing."

Dev appreciated the positive take on things, but..." Regardless of what Luongo decides to do on buying property, he still remains on our suspect list."

"He does," Russ said. "And I'll see what else I can find out for you. But Colin, you should keep on with your internet searches to dig into him and the other suspects."

"I won't stop until we have our shooter behind bars," Colin said.

"Make sure you keep me in the loop, and we can swap notes." Russ cleared his throat. "One more thing before I go. When you meet with the detective at Kinsley's apartment, please tell me you plan to tell him you've been there and removed those binders."

Dev didn't want to answer when he still didn't know what he was going to do. As the time got closer and closer, he was leaning nearer to doing the right thing. He'd thought he could lie to the detective, but Dev just wasn't made for lying. Thanks to his parents. To his faith. He had to tell the truth. He could only hope it didn't result in the detective naming him and Colin as his top suspects and somehow hindering their ability to keep Kinsley safe.

"We need to hang up now," Dev said instead of answering. "We're approaching Kinsley's apartment, and we need all eyes on the area."

"You know I'll ask you what you did, so do the right thing. I'll be in touch." Russ disconnected the call.

"Time for me to lie down again?" Kinsley asked.

"Please." Dev gave her a smile in the mirror, but she didn't return it as she disappeared from view.

Dev checked the dashboard clock. Six forty-five. The detective would meet them in fifteen minutes. Perfect. It would give Kinsley a chance to look around her apartment to determine if anything was missing.

He turned the corner. "We're on your street, Kinsley. Be ready to act in case I need you to do something."

Dev scanned the area, his heart hammering. Colin was on full alert, too. Dev looked ahead to her complex. Everything appeared normal. No sign of a shooter. No sign of danger. Just a few sleepy-looking residents, coffee cups in hand, climbing in their cars to go to work.

He turned into the parking lot and glanced in the mirror to make sure Reid followed. He did, and Dev slowed to let him pass. He would go to the apartment first to check things out before Dev would let Kinsley get out of the car.

Dev tailed his boss at a slower speed, but suddenly slammed on the brakes.

"What's wrong?" Colin asked.

"Her apartment door is standing wide open. We secured it on the way out."

"What?" Kinsley's voice raised. "Has someone broken into my place again?"

"It looks like it," Dev said, letting his shock fade so he could think. "But was it the same person, or are we looking for two different suspects?"

Kinsley sucked in a loud breath, the sound carrying to the front seat. "I can hardly stand the thought of one, let alone two people wishing me harm."

Dev hated that, too. Two suspects could mean double the trouble, something he didn't even want to contemplate. Especially not while Kinsley was out in the open and vulnerable.

11

Kinsley stared at the scene in front of her. Her living room remained trashed, but nothing had changed since the photos. Still, seeing in person the way someone had violated her space in such a forceful way hit her hard. Tears quickly flooded her eyes and rolled down her cheeks. She swiped at the moisture but couldn't stop the flow. The stress of the past few days, coupled with this disaster before her, seemed to hit all at once.

"Hey, now." Dev faced her. "Don't cry. Everything will be all right. I'll make sure of it."

She appreciated his sentiment, and she knew he had the skills to ensure her safety, but he could never make these feelings of helplessness go away. Her tears intensified, and the last thing she wanted to do was ugly cry in front of him, but she was heading down that path.

"Shh." He put an arm around her shoulder and drew her close.

Another sweet gesture and one that moved her further down the ugly crying path she hoped to avoid.

He swung her around to face him and wrapped his arms around her waist. She rested her head on his chest. The solid muscles under her cheek should reinforce her confidence in his strength and remind her how he was doing everything within his power to protect her. It should, but it didn't. She clutched the back of his shirt and lost all control.

"Shh. We'll get through this together. I'll help you in any way I can." He stroked her hair.

She reveled in his touch and moved her cheek against the softness of his cotton shirt. She was in Dev's arms, receiving comfort from the man she cared so deeply for. How could she not forget about the mess here, focus on the softness of his shirt, of his touch, and let go of her worry? Control her emotions and stop crying.

She took a long breath, her chest protesting. She let it out slowly and inhaled more. Over and over until she gained control. After using a tissue from her pocket to make her face presentable, she leaned back. She stared into his eyes. Deeply. Struck by the level of emotion she found there. He cared about her. That was clear. Was it a romantic love for a woman as Jada had said, or was it friendship?

He swiped his thumb under her eyes, drying her tears. He gritted his teeth, then shook his head. "Forget my promises."

He gently cupped the side of her face, then let his fingers tantalizingly slide into her hair and draw her head up.

He returned her searching gaze. "I'm going to kiss you unless you tell me not to."

Kiss her? Not want him to? What was this nonsense he was speaking? Of course she wanted his kiss, more than anything, but was it a good idea?

He drew her closer, his fingers behind her head urgent, his other hand moving to join the first one. "Tell me it's okay." His voice was raspy, and emotion nearly choked off his words.

"Yes, please," she managed to get out when she wasn't even sure if she could breathe.

He tugged her even closer and lowered his head. Slowly, as if savoring the coming moment when their lips would touch. She held her breath. His mouth settled on hers, gently but passionately. She kissed him back.

Savored his touch. Savored the freedom. Savored the fulfillment of years of wanting.

This kiss meant more than anything she'd experienced in her life. Much more.

She intensified the kiss, showing him the deep well of her emotions.

He moaned and deepened the kiss even more.

She wrapped her arms around his back and slid them up to his neck, moving one hand into his hair and pulling him closer. She lost herself, forgetting where she was. Forgetting everything but his touch. His lips. The joy.

"Guess I'm interrupting something," a male voice she didn't recognize came from the doorway.

She jerked back and looked around Dev to see a slender man dressed in a tight-fitting black suit standing by the door and holding a small notepad. He wore polished dress shoes that gleamed in the light, and his hair was in a modern cut, styled to perfection with gel. He looked nothing like a detective, but more like a model.

"Detective Stewart." He glanced at his notes before fixing a penetrating gaze on her. "And you must be Kinsley Pearce."

She brushed her hands down her shirt to straighten it and stepped to the door to shake hands. "I am, and this is my friend Devan Graham."

His eyebrows had gone up at the word friend, but he didn't comment. So the man had restraint.

Dev offered his hand, not seeming at all disturbed by

being caught kissing her. Maybe he was far more used to that sort of thing, but it didn't happen in her world. Was she just one among many women he'd kissed? He was handsome and attractive, so of course he'd kissed a lot of women over the years.

Stewart released Dev's hand. "Since you're both still at the doorway, can I assume you haven't disturbed anything?"

Dev cleared his throat. "Unfortunately my brother and I discovered the break-in earlier, and we looked through a few things. Then we also removed some binders. They're in my vehicle if you would like to look at them."

The detective's eyes narrowed, his gaze sharpened even more. Gone was the model façade. She could now see him on patrol, stopping a vehicle or arresting a suspect. "That's unfortunate. You've likely contaminated the scene and could've disturbed evidence as well."

"We took great care not to do that, but even if we did, we're looking for a person who has twice fired shots at or around Kinsley, and we had to move forward in our investigation at all costs."

Stewart took a wide stance. "Amateurs have no place in an investigation, and it should be left to law enforcement."

Dev lifted his chin. "We aren't amateurs. I'm a former deputy, and my brother was FBI. We're fully versed in crime scene protocol and know what we're doing."

"Then that's even worse." Stewart's nostrils flared. "You knew that you were disturbing the scene and could very well cause investigative problems."

Dev shoved his hands into his pockets. "It's not like we ran through the place ransacking it. We wore gloves and were careful to leave most things where we found them."

"And today? Have you touched anything today besides each other?" His sarcastic grin wasn't a surprise.

Dev cringed and took a step back.

The heat of a blush raced up her neck, and she was sure her face had flushed bright red. But she wouldn't let it sideline her. She cleared her throat. "This is as far as we've gotten today, and the first time that I'm seeing the scene."

"I'll take a closer look at the apartment, and then I'd like you to determine if anything is missing. Other than those binders." He gave Dev a pointed look.

"Like I said," Dev's eyes held a challenge, as if warning the detective to lay off, "the binders are in my SUV, and I'm glad to get them for you."

Stewart shifted his focus to Kinsley. "What do the binders contain?"

"I'm a forensic engineer. They hold my case notes from every investigation I've conducted."

"Oh, right." He palmed his forehead. "I thought I recognized you, but I couldn't place you. You worked the Nico Huff investigation. I was most impressed with your work. Very thorough and yet concise."

That was unexpected and appreciated. Especially after the sarcasm, but... "I don't remember you being on that investigation."

"I wasn't lead, but I assisted." The right side of his mouth curved up as if he planned to smile, but then thought better of it. "Your work was a big help in persuading the jury to convict Huff."

She couldn't agree more. "He deserved to be put behind bars to pay for what he did. His negligence and greed could've killed a lot of people."

Dev took a step closer. "He was just released from prison and is one of our suspects in the shootings directed at Kinsley."

"I wouldn't have pegged Huff as someone who would carry out his threats, but when the prisoner has time to stew about his conviction, things can fester and rupture in unpredictable ways." Stewart turned to Dev. "So you think he's behind this break-in too?"

Dev's defensive posture relaxed. "Could be, or it could be the other suspect."

Stewart lifted his hand with the pen over his notepad. "Tell me about him."

Dev said all he needed to say. "Louis Luongo."

Stewart's mouth dropped open, and he blinked rapidly. "You think *that* guy is involved?"

"It's a longshot for sure, but we can't rule him out." Dev shared what they had learned. "Kinsley will get in touch with the detective who investigated Mrs. Luongo's murder. See if he's had any communication with him in relation to Kinsley."

Stewart bounced from foot to foot. She didn't blame him for being excited. Looking into a connection to a murderer versus looking at a simple break-in had to be a step up in his job. Even more so for a guy like Luongo, who was notorious in the law enforcement community.

Stewart jotted something on his notepad and looked up. "I'm glad to ask about that for you, and I'll let you know what I learn."

Kinsley opened her mouth to argue, but before she could, Dev nodded. "We'd appreciate the help. Can you do your walk-through so we can get out of here? The longer we stay, the greater risk that our shooter will show up."

Stewart closed his notepad and shoved it in his pocket, then without a word picked his way through the mess to enter her living area. Kinsley tracked him as he walked until he stopped at the back wall of bookcases.

Kinsley moved closer to Dev. "I wonder why our suspect came back. Nothing looks different from your pictures, so it's not like he wanted to trash the place even more."

Dev nodded. "It all looks the same."

Stewart glanced back at them. "Maybe your suspect added something to the scene. Like installing a camera or a listening device, or he took something on his first visit and returned it."

"Why would he do that?" Kinsley asked.

"Now that I can't answer," Stewart said. "Could be he thought the missing item might lead you to investigate him."

Kinsley took another good look at the room. "I don't see anything like that or a camera."

"They make them pretty small these days. It would take a very detailed search to locate one."

"We can use a detector to scan the place. It'll pick up any camera or recording device." Dev looked around. "But before we do, let's compare the photos we took to the room, and see if something obvious jumps out at us."

He grabbed his phone from the entryway table where he'd set it on the way in. He opened the first photo containing the items on the back wall of her living space and expanded the picture.

Kinsley glanced between the photo and the room before her, searching for any little detail out of the ordinary. "I don't see any difference."

"Me neither." He moved to the next picture, this one of the end table contents strewn on the floor. A mound of jewelry dumped in front of it glittered in the overhead light.

She glanced up at Dev and lost her focus. She was in her ransacked apartment, but her lips still tingled from the kiss. Having her wish fulfilled after years of longing left her wanting another kiss. Badly. Even now. Here.

Stop it. Focus.

She looked at the screen again. Searched it. Nothing unusual to see in the photo compared to the room. "Ditto for this pic. Next one, please."

"Hold up." Dev's eyes gleamed as he made the photo

even bigger, highlighting the pile of jewelry. "Check this out again."

She compared the space and the photo. "Oh! Oh, I see it now. The picture has a gold piece poking out of the side of the pile, and it's not there now." She looked up at Dev. "Do you think he came back for that?"

"I don't know."

She gave it some thought. "I'd be surprised if he did. None of my jewelry is worth stealing or risking being caught on a second break-in. And the only piece of jewelry I have that would match that shape isn't a very expensive necklace. Why would he take that?"

Dev cocked his head. "What if it's not your necklace?"

She tried to process his comment, but nothing made sense to her. "Then what?"

He looked at her with a pleased expression. "What if the intruder dropped this piece of jewelry the first time and didn't realize it until he got home? Then he came back to get it because it would've identified him."

"Sounds like a good possibility," Stewart said from near the jewelry. "You should go through the pieces to see if the one you think was visible in the photo is still here."

She didn't need any encouragement and picked her way through the mess until she could kneel next to her empty jewelry box and the mound of costume jewelry she'd bought over the years.

She carefully sifted through the top pieces, untangling and placing them in her jewelry box. She neared the bottom of the pile, and the necklace that she thought had been poking out of the pile lay right before her.

She held out the flat gold medallion on a matching gold chain. "It's here. The piece you captured in the photo. If he didn't take this, then he must've taken something else."

"Did you have another piece of jewelry that resembled this one?" Stewart asked.

She shook her head. "Nothing nearly this big."

Dev crossed the room to join them. "So he came back to get jewelry he must've left on his first visit."

"But why leave it in the first place?" she asked.

He squatted and pointed at a tiny, shiny object lying on the laminate floor three feet from her jewelry pile. "Looks like a link from a large chain. Maybe he was wearing the medallion around his neck, it broke, and he didn't know it happened until later."

"Or the link belongs to Kinsley." Stewart peered at her.

"No," she said. "I've never had a chain with such large links."

"Looks like the size a man might own," Stewart said.

"Seems likely." Dev stood. "In either case, we'll leave it here for Sierra to collect as evidence."

The detective tipped his head. "Sierra?"

"The Veritas Center's trace evidence expert." Dev took a wide stance as if he expected an argument. "We're asking her to process the scene."

"The big shot forensics people on the west side," Stuart said. "Kind of overkill for this crime, isn't it?"

"Maybe," Kinsley said. "But we figured you wouldn't even order a forensic review for a break-in. Especially since it doesn't seem like anything's missing. So we had to do something."

Stewart worked the muscles in his jaw. "I haven't decided what I want to do. If it could be connected to our parking lot shooting, then a forensic review is in order. But our teams are backed up, and if you're willing to fork out the money for the Veritas Center, then I say we go for it. Assuming the reports are sent to me first."

"We can arrange that," Dev said.

"Then do it."

"And we should have Nick look at the photos I took to see if he can enlarge them to give us a better idea of the piece our intruder took." Dev looked at Stewart. "He's the electronics expert at Veritas."

"Then arrange that too," Stewart said. "But first, I need Kinsley to determine if anything else is missing so I can complete my report."

She nodded, but anxiety squeezed her chest. The last thing she wanted to do right now was sift through this chaos and discover missing items the creep might've taken.

Another extreme violation of her sanctuary, and she worked hard to keep her thoughts in check. If she didn't, she might imagine the other horrible things their suspect might do if he found her.

12

Kinsley stared at the copious memories spread across the double bed she was sharing with Jada. Her face hurt from smiling and laughing over all the fun stories they'd shared for the past few hours since she'd returned from her apartment, and she could tell her friend was having a good time, too. The time was supposed to help her forget about the shooter, but underneath the fun, she still couldn't let go of the fear that some man was trying to end her life. Of the sight of her apartment. The mess. The turmoil. The stress. The call to Sierra on the way back here somehow making it all real.

All things fighting to evaporate the joy she'd planned to experience with her best friend this week.

Maybe it would be different if they had a solid suspect. Something—anything—to go on. Evidence other than the photograph and a tiny piece of chain. Maybe Sierra would find something when she arrived at the apartment in the morning. Or Nick could enlarge the photo without distorting it to reveal a lead. They'd both been known to pull a rabbit out of a hat, and that's what Kinsley needed right now. One giant bunny.

Somehow, she wasn't convinced that Huff was behind the shooting and break-in, but that could be because she hadn't had any contact with him for years, and his truly ugly behavior directed toward her at the trial had faded some. She loved her job, reviewing plans, site pictures, questioning workers and supervisors, and coming to conclusions on how the items under investigation should be handled.

She didn't like finding wrongdoing. That was the job, but only because she was charged with defending the innocent. Defending people who would interact with defective products where shortcuts had been taken to save money, often resulting in injury, and she felt a real responsibility to these people.

Something she couldn't simply let go of just because she wanted to have a fun week of remembering her childhood. Her childhood had passed. She would never get back the full excitement and joy spending time with this family—this wonderful family—had brought. Wishing they were her true family. Wishing she could live with them full-time. They'd embraced her. Made her as much a family member as possible. And she needed to just accept her role and not constantly worry they would tell her to get lost if she did the wrong thing.

She knew they weren't those kind of people, but that niggling worry had lived inside her throughout her childhood. That two families would reject her and she would be alone. Totally alone.

Jada yawned. "We should probably put all of this stuff away and get some sleep."

Kinsley slipped to the edge of the bed and started to pick up movie ticket stubs, friendship bracelets, letters and postcards, songbooks from camp, journals, pictures, and all the other memories a child and teenager might save into the box.

"I can't believe you kept this much stuff." Jada came alongside her and helped. "Maybe tomorrow we can go to my mom's storage locker and raid the items that I never got rid of."

"Did you ever intentionally keep anything? Or was it just a matter of your mom saving what you left behind when you moved out?"

"No, there's a bunch of stuff I kept in a shoebox for sure. But it was just a shoebox, not a moving-size box like this one." Jada tapped it and laughed. "But then you were always much more touchy-feely than me."

"Yeah, I still am. Which is really funny for my career. It's more of a matter-of-fact, black-and-white kind of thing." Kinsley sat back. "I guess the touchy-feely comes from me wanting to make sure no one is hurt by substandard products."

"I guess we're both crusaders in our own way. Remember back when we were kids and we were so into rescuing every little animal, insect, or amphibian that was in danger?" Jada smiled. "Mom was so patient with us when we brought all the creepy crawly things home."

"One of the many things I love about her is her acceptance and respect for other people and their differences." Kinsley sighed. "I'd like to think I've become the person I am today because of her."

"Dad did that, too." Jada's expression sobered. "I wish you could've met him. Sad that we lost him too young. He could've had a similar influence on us for many more years."

Tears pricked Kinsley's eyes, and she clutched Jada's hands. "I'm still sorry you lost him so young, but I'm glad we became friends and you were able to talk about him with me and come to grips with your loss."

"I'll forever be grateful for that. I don't know what I would've done if we hadn't met."

The kiss came to mind. What had Kinsley done? Behave like a traitor, that's what. She'd met Jada when she was still vulnerable from the loss of their father, and somehow Kinsley connected with her and helped her to talk about her dad in a way that she wasn't able to do with anyone else. They forged a strong bond that no one could break.

No one except Kinsley and Dev if they got together.

Kinsley released Jada's hands and touched her lips—remembered the connection she had with this man. Something she'd never experienced before. Oh gosh, she would love another kiss. Just one. Many. So what? It didn't matter what she wanted. She wouldn't let it happen, and she had to tell Dev that in no uncertain terms. The only way she could consider kissing him again was if Jada blessed their union.

Jada shook her head. "Now listen to us. We've gone from having fun to being weepy." She started picking up items from the bed again and depositing them in the box. "Do you want to put the lamp away or should we leave it for a nightlight?"

"I vote nightlight," Kinsley said without question. "That way if I wake up in the night, I'll have a good memory instead of remembering the bad things that are going on."

Jada plugged the lamp in on the nightstand near the right side of the bed. Her friend had a good memory. Whenever the two of them had shared a bed, Kinsley always had to sleep on the right side. She didn't know why, but if she tried the left, she couldn't sleep.

Jada put the last of the items into the box. "I don't know about you, but I'm going to crash right now."

Kinsley still felt antsy and didn't want to keep Jada awake. "I'll grab a glass of water first." She got up. "Do you want anything?"

"Thanks, but I'd probably be asleep by the time you brought it to me." Jada set the box on the floor, then crawled under the worn handmade patchwork quilt. She rubbed her eyes and plumped up the pillow.

Kinsley went to her friend and tucked the covers up around her neck, then gave her a kiss on the forehead. "Sleep tight, friend. Thank you for always being there for me."

"You do the same thing for me." She closed her eyes. "Don't stay up too late. We have a big day tomorrow."

Yeah, starting with Sierra at the Veritas Center going to my apartment to search for clues on the man who's stalking me.

Of course Kinsley wouldn't say that to Jada just when her friend was dropping off to sleep, so she silently padded to the door and eased out into the family room. She was expecting darkness, but the lights were on.

Dev sat at the dining table when she expected everyone had gone to bed. Her binders and computer were open in front of him. He looked up and caught sight of her, a lopsided smile spreading across his face and reminding her of the teenage boy she'd wished would've smiled at her like that.

Her heart flip-flopped. Somersaulting, over and over. She swallowed to stop the flow of feelings she shouldn't be having. Feelings that could only hurt her best friend. She curled her fingers into tight fists until she had control, then crossed the room to him.

Guilt ate away at her for the hours of enjoyment with Jada while he searched for her shooter. "You're still looking at my files?"

He leaned back and rubbed his eyes. "I couldn't sleep and thought maybe if I reviewed your investigations some red flags would pop up."

"And did they?"

He tapped a legal pad with three items noted and numbered. One of them was underlined with a dark black stroke. "Other than Luongo and Huff, I found a couple things I think we should look at. They date back to when you first started your career."

She tried to make out the details, but wasn't close enough and was hesitant to move nearby in case her tiredness let her ignore the precarious control she had on her feelings for him.

He slid the notepad across the table to her. "The one I underlined is an investigation you worked for the Veritas Center."

She grabbed the pad and perched on a nearby chair. Her heart sank. He'd chosen the Porter Mooney investigation.

He watched her as if she were a wayward criminal. "You didn't tell me you worked another murder investigation."

Oh, no! He thought she'd kept this from him on purpose. Or at least his tone and look said that. As if he didn't trust her.

Was it something she'd said or done, or had being left at the altar left him with trust issues? Maybe he hadn't gotten over the betrayal. If he was unable to trust, it didn't bode well for a future relationship with a woman. She was sorry for his pain, if indeed he had trust issues, but it didn't impact her future. Due to her love for Jada, that woman would never be her.

Didn't mean she still didn't want a future with him. She just couldn't have it and had to find ways to cope.

She gripped the pad tightly to remind herself of that and looked up.

He was studying her carefully. "Tell me about it."

She didn't want to recall the events, not at all, but he deserved her honest response after all the help he was providing to keep her safe. "This happened a little over a year ago. While I was investigating Mooney, an anonymous source told the police he'd killed his business partner."

Dev continued to look at her. "What was his motive?"

"He never admitted to the murder, so of course he didn't say, but the police believed the partner was going to turn him in for cutting corners, so Mooney ended his life. They also speculated that Mooney buried him in concrete on a home addition he was building. He served as the general contractor and could have pulled it off."

"Did they search the site?"

She nodded. "PPB called in Veritas to do X-rays. They agreed, but they wanted to enhance the concrete findings while also using a lower radiation density than conventional human X-ray devices. That's when they brought me in to use my contacts to source a portable machine that fit their criteria."

Dev clamped a hand on the back of his neck. "But it wasn't quite that simple, right? You didn't just provide equipment, but you also assisted in the concrete search."

"Yeah, and found nothing." She rubbed at a sudden chill on her arms. "That was one of the most disappointing days of my career. His partner had gone missing, and he was the only suspect in his disappearance. The victim had three children under the age of seven. I felt so bad for those children not having closure, so I kept working the investigation."

He raised his eyebrows. "Doing what?"

"I tried to think about where and how he would hide the body. Had he chosen to dismember his partner? If so, I needed to find a location where he could've disposed of individual body parts. As I mentioned, he was a general contractor, and his home project wasn't the only active construction site he managed. There were ten others, so I began to investigate each one of them."

His whole body went still, and he peered at her. "Which led you to find something."

She nodded. "Not that it ended up doing us any good. He was never convicted. But there was a large pond—a commercial site where he was building an office complex closest to his home. I thought if he didn't bury his partner in concrete perhaps he disposed of him in the pond."

Vivid visions of the day of the search flooded her brain. The crisp fall air. Dark clouds hanging overhead mimicking the emotions of all the participants. The divers in the water searching and searching for anything that could help.

"So you had the pond searched?"

She snapped herself free of the memories. "Yes, but by that time, nearly four weeks had passed since the partner went missing. Still, the divers found fabric fibers from a section of rug snagged on a rock."

"Wow, after four weeks. It's impressive something like that survived so long in the water. Or wasn't it related to Mooney?"

"It was connected to him, all right. He'd removed a rug from his entryway, leaving a lighter spot on the wood floor. When they'd searched his house, Sierra recognized the inconsistency and lifted fibers found in the area. Turned out to be an expensive Persian rug, and the fibers from the pond were a match."

"That was a stroke of luck when fibers usually don't survive that long."

Kinsley nodded. "I was impressed but I honestly tuned Sierra out when she shared details of how evidence was preserved in the water that long. You'll have to ask her if you want details, but the match was conclusive."

Dev's eyes narrowed. "So it looks like Mooney might've killed his partner, wrapped him in the rug, and dumped him in the pond. But you didn't find a body."

"No, and that's the frustrating part." She gripped her fingers tighter to keep from letting her emotions show. "We had strong circumstantial evidence suggesting exactly what you described, but there wasn't a body. We figured after I started investigating all of his construction sites, that he freaked out, recovered the body, and moved it elsewhere. But the partner has never been found, and you know how hard it is to try a case without a victim."

Dev exhaled sharply. "So Mooney's still a free man."

"He is, but I have to tell you, I periodically review the evidence to see if there's anything that I missed. If I ever find something, I'll go to the detective, who also can't seem to let go of this investigation. Hopefully he could get the case reopened."

"Have you been talking to this detective recently?"

She leaned back in her chair. "Not about the investigation, but I did run into him outside the police bureau one day. We just exchanged small talk for a few minutes."

"But someone connected to Mooney might've seen you." He drummed his fingers on the tabletop. "And might've told him, freaking him out that you were working to open the investigation again."

Could that have happened? Was it really possible? Nah. "Odds are pretty slim Mooney or one of his friends was there that day, and I think it's a real longshot."

He held her gaze. "That's what we're dealing with here, honey. Longshots. And we have to check them all out."

Honey? He'd never called her honey before.

Where was that coming from?

Did it matter where it came from? She liked it. Liked it a lot. So what? Her focus had to be on finding the shooter not falling completely in love with this wonderful man sitting across the table from her.

Ignore the honey and keep to the discussion. "He knew who I was of course, but he never threatened me. Still, you could have a point. If he saw me talking to the detective, he could be worried I've found something, and he might do something rash to stop me."

"Did he seem like the kind of guy who would react this way?"

"I don't think so. When we were closing in on him before, he remained calm. Eerily calm. Freaky calm even. Cold, ice-blue, unfeeling, unfocused eyes staring right through me. I wanted him to pay for killing his partner, but if I never see him again, it would be okay with me."

Dev's body went still, his focus locked on her. "And yet you didn't give up."

"How could I? We were in the right, and if he murdered his partner, which everything points to him doing, he needs to pay for it."

"Didn't mean you were the one who had to make him pay." Dev continued to keep his focus pinned on her. "I get that's who you are. Wanting justice served. I don't like that it can result in someone wanting to hurt you, but I respect you for standing up for justice."

She blushed under his compliment but didn't want his focus to remain on her. "You did the same thing as a deputy. And I know if you were faced with an injustice now, you would do the same thing, too."

"Well, I'm not a deputy anymore, so we'll need to get Russ to look into Mooney to see if he's had any recent charges or convictions."

"I haven't heard anything about that happening, but you never know."

They fell silent, but not a comfortable silence. He was likely thinking the same thing as she was. Mooney killed once, why wouldn't he be willing to kill again?

She averted her gaze, but her gut said his eyes were still on her. She looked back at him. "Go ahead and say what you're thinking. "

"We should talk about the kiss."

Oh, right. Not what she thought he was going to say, but now that he brought it up, she only had one response. "It was a mistake. We don't want to hurt Jada, and if we start something, that's what will happen."

"But we can at least admit that we have feelings for each other." He leaned closer, his gaze heating up. "At least I have feelings for you. Which was obvious by the fact that I kissed you in the first place. I could be wrong, but since you didn't stop me and participated quite enthusiastically..." He grinned at her, a sweet smile that sent her heart racing. "You have feelings for me too."

"I do," she admitted as she couldn't lie to him. "But I'm not going to do anything about it."

Dev leaned even further across the table, reaching out with his hands as if he hoped she would meet him halfway. Should she or would it be another mistake like the kiss?

A loud pounding sounded on the front door. Kinsley jumped and turned to see who might be arriving.

"Stay here." Dev lurched to his feet, drew his sidearm, and bolted for the front door. He didn't open it but pressed his ear against the aged wood. "Micha, is that you?"

Kinsley didn't like Dev leaving her behind. She needed to be closer to him. She got up, her legs shaking as she traveled to the door to stand behind him.

"Hey, yeah, man." Micha's voice came through the solid wood. "There's something you need to see, and you need to see it right now."

Dev faced Kinsley, his jaw set and unyielding. "Stay here. Wait for my return. No matter what, do not go outside."

She couldn't find her words so she nodded.

Instead of leaving, he grabbed her up in a hug and held her against his solid body. A hug she craved, but not under these circumstances. He leaned back and kissed her forehead. His lips soft and gentle. His eyes filled with emotion. "I can't lose you. Promise you'll stay here unless I tell you to leave."

For a flash of a second she forgot about the danger outside and reached up to touch her forehead still tingling from his kiss. A tiny little kiss that probably didn't mean anything to him, maybe even sisterly like he might do with Jada, but Kinsley almost couldn't think straight.

"I promise," she managed to eke out.

He didn't depart immediately, but flashed her a tight smile. His gaze drifted back and forth between her and the door as if waffling on what to do. Suddenly, he turned the knob and stepped outside.

He was gone. Good and truly gone. Walls and doors between them. Panic slithered over her, threatening to take her down.

No. That won't help. Not at all.

She lifted her head in prayer.

Please, whatever danger Micha discovered, don't let the threat hurt any one of us, much less end anyone's life.

Dev stepped into the darkness on the porch. He'd hoped the fire had receded, but the heavy smoke told him otherwise. Even on a moonlit night, the porch kept the floorboards in shadows of darkness, but the cloudy haze tonight helped further conceal Micha's location. His main job was to prevent an attack. Normally that would mean lights on as a deterrent, but he'd left the lights off to keep from drawing attention to himself.

In this instance, if their shooter arrived on site, Micha would still want to catch him and lights off could encourage him to step onto the porch so Micha could detain him. In either case, Micha wouldn't make himself an available target, so even if the lights were on, he would stay out of sight as he was now, snugged against the siding in a deep shadow.

"Can you hear it?" He took a step forward.

Dev hadn't been as focused on the sound as on the visual aspect of his search, but now he tilted his head and listened. A distant hum reverberated through the sky above.

He didn't need to step off the porch and look up to know what he was listening to. "A drone. You get eyes on it yet?"

Micha shook his head. "Didn't want to alert the operator to my position and make him fly off."

"He's flying pretty low," Dev said.

"Could be the smoke is causing him to get closer for clear pictures."

"Makes sense."

"What's your plan?" Micha asked.

Dev had lived in the cabin long enough to know the property well. He could slip off the porch and into the trees where he could get a look above while remaining under-cover. "Stay here. I'll take a look."

He didn't wait for agreement, but eased his way along the building to the far end and stepped off, hugging the cabin's rough cedar siding until he reached the back where he duckwalked between aromatic shrubs to the massive evergreens. Planted long before the cabin was built, the trees towered toward the sky, and their lower branches were thick and wide.

He slipped between them, the rough branches brushing against his arms and snagging his shirt. He emerged on the far side of the long stand of trees planted as a windbreak from the lake. A good thing as the wind was brisk tonight, and not taking the time to put on a jacket, it chilled his body.

He looked up. A small drone hovered above as expected. Someone was watching them. Carefully. Undetected, if Dev hadn't thought to put someone on guard duty out front. They would be blissfully unaware inside the cabin. Likely sleeping. A perfect time to determine the adversary he was facing and plan an attack.

Who was operating the drone?

He didn't know, but he could guess.

From this distance the device looked like a garden variety drone that could be purchased inexpensively online or in local stores. So not likely a surveillance professional.

Certainly could be their shooter, but how had he found them? They hadn't been followed to this location, but as they'd theorized earlier, if the shooter was hanging out after the police arrived at the downtown shooting, he could've overheard Dev's name and then figured out where he lived.

That was a very big unanswered question, but the second question was, where had the drone operator stationed himself? Some drones could fly a distance of a couple of miles from their controller. So the operator could easily be well away from the property. He certainly hadn't breached the fenced perimeter. Which was only three-sided as they couldn't fence the lake and still leave it accessible for Dev's water rescue and safety training.

Could he be down by the lake? Or in a boat on the lake? Or on the road? Maybe across the road, hunkered down on the neighbor's wooded property.

There were so many options. Too many options. But he couldn't afford to waste time waffling between them. He had to decide which location to pursue before the drone disappeared. If he wanted to find and detain the operator, he would have to choose the most likely spot. Now!

He eased back into the trees and started for Micha. A

quick discussion with his teammate might help clarify his decision.

He rounded the corner and stepped onto the porch. Micha spun, his hand clamped on his sidearm, then relaxing when he realized it was only Dev.

"Learn anything? Micha asked.

"Looks like a small inexpensive drone. Nothing professional. Hovering over us. Likely trying to determine if we're asleep inside, and if the property could potentially be breached."

"Hah!" Micha shook his head. "Good luck in doing that. We'd be on him like an ant on a picnic watermelon."

Dev tried to crack a smile at the visual Micha suggested but failed. The impending sense of trouble left no room for comedy. "I'm debating whether the operator is down by or on the lake. Or could be out on the road somewhere. Or on the neighbor's land across the road."

"My guess?" Micha took a step closer. "I'd say on the road or across the road. If he was spotted and had to make a getaway, taking off in a boat could be challenging. The neighbor has logging roads on his property, and the operator could have a vehicle parked on one of them for a quick getaway."

"Okay, then I have a plan. First I wake Colin and then make sure Kinsley knows to stay inside with him, you on the porch."

Micha tilted his head. "And what about you? What's next?"

"Me?" Dev turned to stare at the fenced side of the property that abutted the road. "I'm headed to the neighbor's property to bring this guy in once and for all."

13

The front door opened, and Kinsley spun, searching the opening for Dev, wanting to be sure he was safe and unharmed. He quickly stepped in, not before letting in a heavy whiff of the wildfire smoke before he closed the door behind him with a solid thud.

"Are you okay?" she asked, taking in every inch of his body. "Is everything okay?"

He clenched his jaw as he crossed the room. "We have a situation. I'm going to wake Colin up, and I'll explain it to both of you at the same time."

She opened her mouth to beg him to tell her first, but he marched past her, taking long, sure strides to the hallway leading to his and Colin's shared room and leaving her alone to think.

Situation? What kind of a situation had occurred that he had to wake up his brother to tell him about it? Couldn't be good. Couldn't be good at all.

She resumed pacing, back and forth as fast as she could move, her heart beating erratically. She wanted to talk to Jada, but Kinsley had already gone into their shared bedroom to tell her Dev had to go out to see Micha, and she was sound asleep. Kinsley didn't have the heart to wake her unless she needed to.

Footsteps sounded on the wood floor in the hallway. A sleepy-eyed, but already alert Colin entered the room before Dev. Colin was fully dressed in camouflage cargo pants and a black T-shirt. She had no idea if he had to get dressed or if he was sleeping in his clothes, but if he had to dress, he'd been quick about it.

Dev gestured at the plump sofa. "Go ahead and sit."

She hurried over and dropped down on the cushy couch, her focus not leaving his face. "Okay. Please tell us what's going on."

Colin perched on the arm at the far end of the sofa. "Yeah, bro. What's got you so hot under the collar?"

Dev planted his hands on his hips. "We have a drone flying overhead. It's likely our shooter trying to get a glimpse of Kinsley so he can make another attempt on her life."

Kinsley gaped at him. "But how could that be? There's no way he could've found me, is there?"

"That's what I'm struggling with." Dev gnawed on the inside of his cheek. "I know we weren't followed here, but he might've somehow connected me with you and then connected me here."

"He could've asked around about who was under fire at the shooting scene in town," Colin said. "Your name or even Jada's could've come up."

Dev rubbed a hand over his face. "And if he did, that's pretty brazen, which I don't like. It could be a hint into his character, and he's an even more aggressive adversary than we thought."

Colin planted his feet. "Either way, I'm sure you want to find him."

"I do, and that's why I woke you. I want you to stay here

with Kinsley. Micha has the door. I'll go looking for the drone operator."

"No!" Kinsley bolted upright in her seat, perching on the edge of the plump cushion as she stared at him. "It's not safe for you to go alone."

"Actually, it's safer for me to go without the others," he said. "One guy moving swiftly through the darkness won't make as much noise as two or more. Easier to keep from raising the guy's suspicions."

"But..." Visions of Dev in danger in the dark with an adversary waiting for him took over her thoughts. Her mouth went dry, and she shook her head to clear out the terrifying scenes. "I don't like it."

He gave her what she thought was meant to be a calming smile. "I'm sorry if it makes you uncomfortable, but it's what we need to do. I'll be careful, and hopefully, the next time you hear from me, I'll have detained the drone operator. AKA our shooter."

She wanted to argue, but she couldn't. He not only had her safety to think of, but his sister's as well, and she had no right to tell him not to try to defend his sister. His birth family.

Besides, no matter what she said, he'd made his mind up and was planning to go. She knew him—knew him very well—and there was no way she could change his mind. He was going to head into the darkness to find and apprehend the man who'd been trying to end her life, even if it meant sacrificing his own.

Something rustled in the underbrush ahead. Was it human? *The* human Dev sought? Or was it an animal?

Dev, weapon in hand, slipped silently forward. He

pressed his comms unit earpiece in tighter to secure his life-line to Micha and Colin. He needed to know if their oper-ator approached the cabin or if the drone stopped hovering, zipped away, or landed.

He scanned through the thick air that left his throat sore and had to work hard not to clear it and alert anyone to his presence. The scrub was thick with ferns and hostas growing large on the untamed property. It would be a beau-tiful scene with the moon shining down, highlighting the hostas' large leaves and the feathery ferns. Not tonight. Not with the fire in the near distance and when he was likely hunting their shooter.

The leaves rustled.

Dev shot his focus to the area. A small animal scam-pered through the thick foliage, moving fast. He strained his eyes to get a better look. No human could move that quickly on their hands and knees. Had to be animal, but he couldn't make out the type.

He released a slow, silent breath to calm his nerves. He didn't want to be riled when it came time to confront the operator. No matter that he hadn't yet located the person he was seeking. With the drone still hovering over the compound, he was still optimistic he would find the guy.

He continued forward, silently, as a cool breeze drifted over him. He wished it were strong enough to clear the air. He reached a narrow, rutted service road that his neighbor used for logging and took a step toward it. If he took the road, he could jog ahead faster and find his prey. But he would be too exposed out there. He slipped back into the shadows to take a parallel route.

He reached what he thought was nearing a mile. The drone had to have an extended range, or Dev was on the wrong trail. He rounded a bend.

A battered brown pickup truck had been backed onto

the property. He'd never seen his neighbor drive this truck. Had to belong to someone else. Now he was getting somewhere.

A twig snapped ahead. Movement in the scrub. Not an animal. A human at last. Tall. Six feet or more, and thinly built. His hands clutched an electronic controller as he spun to look at the area where the twig had broken.

Yes! The operator. The man Dev was seeking.

Go. Now. Bring him down.

No. Slow your roll and think.

Dev filled his lungs with tainted air and backed away deeper into the woods to watch.

"Drone took a dive but is back up hovering now," Micha said over the earpiece.

"I have the operator in sight," Dev whispered into his mic. "A noise startled him, and he spun, likely losing control of the drone."

"Roger that."

Dev took in additional details of their operator, looking for a weapon. He was dressed in black from head to toe, including a stocking cap, and he tapped his foot on the leaf litter surrounding him. Light from the controller bathed his face. Too bad he was facing away from Dev. He couldn't make out his identity, but it didn't look like he was carrying.

Dev would have to take this guy down to stop the drone. He'd love to have Micha shoot it down or use radio frequency jammers to jam the signal, but both were illegal, even when a drone invaded your privacy and was spying on you. Dev didn't plan on facing federal charges when he could apprehend the man.

He would distract the operator again by throwing a stick into the scrub next to him. Then he would charge. Tackle him. Disarm him if necessary and bring him in.

He listened. Waited until the adrenaline pumping

rapidly through his body was under control. Counted to ten. Took a deep breath.

It's go time.

He chose a large branch. Heaved it hard. The wood took its own course and flew through the air, spiraling over the operator's head. Not exactly where Dev had planned for it to land, but it startled the man nonetheless.

"What in the world?" He spun, lowering the controller and ignoring the drone.

At this distance, Dev couldn't hear the drone, but he could imagine the device losing direction and plummeting to earth. A crash that wouldn't be heard from very far away, but the drone would be disabled, and Dev's team could legitimately recover it.

He bolted from his cover. The operator took one look at him, threw the controller to the ground, and ran for the pickup.

Dev took off, ignoring everything around him, his focus pinned to the moving man. Racing. Running.

At top speed, the operator was wiry and quick. Dev outweighed him and was less agile. Slower. He muttered frustrations under his breath. Didn't help. The operator gained on the vehicle. Dev fell further behind. He dug deep to increase speed. He couldn't let this guy get away. He just couldn't.

A small animal lurched out from the side shrubs. Brushed against the operator's legs. Dev could finally make out the animal. A small white dog, barking and yapping, nipping at the operator's pants.

Please. Please let the dog trip him.

The operator gave the dog a swift kick. He yelped and backed off, then resumed barking from a distance in tiny little yips. Dev caught sight of the dog's face. Black circles ringed eyes in an otherwise white coat.

Reid's dog, Bandit. What in the world was he doing out here alone at night?

Didn't matter at the moment. Dev had an operator to apprehend.

He picked up his speed. His lungs screamed for air. He lunged forward. Nearly lost his footing and barely managed to right himself before he faceplanted. The man dove into the truck and got it going. The old engine's rumble sounded louder than a rifle crack at close range, announcing that his suspect was getting away. Taunting him with the rumble. Chastising him for being so slow. For failing.

The guy floored the gas and fishtailed on the rutted road.

Dev lunged for the vehicle. Missed the bumper by mere inches and faceplanted. He'd failed. All he had was dirty clothes, a wheezing chest, and the sooty air to breathe. He sucked it in. Sooty or not, he needed to breathe.

The truck raced away and he searched for plates. They didn't have lights around them and it was too dark and smoky to make out the details.

He could run after the truck, but what good would that do? He would never catch up. Nor could he dispatch someone from the compound in time to trail the vehicle.

No. Dev had to face it. Their suspect was gone. Dev had failed.

He slammed a fist into his other palm. Why hadn't he considered waking up one of the other team members and having them at the ready in a vehicle to go after this guy?

Tactical error on his part. A big one.

Now he had to go back to the others—to Kinsley—and tell them he'd failed. He could just see the disappointment in their eyes. Especially Kinsley's eyes, and he didn't want to go.

So what? He had no choice.

He turned to leave. Spotted Bandit sitting and staring up at him.

"Come here, boy," Dev called out as he squatted.

The little dog trotted forward and pawed Dev's knee, then tried to lick his face. Dev scooped him up. "That kick was something else, wasn't it? But you're not acting like you're injured. Let's get you back to where you belong, and your family can take you to the vet to be checked out."

Dev started through the woods, this time not trying to hide, but still avoiding the narrow service road to preserve any potential evidence that the suspect might've left behind. He would make sure one of them recovered the controller tonight to secure it and get Sierra out here to recover anything that could lead them to the operator and also have her check out the drone. This being an outdoor scene, it would take priority over Kinsley's apartment. Unless Sierra had enough staff to do both. He would ask.

What's the worst thing that could happen? She would say no. And he had to do everything as fast as he could. The shooter could know Kinsley was here and find a way onto the property or take long sniper shots from a distance.

He got out his phone and tapped Reid's number as he crossed the main road.

"Hello." His sleepy tone almost left Dev feeling bad for waking him up instead of keeping the dog with him overnight.

But the last thing he needed was to take care of a dog on top of everything else. "I found Bandit wandering in the woods and scooped him up. I'm near the lodge and can drop him off."

"In the woods?" Reid paused. "He's right here in his...oh, man. The little bugger got his crate open and must've made a run for it out the doggie door. Thank goodness you found him or Jessie would've freaked."

"I'm glad to spare your daughter any heartache," Dev said, and meant it.

"Is he all right?"

"He seems to be fine, but you might want to have him checked out by a vet." Dev described the rough treatment by the operator.

Reid muttered something Dev couldn't make out. "You catch the guy?"

"Sadly, no."

"So what are you going to do about it?"

"I hope to get Sierra out here to process the scene, and hopefully Nick will also check out the drone. I plan to look at it too, but an electronics expert like Nick probably would see something in the device that I don't see."

"But what about Kinsley's apartment? I thought you had Sierra going there first thing in the morning."

Dev explained his reasoning regarding the unstable nature of the outdoor scene.

"Good thinking," Reid said. "Sounds like a solid plan. Let me know if you need anything from me. I'll wait on the porch for you to deliver Bandit."

Dev used his passcode to get through the security gate, making sure it latched solidly behind him. He marched down the compound's driveway. Took three minutes of crunching over gravel and sustaining copious licks from Bandit to reach the big lodge. Reid and his brothers had grown up in this house. Now life had come full circle, and Reid, along with his wife Megan, were raising his nine-year-old daughter and Megan's seven-year-old daughter, Ella. They seemed to be the perfectly blended family. Dev had to admit to being jealous at times of their close family unit.

Despite always backing away from his feelings for Kinsley, he wanted to get married. He wanted kids. Hence his big mistake with Hailey. He'd given up on a future with Kinsley and had gotten engaged, but Hailey suspected he was holding back. She ignored her gut feelings, but when the big day came, she couldn't walk down the aisle until she had it out with him. She pressured him until he told her that he still had feelings for Kinsley and he doubted they would ever go away. But he loved Hailey and tried to convince her of that. She didn't believe him and left him at the altar.

He deserved it. He could love and commit to another woman, but not in the way he loved Kinsley. Any woman deserved more than that from him. He had no business getting engaged and cheating her out of what she deserved. But Hailey bailing on him as he stood waiting at the altar still stung and was almost as difficult as not being able to explain it to his family. He couldn't. Not without making Jada feel bad for eliciting the promise from him. So despite his mother hounding him for months, he kept silent and simply took the blame so they didn't think badly of his fiancée.

After connecting with Kinsley again, he knew he wanted her more than anything, but that changed nothing. He couldn't have her.

Reid eased out of the shadows cast by a large wrought iron light fixture hanging near the heavy wooden door. Bandit started whimpering, and Dev hurried up the steps to his boss.

He reached for the dog and held the little thing out to give him a good once-over. "He doesn't seem to be suffering. Did he walk okay?"

Dev nodded. "I didn't notice anything unusual."

Reid drew the dog close to his chest, and Bandit snuggled up against his neck. Reid rested his cheek on the dog's head and cooed in baby tones. If Dev didn't have a suspect to follow up on, he would stay here and razz his rugged boss about being so smitten with a little puppy dog.

"Got to go." Dev turned to leave. "I'll let you know what we find."

"I'll still make sure we have a protection detail at your cabin twenty-four seven," Reid called after him. "Let me know if you need anything else."

Anything else? His boss was just trying to help, and Dev appreciated that, but needing anything else, anything at all, to bring this investigation to a close made the solution seem very far off.

Right now he didn't have the capacity to deal with what was right in front of him, much less try to predict his future needs. Especially not with an adversary who seemed to be cunning and persistent. Very persistent indeed.

14

The online church service Kinsley was watching in Dev's cabin with his mother, Jada, and Colin was winding down, and a knock sounded on the door. *Sierra.* Had to be her. Or at least Kinsley hoped it was her and not another problem. She had seen Dev glancing at his phone during the last song and tapping his screen a few times, most likely opening the gate for Sierra.

Dev flashed Kinsley a look that she took to mean stay put, and he strode to the door.

"Has to be Sierra from the Veritas Center," Kinsley said so the others didn't worry. "Dev somehow succeeded in getting Sierra to hop in her van first thing this morning and drive directly here. How he did it, I don't know. Especially on a Sunday."

"My boy can be very persuasive." Sandy smiled. "Especially when he turns on the charm with women."

"Yeah," Jada said. "He's the charmer of the family all right, but he's still single, so apparently he isn't succeeding with the women." She chuckled.

Sandy swatted her hand at Jada, but Colin laughed along with her.

Kinsley had no desire to laugh and kept her eyes pinned to the doorway. However Dev got her to come here, Kinsley was thankful. Plus, she was thankful that Sierra had assigned a team to process Kinsley's apartment. And on top of that, Sierra refused to take any money for their work. That didn't mean Kinsley wouldn't find a way to pay them back. She would. She just didn't know how yet. Maybe she'd give them free work on any projects they needed her on in the future.

Dev opened the door a crack, looked out, then stepped back. "Thanks for coming."

Wearing jeans and a navy blue sweatshirt that highlighted her blond hair, Sierra entered in quick steps. She strode into the family room and stopped near the fireplace where she turned her back to the roaring flames.

She didn't look tired from the long drive, but her eager expression said she wanted to get to work, and she quickly introduced herself to everyone.

"Thank you for coming," Kinsley said.

Sierra waved her hand as if it were no big deal, but Kinsley knew she was leaving her family behind to be here. She held her hands out to the fireplace. "This fire is wonderful, but the wildfires not so much. Looks like they're approaching here."

Dev joined them. "So far, they haven't issued any evacuation alerts for our area, but we're keeping an eye on it."

"I've never seen the glow from the flames this close." She shuddered. "And I hope never to see it any closer." She took a deep breath and let it out. "So tell me more about what happened last night."

Dev described the incident in detail.

Kinsley watched Sierra's expression as she took in the news. The forensic expert had always impressed her, but she could often look unassuming. Pretty, but almost forgettable. With her long blond hair and bangs, she appeared to be in her early twenties just starting out in a professional career when in reality she was in her thirties and headed up one of the nation's top crime forensics labs in the country.

Of course, her inconspicuous presence was only true when she was dressed in civilian clothing, standing still and not in action. The moment she put on her white Tyvek suit, her focus became laser-sharp, and she tuned out everybody but her workers to do the job.

Dev picked up the plastic bag with the drone controller and handed it to Sierra. "This is the controller our suspect dropped so you can run it for prints and DNA."

Sierra took the controller and looked at it then nodded. "And is that all that happened?"

Dev shook his head and described the suspect fleeing in a truck. "I hoped the dog would take him down, but no such luck. The suspect fended him off."

"A dog." Her eyes lit up. "Did you say the dog touched the suspect?"

Dev nodded. "He almost tripped the guy up, and that's when he kicked the poor little fella in the side."

"Then I need to see the dog." She planted her hands on her hips, which were made curvier by the birth of two children. "Now!"

"But why?" Kinsley asked.

Sierra looked at her. "Human DNA can be transferred to dogs."

Dev gaped at her. "Do you mean Bandit could be the source for our suspect's DNA?"

"It's a distinct possibility. Researchers have determined that DNA collected by a dog's contact with humans is retained on the surface of the fur, not deeper in the fur and closer to the skin. That also gives it the potential to be easily disturbed, and I need to see the dog right away before that happens."

"If I take you to Bandit's house, you can swab him for DNA?"

"This information is very new and cutting edge. I haven't tried it before, but the researchers tell me that if Bandit touched your suspect, and he hasn't rubbed away all of the evidence, I should find touch DNA on his fur."

Dev's expression lit up. "Then let's get over there before he does rub it away."

"I wish I could come with you," Kinsley said as she looked at Dev. "But I know I have to stay here. Will you let me know if you locate anything?"

"It's okay if you're not there," Sierra said. "We won't learn anything today anyway. I'll take samples, but I won't know anything until I get back to the lab and Emory and I process them to determine if DNA is present."

Kinsley had met Emory, the center's DNA expert, before. She was extremely qualified and talented, too. "Emory's the best, and if DNA exists, she'll find it."

"Indeed." Sierra pivoted toward the door. "Let's get after this."

Gone was her laid-back demeanor, replaced by a single-focused drive that gave Kinsley hope. Hope that they would indeed find DNA on the dog.

Great news, but now came the waiting. Hours? Days? How long?

Kinsley really didn't want to wait even a minute, but maybe if she knew how long the process might take, she wouldn't fret the whole time.

"When will you have results?" she called after Sierra before she got out the door.

She tossed her hair over her shoulder and glanced back. "First, we have to finish the crime scene and drive back to

Portland. I don't expect that to occur before the end of the day. Then, it could take a half day or more for us to isolate the DNA and get it running. Once we get the samples on the PCR machine, it takes a minimum of twenty-four hours to complete." She put her hand on the doorknob. "Does that give you a good enough idea of what to expect?"

Kinsley calculated the wait time in her head. "So by the end of the day on Tuesday, I should know who kicked Bandit and who operated the drone, likely our shooter."

"No," Sierra said. "You'll know if we have a DNA profile, but I won't be able to give you a name. To give you a name our profile has to return a match in the Fed's DNA database."

"What are the odds that his profile will be in this database?"

"Good, if he's a known criminal. The database contains most every offender arrested in the past twenty-four years. So if your guy has been arrested in that timeframe, he's likely included in the data. Perhaps even earlier, if the state adopted a DNA law sooner. However, without an official police investigation, I don't have the right to access that database. So if you want a name to go with the DNA profile, you'll need to get the police involved and have them officially request me to process the sample."

Kinsley's heart fell, and she swiveled to look at Dev. "What about Russ? He's a sheriff. Can he do this for us?"

Dev frowned. "He could, but I don't know if he will. If it compromises him in any way, he won't agree."

Sierra twisted the doorknob. "He's right. I've worked with Russ before. He's by the book and won't make any exceptions."

Kinsley wouldn't be deterred by Russ's straight-laced approach. She had to at least try to get him on the scene to convince him to order the test they needed. "Then we better get him out here to file an official report. And let's hope there aren't any exceptions that would prevent him from requesting DNA tests for the creep who seems determined to kill me."

~

Dev appreciated Reid and his family's cooperation with Sierra as she swabbed Bandit. Reid looked on as nine-year-old Jessie clasped the dog's short leash, and her stepsister, Ella, held the dog's rump so he couldn't wriggle away from Sierra's swabs. Dev wasn't surprised by the number of swabs she'd taken. She said foreign matter was clinging all over his short hair, and she didn't want to miss the important samples.

She paused and looked up at Jessie. "And you're sure he's only been in his crate since he came home?"

"Positive." Jessie met her gaze with a confidence beyond that of a young child. "He spent so much time outside last night that he was exhausted, and all he's done is sleep." She stared at her dog. "Besides, he deserves to be in time-out for taking off like he did last night. Something could've killed him in the woods, and then where would I be?" Her voice wavered.

Sierra reached out as if to pat the child's hand, but pulled back. She wore gloves, so maybe she thought twice before contaminating them.

She smiled instead. "But he didn't get hurt, and there's a positive in all of this. He could very well have helped your friend Dev here find the man he's looking for."

"Yeah," Ella said. "My mom always says God makes good things come from bad. Maybe that's what happened here."

Ella would know all about making good from bad. The child had suffered from a brain tumor and survived life-threatening situations. Dev found it amazing to see such a positive attitude coming from her. He could learn a thing or two from the sweet child.

Sierra leaned back and ripped off her gloves. "I'm done with Bandit, and you can release him, but I'll need to take the dog bed from his crate."

Jessie narrowed her eyes. "He's not gonna like that, but if he stayed home last night it wouldn't have happened."

Ella let Bandit's back half go and cuddled his head. "He's just a dog, Jess. Give him a break."

Jessie wrinkled her nose at her stepsister. "You're such a softy."

Ella lifted her shoulders. "And proud of it."

Their banter reminded Dev of his childhood with his brother and sister. And with Kinsley. He didn't often argue with her, but he remembered hiding his real feelings by making sure she didn't think he liked her. Stupid boy things, like pretending she had cooties and germs. Or watching her all the time, then looking away when she caught him. Acting all tough and mean when all he wanted to do was be nice to her.

In some respects, he was doing the same thing right now, only more subtly. Or at least he thought he was being subtle. Maybe to Kinsley he was still behaving like a teenage boy.

Sierra shoved the gloves in a plastic bag she'd gotten out of one of her pockets and stood. "I don't have a bag big enough for the bed, so no one touch it. I'll send one of my assistants back to bag it. Any questions?"

"Yeah," Reid said. "Is there any hope that the DNA process has been sped up in the last few years?"

"We do have rapid DNA for buccal cheek swabs, but in this case? No, nothing has changed. We still have to manually isolate the DNA before running it on a standard PCR machine."

"Kind of figured that." He shoved his hands into his pants pockets. "But thought I'd ask, just in case things had changed since I retired from the bureau."

Sierra turned to Dev. "Time for me to get a look at that drone that was spying on you."

"Spying?" Jessie glanced up at her father. "Dad, are we in danger here?"

Reid rested his hand on her shoulder. "Do you think I'd let my favorite little princesses be in any danger?"

"Princess?" Jessie stuck her finger in her mouth and mocked gagging. "Ella might be a princess still, but I'm way too old for something like that."

Reid gave a sage nod. "Oh, yes. Nine years old is very mature, but remember in royal families you can be a princess your entire life."

Jessie's eyes narrowed as she studied her dad. "Is that true or are you just making it up?"

Reid held up his hand. "Scout's honor, bug."

"Okay, then I guess I can be a princess still." She jumped up and flung her arms around Reid's waist. "Which is a good thing, because I do still have that princess dress Megan picked out for me, and I really do like wearing it."

Reid gave her a fond look, then focused on Sierra. "I'll make sure no one goes inside the dog crate, and we'll wait for your assistant to pick up the bed."

"Thanks, so much for your cooperation." She turned her attention to Jessie and Ella. "And to the two of you for being such great assistants. You were a big help."

"I want to solve crimes when I get older." Jessie's expression turned serious. "Maybe even do what you do."

Reid's mouth fell open. "You never told me that, bug."

"Because I knew you wouldn't like it." She stuck out her chin. "But it's what I want to do."

Dev had no idea that coming by here was going to cause

Jessie to reveal her choice of careers to Reid. But she'd just turned nine, and she probably would want to be a lot of different things before she was old enough for a career.

"Then when you get older, if you still want to do that, you can come see me for a tour of our lab." Sierra patted Jessie's shoulder and headed for the door, her tennis shoes thudding on the old wood floor.

"Catch you all later." Dev took off after her.

Reid followed them outside onto the large, wrap-around porch and addressed Sierra. "You do know I'm going to do my best to change her mind about the career she wants to have, don't you? She might be young and could change her mind over the years, but law enforcement in any capacity isn't an easy career, and I want her to know that."

"Figured as much, but please know I'm a worthy adversary." She laughed and jogged down the wide steps.

Reid had left the door open, and Jessie came barreling out to fling her arms around Dev's waist. "I forgot to say thank you for saving Bandit last night."

Heat rushed up his neck at her extravagant display. "No biggie."

"You're my new hero." She looked up at her father. "Sorry, Dad. You're my hero, too, but he rescued Bandit."

"I'm not bothered by it at all," Reid said, his tone sincere. "Rescuing Bandit is definitely worthy of hero status."

"Besides." Jessie smiled up at him. "You'll do something before the day is over to take your place back. That's just who you are."

Reid ruffled her hair. "Maybe I will. Maybe I won't, but either way I love you, and I know you love me. That's all that matters."

She flung her arms around him and held him fast.

"On that happy note, I'll take my leave." Dev started off

toward his cabin and tried to keep in his heart the joyful spirit that Jessie often displayed.

Sierra fell into step next to him. "I hope my kids turn out as sweet as Jessie and Ella. But then, they're both boys. Rough-and-tumble. As they are now, I won't expect a lot of sweetness."

"How old are they?" Dev asked.

"Asher is four and Mason is just over a year old." Her wistful tone spoke to missing them.

"I'm sorry to take you away from them."

She waved a hand. "I'm the one who chose to continue to work. You're just providing that work. Besides, by bringing my assistants with me on this trip, I hope to be home tonight."

"There's one thing I wanted to ask you about, before we get to the drone."

She cast him an inquisitive look. "Go ahead."

"Kinsley told me she worked with you on the investigation into Peter Mooney."

"That's right." She frowned. "The guy who allegedly killed his work partner."

"She said you found evidence in the pond that still had DNA after an extended period of time."

"Oh that. Don't tell me you're one of the skeptics."

"Skeptic? No. Kinsley didn't remember the details, so I couldn't be skeptical if I wanted to." He shortened his normal steps to remain next to her. "Were others skeptical, and that's why the evidence didn't help?"

"A majority of crime scene professionals believe that after seven days in an aquatic environment, zero remaining fibers would be recoverable as possible evidence. That means a majority of agency protocols don't allow them to search and recover this form of evidence after a week."

"But you believe otherwise."

She nodded. "My belief is based on recent research, but there aren't any precedents set to admit it in a court of law."

"Tell me about it."

"It's simple really. The partner had gone missing four weeks prior to my search, and the skeptics couldn't believe that there would be any evidence left after that long of time, but we located the carpet fiber. Research told me to expect a high initial loss of fibers in the first twenty-four hours in the water—up to eighty-one percent in moving water regardless of the textile type. But after the first twenty-four hours the persistence rates plateau. Then at forty-eight hours, the effect of textile type became important." She cast a glance at him. "Are you with me so far?"

Dev nodded. "But you were way beyond the forty-eight-hour mark."

"I was." She got a gleam in her eyes. "But that's when the textile type came into play. Carpet shows the highest persistence and the respective roughness of surface texture make a big difference. These textile types keep the same order of highest to lowest persistence even over four weeks, illustrating the overarching effect of fabric construction."

"So the moral of the story is law enforcement shouldn't give up too soon, and it's always worth searching. Or at least it will be once the courts catch up to the research."

"Exactly. Which is one of the reasons why the DA chose not to prosecute." Her attention shifted ahead, probably studying the drone that remained in the same position where it had fallen, about twenty feet from his cabin's porch.

She closed the distance to it and set down her portable kit that resembled one of his large fishing tackleboxes. He hung back a bit and watched her in action. She took out a stack of yellow, numbered evidence markers and placed one next to the drone and a second near a section that had broken off the drone when it crashed.

She slipped her fingers into disposable gloves and lifted her camera from around her neck. She snapped pictures of both items, the click of the shutter breaking the silence. Releasing the camera to let it hang around her neck, she squatted and picked up the large piece of the drone that held a camera.

She turned it over and studied the device. "Are you familiar with remote ID?"

Dev nodded. "A registered drone in flight has to provide identification and location information through a broadcast signal so it can be received by others."

"Exactly. It allows the person receiving the signal to locate the control station."

"So, for example the FAA could find a drone that is flying unsafely," Dev said.

"Correct." She peered at the drone again. "Newer models have the broadcast signal built in, but this looks like an older model drone. If I'm right, it would have to be retro-fitted with a remote ID module. I don't see one, but Nick can tell us if it had any earlier broadcasts. I'm not sure if he can access the data or if it's only restricted to the FAA and law enforcement."

"Come on now." Dev grinned. "I've heard Nick is the wonder boy, and he can do anything, just like the rest of you."

Sierra rolled her eyes. "You all may think we're super-human, and we come close." She chuckled. "But we're just hard workers using the most current technology possible to help solve crimes, like any other forensic expert."

"If you say so, though I've never seen other experts contribute to resolving investigations like you all do." He smiled. "Is there any way to tell if the drone is registered but just failed to add the module?"

She turned it over again, then grimaced. "No registration number on the device, which is required by the FAA."

Dev resisted letting his frustration get to him. "So we can't track it that way."

"Nick might be able to. Each drone has a remote ID serial number, so if it's registered with the FAA, Nick might be able to use that number to do a reverse lookup in the registration database."

"Odds are good, if we're dealing with a criminal here, he won't have registered the device."

"Probably not. Happens more often than we like." She went back to studying the aircraft. "I wish I could say there was something unique about this one, but it's the sort of drone you can buy pretty much anywhere. One thing I will say for it, though, is that it's on the pricier end of your routine drones and has a much better camera. If the memory card survived the fall, Nick should be able to read it and maybe find additional footage."

"If this guy is as sharp as I think he is," Dev said, "would there be any footage other than what was recorded of our compound last night?"

"You'd be surprised." She set the drone back on the ground, likely for her assistant to bag. "It's illegal for someone to take down a drone even when its violating the law, so drone operators can be pretty sure no one is going to shoot it down or otherwise bring it down."

"Yeah, I thought of taking it down that way, but not as related to the kind of footage the memory card might contain. I just didn't want it recording us."

"Drone operators often do a test filming before launching their device. Criminals can be lazy by nature and not delete that footage. Sometimes it provides us with images of a building or landmark that can help direct us to them. We've even had it contain photos of the suspects themselves."

Sierra was putting a far different spin on the information they could get from the drone than Dev had heard of, and his gut burned with excitement. "Why wait for Nick? Let's go ahead and take the card out now and get a look at it."

She studied him as she would evidence under one of her microscopes. "I know you're eager for information, and I'd like to help you out. I really would. But the camera will have to be removed to reach the memory card, and manipulating the device runs the risk of smudging fingerprints or contaminating DNA. It first needs to go back to the lab for Emory to process DNA, and I'll lift any prints. Only then will we give it to Nick."

Dev wanted to ignore her answer. Scoop up the drone and pop out the memory card. But she knew what she was doing. The very reason he'd brought her here, and he had to trust her. "Then let's get going so you can give this thing to Nick as soon as possible."

She closed her evidence kit. "We'll get your scene processed, and then I'll take it back with me when we're done."

Dev nodded, but that wasn't soon enough for his liking. Not nearly soon enough. They were going to waste the rest of this day with nothing happening with the camera when their suspect was out there, perhaps planning his next attack on Kinsley.

15

Kinsley held her phone to her ear as she watched the Shadow Lake Survival team enter the cabin. She wanted to know what they had to report, but she wouldn't end her call with Detective Stewart.

Stewart cleared his throat. "I got a hold of the detective who investigated the disappearance of Luongo's wife."

"And?" she asked, keeping an eye on the team as they moved into the dining room.

"And he hasn't had any communication with Luongo in relationship to you or anyone else." Stewart cleared his throat. "He hasn't recently talked to anyone about it. Nor has he heard that Luongo was sniffing around for info either."

"So could be a dead end."

"Could be, but you can never rule this guy out." His tone was filled with grit and determination. "I'd say keep your eyes open and your protection team nearby."

She thanked him for checking into it and ended the call. She joined her protection team as they gathered around the dining table in the small cabin. Dev had called them, and they'd come immediately. All except Russ, who was on duty, and Ryan and Micha had delayed their trip to Portland after the drone incident so they could participate in this strategy meeting before they departed.

The guys got settled, and their larger-than-life presence filled the space with masculinity that was somewhat daunting. Thankfully, she'd had a chance to work with or interact with each member of the team so far and knew, despite their intimidating outward appearance, they were all caring men with hearts of gold who would do anything to help her. Anything at all.

And here they were, gathered together to figure out what they could do before their shooter and likely drone operator succeeded in making his way onto the property to injure her.

"Let's get this party started so we can all do what we need to do." Ryan leaned back in his chair and clasped his hands behind his head.

"Before we get started," Kinsley said, "I should mention that was Detective Stewart on the phone." She shared the conversation.

Dev's eyes narrowed. "He's right. We don't rule Luongo out. We'll keep our eyes open."

"What did you learn from Sierra?" Ryan asked.

Dev planted his feet wide. "They're nearly done with the scene, plus she took DNA samples from Bandit and his crate and will take those back to their lab at the end of the day for Emory to run."

"Bandit?" Ryan popped his chair forward. "What's he got to do with this?"

Dev explained Sierra's experimental approach to collect DNA from animals.

Ryan shook his head. "Just when I think the geeks at Veritas can't surprise me anymore, there's something new. Good thing they're on the side of good and not evil."

"You got that right," Reid said.

"She'll take the drone back to their lab to run it for prints and DNA, then give it to Nick to pull the video card." Dev frowned. "Fingerprint results could be back sometime tomorrow, but she won't be able to give us names without the help from law enforcement."

Reid took over, explaining why Sierra couldn't access any official databases. "We'll ask Russ to help, but, knowing our brother, he's going to be a real stickler about it. We better be on our best behavior when he gets here so we can talk him into it."

"He might be a tough guy on the outside, but he's a sucker for a damsel in distress." Ryan made eye contact with Kinsley. "You should turn on the waterworks if you can and add anything that you think might convince him to give Veritas his blessing to move forward."

They were expecting her to help here, and that wasn't an unreasonable request. Until this moment, she really hadn't done much to help herself out, but she wasn't sure she could pull off fake tears. "I'm afraid I'm not much of an actress. I'm a *what you see is what you get* kind of person. I'll do everything I can, but it'll have to come from the heart."

"Just do your best," Dev said. "That's all we can expect."

Colin pressed his hands against the table. "While we wait for Russ, let's go back to the beginning and try to figure out the identity of our most likely suspect."

"And how do you suggest we do that?" Dev asked.

Colin locked gazes with Kinsley. "You honestly can't think of anyone who might want to hurt you other than the men who've cast ambiguous threats at you?"

"Ambiguous?" Dev shot to his feet. "How can you say that? Just because these guys haven't acted on them before now, doesn't mean there isn't fire behind the threats."

"Relax." Reid held out his hands and directed Dev to lower his voice. "Your brother isn't downplaying the threat, he's just trying to figure out if someone has a stronger motive to hurt her than the threats issued by these men."

Dev didn't relax. If anything his shoulders tensed more. "But we've been over this. She doesn't know of anyone."

She didn't like being discussed like this when she could speak for herself and had to step in. "Dev's right. I live a very simple life. Mostly working, and there's no one in my personal life who would want to hurt me."

Dev gave her a long, piercing look. "No jilted boyfriends who might want to get back at you?"

She tried not to wilt under his intensity. "I've had a few relationships that ended, but nothing in the way you're describing. I'd like to think I'm friends with my exes."

"Any of them into guns?" Colin asked.

She shook her head. "At least not when I dated them."

"Still wouldn't be a bad idea to check them out," Reid said. "In any case, get an alibi for the times you were shot at and also last night with the drone."

"Are you sure that's necessary?" She looked around the table and tried to lighten her tone. "I can't imagine you would like it if I tried to contact all your past girlfriends."

"Oh man, the stories they could tell." Ryan laughed.

The others, except Dev, joined him.

The door opened and every one shot a look in that direction, but Dev's hand also flew to his weapon.

Russ strode through the door. He wore his uniform of khaki pants and a black polo shirt, a badge clipped on his waist. He glanced around the room. "You're all acting like you're going to meet a girl's parents for the first time. Relax. It's just me."

Dev released his weapon and let his hand fall to the table. "Glad you could make it."

Russ jerked out a chair to straddle it, then leaned his arms on the back. "What did I miss?"

Dev brought him up to date, but didn't ask him about his official role as related to the DNA and fingerprints. "What about you? Did you learn anything about any of our suspects?"

Russ sat back and clasped the back of the chair. "I got the same Portland address for Huff as your buddy shared. Lives with his mother. He's checked in with his parole officer and is in good standing. The officer didn't think he was up to anything illegal, but then he added, 'there's no one better than an ex-con to try to pull the wool over your eyes.' He said he'd keep me in the loop if Huff's status changed or if there was any reason to believe he was out to hurt anyone."

"Did he mention Huff's wife?" Kinsley asked.

"No, but I asked about her. She *does* live out of state with the kids like you thought. Idaho. He hasn't asked to go visit them. He has to check in every week, but Idaho is close enough for an unauthorized trip between check-ins."

"Then we should call the wife," Dev said. "Make sure she at least knows he's out."

"She should be notified by the corrections system if she asked to receive a notification," Russ said. "But I've seen them screw up and miss telling people."

"I want to call her." Expecting an argument, Kinsley looked at each man. "She should identify with me more than with any of you, and I think I could get information from her that she might not share with you guys."

"Agreed," Dev said but looked at Russ. "What about Huff's sidekick?"

Russ sat up straighter. "Now Caldwell's an interesting story. No sheet, but he's known to PPB. At least he was, for burglary and fraud, but he's in the wind now. He no longer lives at the Portland address in DMV. Been gone since shortly after the trial and left no forwarding address with the complex management. Finding him might take some good old-fashioned legwork, like checking in with neighbors to see if anyone knows where he went. Trouble is, he lived in a sketchy area and the neighbors are most likely transient."

"Still, it's something we need to do." Dev grabbed a notepad. "I need the address, and I'll put it on the list so when we send someone to Portland, they can check it out."

Russ rattled off an address in the northeast part of the city, which could be sketchy, as he'd said.

"There's another option," Colin said. "Do you guys remember my friend, Nolan Orr?"

"The former Secret Service Agent?" Ryan asked. "The one who resigned from the presidential detail to start an investigations agency in Lost Lake?"

Colin nodded. "He's the one. So anyway, he's hired a team of five other investigators and has focused his agency on finding missing people and things."

Russ scoffed. "There can't possibly be enough work for an agency with one investigator, much less six of them, in a town the size of Lost Lake. And especially one dedicated solely to finding missing things and people. The town is smaller than Shadow Lake, and we don't even have one investigator here."

"They're not focused only on local investigations," Colin said. "They take cases all over the country."

"You think Nolan would be willing to try to locate Caldwell for us?" Dev asked.

Colin rubbed his hands together. "I'm sure he would."

"Then ask him to come see us as soon as possible." Dev shifted his attention back to Russ. "Any word on Peter Mooney or Louis Luongo?"

Russ cocked his head. "You mean besides that they're both a piece of work?"

"Yeah." Dev rolled his eyes at the lawman, surprising

Kinsley that he would risk irritating the guy she was coming to see as sort of grouchy when they needed his help. "Besides that."

"I've really only had time to pull their sheets, but neither one has been in trouble with the law since they were investigated for the suspected murders. Well, sort of. Luongo has been picked up on questionable charges, likely officers trying to pay him back for getting away with killing his wife." Russ's shoulders slumped. "I also put a call in to the respective detectives, but haven't heard anything yet."

Dev tapped his finger on the table as if releasing nervous energy. "You'll keep after them and keep us up to date on what you find, right?"

Russ nodded.

"And you'll forward me their sheets?" Dev asked.

Russ lifted his chin, his expression stony. "Only if you promise not to share them with anyone."

Dev nodded his vigorous agreement. "You got it."

"No way I'll send them electronically," Russ said. "Don't want them traceable back to me. Give me your printer login, and I'll print out a copy for you."

"Thanks, man."

"Just be sure nobody finds out about it." Russ looked around the room. "And that goes for the rest of you. Keep your traps shut, and if somehow someone figures out you have them, you make sure you never tell them who gave them to you. You know I won't be a happy camper if you do."

The guys muttered something under their breath, but she couldn't make out what they were saying.

"Moving on," Colin said and eyed Dev.

Dev dropped onto his chair. "I'd hoped we could've eliminated at least one of them tonight, but Huff, Mooney, Luongo, and Caldwell all remain on our list."

"I'm doing my best," Russ said.

Dev waved a hand. "I know you are. I'm just letting my frustrations get the best of me."

Russ squeezed the back of the chair. "Normally I'd be the first to say we need to get in front of each of them to obtain an alibi for the time of the shootings, but I still think we should lay low and just get eyes on them. Where do we stand on that?"

Ryan snapped his chair forward. "Micha and I are departing right after this meeting ends. After we locate Luongo, one of us can tail him and the other one can try to find the inspector Luongo had in his pocket to see if Luongo has made contact with him. Then we can surveil Huff."

"You'll have to find Wacker before you can talk to him," Russ said. "He could be fearing payback from Luongo for testifying against him and is long gone."

"Then I need you to look up Wacker's DMV record to find his address and give me a good place to start." Ryan set his jaw and stared at his brother.

"No need to blow a gasket," Russ said. "Stop by the office on the way out of town, and we'll see what we can see."

"Well good, then." Ryan relaxed back in his chair. "That should save me some time, and I can get to Huff's place sooner."

"I'll call Huff's wife," Kinsley said. "Hopefully she has the same phone number as the one I have in my file."

"You have a good possibility of that," Russ said. "With most people only using mobile phones these days, they don't change numbers like they used to. Makes it easier to track people down when you need to talk to them."

"Then we should finish up here so you can do that and the guys can go to Portland," Dev said.

Kinsley looked at Russ. "You're already doing so much for us, but I need to ask if you can do one more thing."

He raised an eyebrow. "And that is?"

She explained about the DNA and fingerprints. "So you see, only law enforcement is privy to this information, and if we want to learn about the drone operator, you'll have to open an official investigation to authorize them to access the databases."

"As well it should be." Russ crossed his arms.

Was he going to say no?

"I'm glad to see Veritas is following the law," Russ continued. "You should first understand the law as it relates to drones before we talk investigations. You can fly a drone over someone else's property in Oregon one time as long as the drone operator has notified the property owner of their intent and the owner agrees."

"Which didn't happen here," Reid said.

"Correct," Russ said. "And even if you had agreed, Oregon statutes forbid someone from flying multiple times over the property when the drone has flown over it once."

"So our suspect definitely broke the law." Dev's statement came out emphatically.

"He did," Russ said, his expression tightening. "And if Reid or Ryan, as property owners, filed a complaint, I could open an investigation and give the Veritas team the go-ahead. Assuming you all are covering the costs."

"I am." Kinsley smiled at him. "Thank you so much, Russ. You don't know how much your help means to me."

"My thanks, too," Dev said.

Russ waved a hand. "All in a day's work."

"So if no one has anything to add," Dev said. "The final thing that I want to talk about is security and Kinsley's safety."

Dev glanced around the room, pausing his gaze on each person, but no one spoke. "I have to admit the drone has freaked me out a bit. We'll be two men down with Ryan and

Micha in Portland and another man down with Russ needing to be on the job so often."

"Let me see if I can do the math." Ryan laughed. "That leaves the three of you. And it'll take at least two people to staff the cabin's front door for twenty-four seven coverage, never mind needing someone to handle our guests' training."

"Not really a laughing matter," Reid said. "We've got to keep this place running or all but Russ could be out of a job."

"Then we need some help," Colin said. "I know it's not in Nolan's job description as an investigator to provide protection, but his team members are all former law enforcement officers. We could ask them to help on our protection detail."

"You think they'll do that?" Ryan asked.

"Yeah," Colin said. "If they're not fully booked."

"Then if he agrees to meet with us, we can ask." Dev peered at the group again. "We'll table the security discussion until we find out the availability of his team."

"I'll call him right away," Colin said.

"I've got a class to teach right now, but then I can take door duty," Reid said.

"Hey man, thanks for being there for us when you already have a full plate." Dev fist bumped with Reid.

"No worries. It's what teammates are for."

Teammates. Not something Kinsley was. Ever. She worked alone. She lived alone. She had a lonely life, and she was now just realizing it. She wished she had something to offer the team, other than making that phone call to Huff's wife. But besides that, her only priority was to remain in this cabin and not go outside where she might put one of these men who were giving so much to help her in danger.

Kinsley sat across the dining room table from Dev after a long lunch with Colin, Jada, and Sandy in what should've been a relaxing meal, but tension permeated the air. The women had insisted on being brought up to speed on the investigation, and neither liked the ongoing danger. Kinsley felt bad about ruining lunch for two people she cared about.

Thankfully, Jada picked up on her mother's distress and opted to take her into the den to read, which had always been one of Sandy's favorite things to do. It was also where Kinsley had learned her love of reading. Sandy made sure to take Kinsley to the library so she had books to take home with her to fill the hours when her parents were gone. To this day, she spent her free time devouring all manner of fiction books, living vicariously through the characters. Maybe trying to erase the loneliness she'd just discovered she lived with when she'd thought she'd left all of that in her past.

Dev looked up from reviewing Huff's rap sheet. "If you want to talk to Marianne Huff before the other team arrives, you'll need to make the call now."

Colin had gotten a hold of Nolan and impressed upon him their sense of urgency. He agreed to come right away to discuss looking for Caldwell. He was bringing part of his team too. They worked all investigations as a team, and he wanted them to hear the situation firsthand.

"I'll call her right now." Kinsley tapped in the number and pressed her phone against her ear. She half expected to get a message that the number was out of service, but it was ringing. On the third ring, a woman answered with a questioning hello.

"Mrs. Huff?" Kinsley asked, opting for formality instead of calling the woman by her first name.

"Who is this?" Her suspicious tone didn't bode well for the conversation.

"My name is Kinsley Pearce. I was the investigator who discovered your husband's illegal business dealings."

"You!" Kinsley felt the force behind her word even on the other end of the call. "If it hadn't been for your interference, I wouldn't be slumming it here in Idaho with my parents. I have nothing to say to you."

"Wait, don't hang up. This is important. Life and death important. Did you know that your husband was released from prison?"

"Yeah, sure I did. But he's not my husband anymore. I divorced him."

"Has he tried to contact you since he was released?"

"I haven't heard from him, and I don't expect to. I made it perfectly clear when we signed the divorce paperwork that he was out of my life and my children's lives forever."

"And how did he take that?" Kinsley held her breath as her personal questions could cause Marianne to hang up.

"Not that it's any of your business," she said and let silence linger. "He lost it, just like he lost it so many times at his trial. That shouldn't surprise you, right?"

No, it didn't surprise her in the least. "Did he threaten you?"

"Kind of, but I really don't think he'd ever hurt the mother of his children. Despite being a felon and his crazy temper, he loves his kids and wouldn't want to see them hurt by losing their mom." She fell silent again and Kinsley waited it out. "Why are you asking all these questions all of a sudden? It's not like you ever cared about our family. If you did, you would've never given the DA evidence so he could bring charges."

"I was just doing my job, ma'am."

"Don't ma'am me. You and your job ruined my life. I should be the one threatening you."

Kinsley pulled back from the force behind the threat. She'd never thought to suspect Marianne as the shooter, and she really didn't, but she would be a fool not to try to get an alibi for the shooting times. "You wouldn't have happened to come to Portland in the past few days, would you?"

"How in the world could I afford that?" she screeched. "My crappy waitress job doesn't give me enough money to even support my kids, much less pay for a trip out of state. If we didn't live with my parents, we'd be homeless."

"And they can verify that you were in Idaho this past week?"

She didn't answer right away. "That's sounding a lot like you want an alibi for something."

"It's just that your former husband might be mixed up in something illegal again, and we want to make sure that you weren't involved in it, too."

"Of all the nerve. You don't deserve to talk to my mom, but I'll get her so you don't go accusing me of something and putting me behind bars."

"Hey Mom!" she yelled. "Come here and tell this lady where I was last week. She thinks I was helping Nico with something illegal."

Kinsley felt bad about having to involve both Marianne and her mother, but she had to do her part to rule her out and find out if her ex had been threatening her. So she held the line and had a brief discussion with the mother, who confirmed Marianne's alibi.

"Would you please call me if you do hear from him?" Kinsley asked when Marianne came back on the line.

"I wouldn't hold my breath."

The call disconnected.

"That didn't go so well." Kinsley told Dev about her conversation. "But hopefully if Huff does contact her, she'll let us know."

He rested his hands on the pages Russ had printed. "That's all we can do then."

"It just seems like there should be something more." She shook her head. "I know all of you are doing everything you can, and everyone is stretched thin, but I wish there was something else that could be done."

He leaned back and studied her. "Sounds like you're eager to leave here."

"Leave? No, I would just like to spend my week at the Bluebird with Jada without all the worry. And all of you could go back to your lives, too, and not put yourselves in danger."

He tilted his head. "And here I was thinking that you were trying to get away from me."

"Why would I want to do that?"

He shrugged. "I just got the feeling since we reconnected that you'd rather be with anyone else but me."

"No, that's not it." She paused while she tried to think of how to explain what she was feeling. But then, she really couldn't tell him, could she? Not unless she wanted to tell him about her promise to Jada and go against her best friend's wishes. Which she would never do. Ever.

Jada had been with her through thick and thin. Through the rough times with her parents. The way they ignored her, and she'd wondered at times why she'd ever been born. Then, when she escaped her family and went off to college, she thought things would be easier, but after the first semester, her mother didn't approve of the field of study Kinsley had gone into and cut off all money for her education.

Jada was there for her. Working late into the night

helping Kinsley fill out scholarship applications. Helping her apply to different colleges that offered her major and could perhaps provide funding for her. Hours and hours they'd spent in front of a computer until finally she received a full-ride scholarship.

So she not only owed Jada for years of solid friendship, she owed Jada her career.

She opened her mouth to explain to Dev, but Reid poked his head in the front door, taking the attention.

"They're here," he said.

Perfect interruption. No need to explain her feelings to Dev. But now? Now she would meet with another team of men who could end up putting their lives on the line for her. She was glad for any help they were willing to provide, of course she was, but her heart sank.

Going against her friend's wishes would be a heavy weight to carry. But potential death of these fine men? She wasn't sure if that wasn't the very weight that would crush her.

16

Kinsley's thoughts held her in place, and she hadn't reacted as rapidly as Dev. He shot to his feet and raced to the door, tapping his foot as he let a cold, smoke-filled breeze blow in while he watched outside. He was transmitting his nervous energy to Kinsley, and her palms began to sweat. She rubbed them down her pant legs. If she had to shake hands with these team members, she didn't want to gross them out and embarrass herself.

Colin joined his brother at the door and shook hands with a tall guy with dark hair and a close-cut and perfectly groomed beard. Colin released his hand and gestured at Reid on the porch. "Nolan Orr, meet Shadow Lake Survival owner, Reid Maddox."

"We need to swap horror stories about starting a business sometime. I'd love to learn from your mistakes." Nolan chuckled then moved inside.

"My little brother, Devan," Colin said. "We call him Dev."

Nolan gave Dev a once-over and shook hands. "Not so little."

"Thanks for coming." Dev pumped Nolan's hand for

only a fraction of a minute, then stepped back to let him in while the next person entered.

"Abbs, is that you?" Dev's voice rose as a petite woman with reddish hair, a cute nose, and big eyes stopped next to him.

"In the flesh." She laughed.

"Abby Day." Dev shook his head. "I almost didn't recognize you with the short hair and color change."

She ran a hand through her cute pixie haircut with wispy bangs. "A change of hair for a change of job."

He blinked at her. "No more sheriffing, and you're on the team now?"

"Not sure sheriffing is a word, but yeah." Her smile disappeared. "I resigned from my position to work with Nolan a couple of months ago."

Dev opened his mouth as if he wanted to ask additional questions, but another dark-haired, bearded guy stepped up behind her and eased her forward.

"Come on, pipsqueak. Quit hogging all the limelight." He held out his hand. "Gabe Irving at your service. Never a big-shot sheriff but a former Oregon State Trooper."

"Then you're more in my league," Dev said. "My brother might've been a fed, but I was a Clackamas County deputy."

"Then you speak my language, bro, and we should get along just fine." Gabe clapped Dev on the back and stepped into the room, his gaze instantly taking it all in, including making brief eye contact with Kinsley. She felt the intensity of his assessment clear to her toes. This guy had very likely been an excellent state trooper.

The fourth team member, another guy with dark hair and a beard—what she was beginning to think was a prerequisite for the men who worked on this team—shook hands with Dev. "Hayden Kraus. Former Customs and

Border Protection. And the last one in, so you can close the door and keep some of that smoke outside."

Colin gave a quick nod to Reid, then closed the door tightly. "We'll be meeting at the dining table. Go ahead and have a seat."

Dev crossed over to Kinsley and rested his hands on the back of her chair. "This is Kinsley Pearce. We're here not only to talk about finding Caldwell but about her protection too. Nolan, you can do the introductions."

"No need for that." Kinsley made sure to smile, even if her nerves were threatening to get the best of her. "I caught everyone's name on the way inside."

The team members looked her over, eyes burning with interest. She'd expected a bunch of buff guys, but she hadn't thought one of them would be a woman. Based on her petite stature, Kinsley wouldn't peg her as a law enforcement officer, except for the look in her eyes.

The same look the three men had in spades. All three had dark hair and close-cut beards but none of them wore wedding rings. All three had dressed in the same basic uniform as the woman—a black, long-sleeved T-shirt with the team logo on it, and black khaki cargo pants. And all three had that look about them. The look Kinsley had seen time and again when she worked with law enforcement officers, male and female, on the job.

She'd never been able to put her finger on what *it* was, but she did know that it indicated they were always on. Always looking at their surroundings. At the people they met. Assessing and evaluating. They had to be that alert on the job if they wanted to stay alive.

Most people didn't think about the danger law enforcement officers faced on a daily basis. They didn't realize that a routine traffic stop could go south in a minute, and their lives could be snuffed out just like that. Just from not reading the situation right. Just from being tired or getting lazy.

And in her experience, even if they left the job or took time off, they never lost that level of situational awareness the average person didn't carry. Added stress to their lives for sure. And stress for those around them. But thank goodness there were men and women like these four sitting in front of her, the Shadow Lake team as well, who were willing to risk their lives and live with that stress.

Nolan clasped long fingers together on the tabletop and glanced between Dev and Colin. "So, what do you need from us?"

Dev stood upright and provided details on Kinsley's overall situation and specifics on Spencer Caldwell. "We have no idea where he's gone, and we don't have the resources to locate him. We thought since your agency specializes in missing people, that you might be willing to locate him for us."

"Well, you're in luck." Nolan gave Dev a smile. "We have a light caseload right now and would be glad to help you. Just know, missing persons investigations are obviously not planned in advance, so if one comes up, we might have to back off to take the job."

"Understood." Dev's shoulders dropped, belying his words. "Did Colin talk to you about your rates?"

"You mean will we do it for free?" Nolan chuckled. "Yeah, we'll do it basically for free as long as you pick up any expenses. It'll be good experience and help our team gel even more."

"As long as you don't have five-star restaurant steak dinners, we got your expenses," Colin said.

Nolan laughed again. He had a good sense of humor even though he also seemed to be a detailed and an in-charge kind of guy.

"Abby would never allow that," he said. "She's vegan all the way and is doing her best to convert all of us."

She wrinkled her cute button nose, looking nothing like a former sheriff. "Well, it *is* the way to go."

"*Go where* is the big question." Gabe gave a shake of his head. "I mean, a life without meat isn't a life worth living."

"Exactly what will you do to find Caldwell?" Colin asked, bringing them back to task.

"First, I'd like to ask if you've done anything to try to locate him," Nolan said.

"No," Dev said. "All we have is his last known address, and we know he doesn't live there anymore."

"What about his date of birth?" Hayden asked.

"We don't have it, but we can get it from his DL information." Dev glanced at Colin, who gave him an almost imperceptible shake of his head.

Ah, yes. Colin was warning him to keep quiet about the details. They would get Caldwell's birth date from his driver's license information, which they could get from Russ. But they had to protect Russ. They weren't about to tell these guys where the information had come from.

Nolan sat forward in his chair. "Get it to me, and the sooner the better. We'll need it to get started on the first part of our two-pronged approach."

"Two-pronged?" Dev asked. "What's the first part?"

"Online and database tracking," Nolan replied. "As private investigators, we have access to a selection of databases that can help us find him."

Kinsley's ears perked up. "What kind of databases?"

Nolan focused his intense gaze on her. "With his name and DOB, we can get a ton of information on the guy, including his Social Security number. Cars registered to him. Relatives—their names, dates of birth, and contact info. And info on other people who know him as well."

"We can also run a statewide bank account search and see where he banks," Hayden added. "This is just the tip of the iceberg."

"Wow," she said. "I'm glad you know Colin and are willing to help us."

"Always willing to help a woman at risk." Gabe bowed toward the table, and a flirtatious smile captured his mouth, leaving him looking impossibly handsome. No doubt women fell for him all the time.

But not her. Not for any of these men. Her heart was taken, plain and simple, and it was time she admitted it.

Abby looked at Gabe and put her finger in her mouth to mock gagging. "Kinsley is in serious danger, dude. Leave the flirting up to Jude. He's so much better at it than you."

"Yeah, well, our charming teammate isn't here, so someone's got to do it." Gabe laughed.

Kinsley laughed with him.

Not Dev. He glared at him, then faced Nolan. "Sounds like you have that under control. What's your second prong?"

"Even if we find a current address, we'll still physically canvass the old neighborhood to see if anyone is willing to talk about him. To see what we can learn, and how he might try to evade our search or any attempt to make contact with him."

"That might be a problem," Colin said. "His last known address puts him in a pretty sketchy neighborhood, and there might not be anyone left who knew him."

"Or even if they do," Abby said, "my experience says if the neighborhood's that sketchy, they might not be willing to talk to us."

"But that doesn't mean we won't do our best." Hayden's determination deepened his tone. "Hopefully, we'll stir the pot and make some people jumpy enough to talk."

Gabe leaned forward to look at his teammate. "Exactly what you like to do. Rile everyone up to create some excitement when we might've been able to get the same information without the risk."

Hayden grinned and shrugged. "What can I say? Excitement is my middle name."

"You'll have to excuse my team." Nolan eyed them. "They haven't learned not to air their dirty laundry in front of a client yet."

"No worries." Colin waved a hand. "We're not paying clients, so feel free to say whatever you want to say." He looked at his brother. "After all, when you start working with our team, you'll hear some dirty laundry too."

"Thanks for understanding," Nolan said, his focus still pinned to his team. "Maybe they'll remember for the rest of the meeting not to make unnecessary comments."

Gabe ran a finger across his lips, zipping his mouth closed.

"I won't want to be unprofessional and mention that Gabe's the sarcastic one of the team, so you should ignore him." Abby grinned.

Kinsley laughed. Poor Nolan. He had his work cut out for him to manage this impetuous team. A challenge, but she thought it would be fun, too.

Nolan let out a long breath. "If you would get me the name and date of birth before we leave, we could get started the minute we get back to our office."

Colin stood and dug his cell phone from his pocket. "Let me make a call, and I should have it for you in a matter of minutes."

He stepped outside and closed the door firmly behind him.

"I know we're pushing our luck here," Dev said. "But with sending two of our teammates to Portland to surveil suspects, we're short-staffed here in protecting Kinsley and could use one more guy on the ground in Portland."

Nolan clasped his hands together on the table. "And you'd like us to supplement your details."

"Yes, if possible."

Hayden—Mr. Excitement—got a gleam in his eyes. "I'm down with that."

"I'd be glad to help, too," Abby said.

"If you have a workspace for us here," Nolan said, "I don't see why we can't all work here for now and help you out."

Gabe leaned forward. "I'd be happy to go to Portland if you give me an interesting suspect."

Dev cocked his head. "Ever heard of Louis Luongo?"

Gabe's eyes widened. "Who in the state of Oregon hasn't? Don't tell me he's one of your suspects."

Dev explained. "So you can see, he's loosely connected, but we can't cross him off our suspect list, and we're not quite ready to press him for an alibi and send him into hiding. So we need someone to keep eyes on him."

"I'm your man," Gabe said, his eager expression brightening his eyes. "Just give me his address, and I'm out of here."

"Not so fast." Nolan looked at his teammate. "We came in one car, and you'll need wheels."

"He'll get to Portland faster if he uses one of ours instead of driving back to your place," Dev said.

Gabe rubbed his hands together. "Then point the way."

Dev stood. "Let me ask Reid about office space for you all and for the use of a vehicle." He hurried out the door.

Nolan looked at Kinsley. "Dev referred to several suspects under surveillance. Would you mind telling us about them so we know what we're facing?"

Mind? Yeah. Kinsley would rather not talk about these men. She'd rather Dev or Colin would bring them up to date, but this was something she could do, and she had to do her part. She took a deep breath and launched into a description of why Huff and Mooney were considered suspects. She tried to be thorough and share every detail she possessed. She was just finishing when both Colin and Dev returned.

Colin ripped a piece of paper off the notepad Dev had left behind, scribbled a note, and shoved the paper across the table to Nolan. "Caldwell's details. Name, date of birth, and driver's license number. And by the way, he doesn't have any vehicles registered to him in the state."

Nolan picked up the paper to study it, then folded the yellow page, and shoved it into a large cargo pocket. "Thanks for saving me some time with the additional information."

Dev returned and dropped onto his chair. "Reid said it's okay to use an SUV for Portland and the conference room as an office. Once we get you set up, just ask for anything else you might need."

"Then Gabe will head to Portland and give the rest of us time to get back to our office to pick up our things. Also to bring the rest of the team up to speed so they can continue their current investigations, then make the drive back here." Nolan stood. "And we'll be at your disposal."

Dev sighed. "You don't know how good that sounds and how thankful I am for your help."

"Maybe save your thanks until after you've worked with us for a few days." Abby pushed to her feet. "You only got a hint of our joking. It gets much worse when you add Jude and Reece to the mix. It's probably a good thing they stayed home to hold down the fort."

"I for one think it'll make things interesting and could

relieve some of the tension," Kinsley said, trying to sound positive and brighten the mood.

She got a wan smile from Dev instead. Okay, so the tension wouldn't really go away until they arrested the person who wanted her dead. And made sure the shooter was locked behind bars before any of these fine men and women got hurt or worse yet, lost their life.

~

Dev ignored his brother sitting next to him and kept his eyes on Kinsley from across the dining table. She'd sounded optimistic at the end of their meeting, but was she really? She'd been quiet for the rest of the afternoon and through dinner, not really participating in the conversation. Now, hours later, her slumped posture would say she wasn't handling things so well.

Maybe she was just going stir-crazy, being cooped up in this cabin all the time. He would be for sure, but even if he felt a whole lot better with Nolan and his team partnering on her protection detail, he didn't feel good enough to let down his guard.

Or good enough to let her move about the property without proper supervision. He wasn't about to let her go down by the lake. With no way to close off the area, it remained vulnerable to attack. He would allow her to join them in the conference room when they held update meetings with Nolan's team. As a bonus, she could at least get away from the cabin for a while.

His phone rang, and seeing Ryan's name, he put the phone on speaker for Kinsley. He set it in the middle of the table and leaned closer. "You're on speaker, Ryan. Kinsley and Colin are here. Please say you have an update for us."

"I do," Ryan said. "First, Russ came through with Wacker's current address. Not that he will admit it."

"Russ who?" Dev laughed.

Ryan's chuckle came over the speaker. "So I talked to Wacker. He hasn't heard from Huff and nothing out of the ordinary has happened."

"Did you warn him to be careful?" Dev asked.

"Yeah, and I also gave him a business card. He promised to call if Huff contacts him."

"And you believed him?"

"As much as one can believe anyone affiliated with a criminal, yeah, I did. He was pretty laid-back when we arrived and seemed genuinely shocked when I told him Huff was out on early release."

"So you moved on to surveilling Huff, while Gabe and Micha took on Luongo and Mooney."

"Correct," Ryan said. "Both of the other guys have been going about their everyday lives. Pretty boring actually, but I've got something on Huff."

Kinsley bit her lip. "I hope it's not bad news."

"It's not good." Ryan stopped talking, letting a dramatic pause fall over them.

Drama wasn't something Dev needed in his day. "Go on."

"He left his house to take a phone call in the front yard. I heard him talking to a private investigator. Sounded like he'd hired the guy. He was yelling at him for not finding Kinsley and Caldwell." Ryan cleared his throat. "He threatened to fire the PI if he didn't locate them by the end of the day."

Dev ran a hand across his face, wishing when he took it away that he wasn't looking at a terrified Kinsley. "Then the PI is probably motivated to hunt them down. Did Huff indicate which of the two was his top priority?"

"Sorry, no."

He didn't like that answer. One more ambiguous thing to deal with. "If I was the PI, I would go after the person I thought was the easiest to find."

Ryan didn't respond right away. "Which would be who, in your mind?"

Colin leaned into the phone. "If the PI has done his research, he knows that Kinsley still had a residence in Portland and likely hasn't fled the area on a permanent basis. If he finds out about the shooting, he can surmise that she left due to that and might not have had a chance to hide her trail, whereas Caldwell has been gone for some time and could've covered his tracks better."

"I don't know," Ryan said. "Are you reaching that conclusion because of the information you have, that he wouldn't be privy to?"

"Could be." Colin looked at Dev.

Dev met his gaze. "And he could've already located information on one of the two and just has to follow up."

"Odds aren't good he can find me here, are they?" Kinsley's words rasped out as if fear was strangling her.

Dev didn't know how to answer in a way that would comfort her. Especially if the PI could discover Dev had been at both shootings. If he coupled that with a lifelong friendship, he could guess she was hiding out at his place. Dev's address wasn't readily available, but a good PI could find it.

He gripped his knees under the table. "I guess the question is how good is the PI Huff hired? Having just come out of prison, I wouldn't think he'd have a lot of cash to spend on a top-notch investigator, so maybe the guy isn't very skilled."

"He could've gotten money from his mother," Colin said.

"I got the PI's name," Ryan said. "We can ask Nolan if he's familiar with him. See if he's legit."

"Text it to me," Colin said. "And I'll ask him right away."

"You got it," Ryan said.

"One potentially positive thing." Dev looked up from the phone to peer at Kinsley. "If Huff is still looking for you, he doesn't know where you are and couldn't be the drone operator."

"Or he really does know," Ryan said. "And he held that conversation outside because he knows or suspects he's under surveillance and is trying to throw us off track."

"Do you think you were made?" Dev asked.

"No." A one-word answer, but Ryan filled it with confidence.

"But you never know, right?" Colin asked.

"Yeah."

Eyes wide, Kinsley grabbed her water and chugged it. "If he really doesn't know where I am, but is looking to pay me back, that means I have two people who want to hurt me."

Dev gritted his teeth and didn't want to say anything in response to her comment. Not when she could be right. Two men could be after her. Not just one. Two! They hadn't worked out the identity of one guy, much less a second one. They had to figure out which of their suspects might fit the bill before something else happened and Kinsley was harmed.

"Anything else you learned from him or the other suspects?" Dev asked.

"Not at the moment, but I'll keep you updated." Ryan ended the call.

Dev's phone dinged with the text Ryan had promised. He glanced at the private investigator's name. *Greg Egan.*

He held his phone out to Colin. "See what you can dig up on this guy."

"On it." Colin opened his laptop and shifted in the padded dining chair as if getting comfortable for a long search.

Dev turned his attention to Kinsley. She'd hunched her shoulders and crossed her arms. He wanted to go to the conference room to talk to Nolan and ask him if he might know anything about this Greg Egan guy, but he didn't want to leave her in this kind of state. He shouldn't leave her at all. He could accomplish his same goal by having Nolan come to the cabin.

He sent Nolan a detailed text.

On my way, came his immediate reply. *I have news for you too.*

News? It had to be positive, didn't it? He needed something encouraging, but Kinsley needed it even more. It would take Nolan a few minutes to get to the cabin. Dev had time to talk to her about how she was feeling about the most recent developments and maybe restore her earlier optimism.

He smiled, but she didn't respond. Not a good sign as he'd pretty much always been guaranteed one of his smiles would elicit a positive response from her. "How are you handling Ryan's news about Huff?"

"I guess hearing that he's actually looking for me has given me something real to fear from him." She shivered and looked down. "He's a terrible man, and if he finds me, I don't know what might happen."

Dev settled on the chair next to her and took her hands. Her skin felt like she'd just climbed out of an ice bath. He held her hands between his to try to warm them up and also to convey his sincerity. "To find you, he'll have to find me first, and I'll neutralize any threat before it reaches you." He bent lower to make sure she looked at him. "I promise not to leave you until our suspect is in custody."

"That makes me feel better." She bit her lower lip. "I have confidence in you, but I have to admit I'm still afraid. Not just for myself, but for you too. Whoever's coming after me only has to fire one bullet and it could take you out."

"You're right, that could happen, but we're doing our best to make sure it doesn't." He tried to look confident, but her comments left him wondering if he was up to the task of keeping her alive.

He couldn't do it on his own. He needed his team. But more importantly, he needed God. That would mean trusting Him to protect them all. Was Dev there yet, or was he still letting Hailey's betrayal at the altar impact his actions?

He would have to figure that out, but right now his job was to try to encourage Kinsley.

"You'll just have to trust me on that." He almost snorted as he said the words, expecting her to trust him when he was the king of distrust.

She didn't pick up on his internal conflict and gave a firm nod. "I do trust you. All of the team. I'll also pray about it."

He forced a smile, hoping she thought he believed God would be there when they needed Him. Too bad he still wasn't certain.

Kinsley couldn't take her eyes off Nolan as he raced past Dev at the door and into the room. He approached Colin at his computer across from her.

Nolan stopped at the end of the table and turned to look at Dev, who was closing the door. "I know you need to see me, but you won't believe what we found."

Dev came to sit by Colin, but enthusiasm about the

potential news she expected Dev to have was nowhere in his expression. "You struck out on Caldwell this soon?"

Nolan gave a throaty laugh and bounced on his toes. "Not hardly. We found the guy."

"You did?" Kinsley resisted shooting to her feet in excitement. "Where? How?"

"Believe it or not, he's big into poetry." Nolan's face beamed, but he stopped bouncing. "Gabe talked to Caldwell's former neighbors before going to Luongo's residence. An older lady remembered the poetry connection."

"Poetry?" Dev shook his head. "I would never have guessed that."

"Odd for sure," Nolan said. "But something unique enough to help us locate him pretty quickly."

"How can it help?" Kinsley asked. "Other than looking for something he might've published."

A confident, almost cocky smile crossed his face. "We joined a poetry association—be prepared for the bill—and their directory contains their members' names and cities where they live. His name was listed in their directory. Lives in Eugene. Didn't take much after that to find his address and also discover that he would be reading at an open mic night where we can intercept him if needed."

Colin looked over his computer. "If he's listing his city in the directory, he must not be trying very hard to hide out."

"Could be," Nolan said. "Or he's kept his poetry a secret and doesn't figure Huff can find him based on that."

"I could see that happening," Kinsley said. "Especially since he was in the construction trade. I wouldn't be surprised at all if he hid it from everyone."

"Ryan told us Huff hired a PI to find Caldwell and Kinsley," Colin said. "If you found Caldwell so quickly, then another good PI can find him too."

"That's why I called you up here," Dev said. "I wanted to

see how much of a threat we had with this PI potentially finding Kinsley, and I wanted to know if you'd heard of him. His name is Greg Egan."

Nolan rested his hands on the table. "I'm not familiar with the guy, but I can ask the team and see if anyone else recognizes his name."

"Is there a PI directory that you can check to see if he's even official?" Kinsley asked.

"I can do that right now." He got out his phone and tapped the screen.

She shifted her attention to Dev. "Odd turn of events for sure, but at least it led to his whereabouts."

He nodded. "Let's hope Egan doesn't figure this out."

Nolan looked up from his screen. "Egan's licensed. He's been licensed for nine years. The database contains his address and phone number. Lives in Portland. The records were updated earlier this month, so his information should be current, and we can pay him a visit to ask about an alibi for the shootings."

"But first," Dev said, "we need to warn Caldwell that Huff could be coming for him."

Nolan frowned. "If we're not already too late. Do you want us to approach him?"

"Yes," Dev said. "And the sooner the better. I don't want someone's death on my conscience."

Kinsley couldn't imagine living the rest of her life feeling responsible for someone's death. If only she could do something to stop Huff, and yet, all she could do was pray that Egan hadn't located Caldwell or didn't find the man before Nolan had a chance to warn him.

17

Dev watched his family and Kinsley set up a game of Monopoly on the coffee table. He remained in the dining room, trying to decide what to do after the information they received. The day had started off far too uneventful for his liking and had remained that way all through the tense coffee break he'd just shared with Kinsley and his family.

Uneventful when it came to Kinsley's safety was good, but Sierra had said the fingerprint information for the drone would come in today. He'd hoped she would've called him by now and had identified Huff as their suspect, as he was their most logical one. That was, if his conversation on the lawn wasn't staged. But Dev would be glad for anyone's name. That would give him a lead to go on. A solid lead.

He would far rather have that than go into the living room and join in a game. Usually he loved Monopoly. Most times he won when he played his family, but today he couldn't concentrate.

His phone chimed a text from Nolan. *Located Caldwell. He didn't hear from Huff and didn't seem concerned. Tried to get him to understand the danger he was in, but he didn't believe*

Huff would come after him. Claims he's never heard of Kinsley, so had no reason to want to kill her.

You did your best to warn him, Dev fired back. *Would be good if you kept an eye on him. For protection and in case he's lying and has it out for Kinsley.*

Roger that, but man, you'll owe me for making me sit through poetry readings tonight.

Dev replied with a *ha-ha* but hoped he could find some way to pay the guy back.

Should he have had Nolan come back instead of keeping an eye on Caldwell? Dev really needed all the help he could get with Kinsley's protection detail and couldn't afford for Nolan to stay in Eugene. Would Dev come to regret that decision? Only time would tell. Something else to weigh heavy on his mind.

His throat seemed to close on him, and he needed some air.

"I'm stepping out on the porch for a minute." He didn't wait for anyone to reply but opened the door and joined Abby, who had the dayshift.

"All's quiet," she said. "I'm not hoping for anyone to break into the compound, but this is getting a little tedious."

Dev felt sorry for her and appreciated her even more right now. "Better than sitting at the sheriff's desk and doing paperwork, right?"

She stared into the distance. "Pretty much anything trumps that part of the job, and the higher I climbed in the ranks, the less action I saw. I was only called in when the problem was so big my sergeants and lieutenant couldn't handle it. Often a disaster by then, and I had to make sure the public didn't lose confidence in us." She shook her head. "The job ended up being far more about politics and putting out fires than actual law enforcement."

Dev would've hated that kind of job. "Is that why you left to join Nolan's team?"

She shifted to look at him. "Actually, you got it wrong. It's not Nolan's team. Not really anyway. It was his idea, and we voted for him to be in charge, but each of us ponied up our fair share to start the business."

"Seems like you know each other pretty well for having just formed the company."

"We do. Went to college together, studying law enforcement." Her eyes took on a fond look. "We formed a study group our freshman year to get through science prereqs and became friends. We had jobs with different agencies before we graduated, but we managed to go to police academy together too."

"Sounds like you have a pretty tight bond."

"We do, even though we went our separate ways and lived in different cities. But then Nolan contacted us and offered to provide the property where we live and work out of—an old inn with an attached lighthouse sitting on the point. He paid for it, and we're renovating the main areas together, but doing our own rooms."

"How's that going?"

She shook her head and laughed. "Some of us are doing better than others."

"The place sounds amazing. I'll have to come by and see it."

"It'll be great all right." Her lips turned down. "*Once* we get the renovations done. We're doing them between jobs, and it's taking longer than we hoped."

"I'm sure Reid would agree to pay back your help here by our team coming to work on the place with you for a day."

"There's no need to repay us, but we wouldn't turn it down." She wrinkled her nose. "Took me a long time to accept help like that. Until God taught me a valuable lesson about trying to always go it on my own. And before you ask, it's a long story. Just trust me when I say, I now know that accepting help is a good thing."

Dev could take a page out of her book. He didn't like to ask for help. Something he rarely did. Probably came from being the younger brother of an overachiever and wanting to prove himself. But protecting Kinsley had been an exception. He would take all the help he could get if it meant he could keep her alive.

So far, he and the others had succeeded in that area—the most important area—but they hadn't moved very far in the investigation.

"Excuse me a minute." He walked around the other side of the cabin.

He'd had enough of waiting and dug out his phone to text Sierra. He started typing, then stopped, letting his finger hover over the keypad. She and her team had gone out of their way to get here and to Kinsley's apartment right away to collect forensics. It would be rude of him to try to push her along when he knew she was doing the best she could do.

He pressed the X on the keypad until the text disappeared and stared at the screen until it went black. What should he do now? Not go inside and play games. Or should he take the time to relax and rejuvenate with the others?

Problem was, he was too amped up to relax, and he didn't want to bring them down. So then what? What could he be doing to follow up on any of the suspects? Maybe he should review all the files again just in case he was missing something. He could take them to the bedroom he was sharing with Colin so no one was distracted by his foul mood.

He rounded the corner again. His phone rang in his hand. His heart lurched.

Could it be Sierra?

He woke up the phone and checked the caller ID. Sierra. Perfect.

"Please tell me you have news," he said into his phone.

"I do, but probably not what you're waiting for," she said. "We cast the footprints we found near the drone operator's truck. One of my assistants has already identified the footwear."

"And?" Dev asked, though honestly he wasn't all that excited about the lead as they would have to go to the suspects' houses to get a close enough look at their shoes to match it.

"It's a Nike Cortez."

"That doesn't narrow it down much, does it?" Dev asked. "Pretty much everyone in Oregon knows that's the most popular running shoe ever made, and most people have owned a pair over the years."

"You're right, since Nike is headquartered here, we're all familiar with one of their most iconic shoes." She didn't speak for a moment. "But we all wear our shoes differently, so the wear pattern on the heels and toes are unique to each individual. Think of it as a shoe fingerprint. Find me a pair of Nike Cortez from one of your suspects, and I can tell you if it's a match to our impression."

"If we ever get to the point where we have a single suspect, I'll take you up on that. Until then, I'll have our guys in Portland keep an eye out for one of our suspects wearing those shoes."

"Odds are good if he wore them that night, he wouldn't wear them again in public. But then, he might not be as smart as we're giving him credit for."

"Yeah, he's been pretty clever."

"I need to get back to work, so I'll let you go."

"How are the fingerprints and DNA coming?" he asked quickly before she disconnected.

"Not as fast as I'd hoped, but I'll let you know the minute I have anything. Should be before the day is out." She ended the call, preventing him from asking additional questions.

His phone rang again before he had time to process the call from Sierra. He glanced at the screen. *Micha.*

He could have something on Luongo that would help move them forward.

Dev tapped the button to accept the call. "Our boy behaving himself?"

"You're not going to like this," Micha said.

Dev's gut clenched. "Go ahead and spit it out."

"I talked to Luongo's neighbors on the down low. Found out he belongs to a shooting club and goes there frequently."

Dev shoved his fingers into his hair. "Not the kind of news we want to hear."

"No. He could be our shooter."

"Yeah," was all Dev could say without letting Micha hear his worry.

"Do you want me to keep on his house?" Micha asked, thankfully moving on. "Or should I head to his club to see what I can learn about him?"

"Stay at the house. It's too risky to talk to these club members. They're usually pretty tight, and if you ask around, you might alert Luongo to the fact that you're tailing him."

"Makes sense. I'll hang here."

Dev told him to watch for the Nikes and explained why, then took a deep breath before his next question. "Anything else of interest there?"

"Nah, the dude hasn't even left home."

"Don't let that lull you into a false sense of security. Keep your eyes open. If he's our shooter you're our first line of defense."

∾

Kinsley sat down with Dev in the dining room. Jada had gone to sit with Sandy until she fell asleep leaving Kinsley and Dev alone. He shared the conversations he'd had with Sierra and Micha and now they were reviewing Kinsley's investigation files again. A last ditch effort while they waited for Sierra to call again, and time dragged like a heavy suitcase on a long airport walk. They didn't locate anything new, and tension filled the cabin along with the lingering smell of the rosemary-infused chicken they'd had for dinner.

Kinsley's phone rang with a video call, the caller ID said the Veritas Center. She showed Dev. "Could be Sierra."

"Answer!" He jumped to his feet.

She tapped the accept button and then joined the call. Nick Thorn's face showed on the screen. He still looked the same as she remembered and had a close-cut beard in a reddish-brown color that matched his hair.

"Nick!" She smiled. "Long time no see."

"Hey, Kinsley," he said, his tone deep and husky.

"Good to hear from you." She glanced back at Dev who'd come to stand behind her. "My shadow is Devan— Dev—Graham."

"We know each other," Dev said. "And even if we didn't, all the great things Sierra has to say about you makes it seem like we do."

"They're all true." He blew on his fingernails and polished them on his shirt, then laughed. "I got the drone from Sierra and ran the ID through the registration databases. I'm sorry to say the drone isn't registered, so it didn't provide any contact information."

Kinsley's hope evaporated. "Then we're out of luck in finding him that way."

"Yes and no." Nick tilted his head. "True the registration database was a bust, but we can still use the serial ID number for a few things."

He held up his index finger. "First, I left a message with the manufacturer to find out where they sold this model drone with our ID lot. If we can find out where it was sold and narrow it down to a single location, we might get lucky and recover security footage of the purchase. Or if the drone was sold online, we can find out where it was shipped."

"What are the odds that will happen?" Dev asked.

"Honestly..." Nick paused, and she couldn't help thinking that he didn't want to answer. "With this older model drone, it's a longshot. Businesses often don't keep security video for long. And we have to consider the fact that it could've been bought at a garage sale, on eBay, or other selling sites. If our suspect is smart, he might have bought it this way so no one would be able to trace it to him."

Kinsley felt Dev's posture stiffen behind her.

"So, really, we shouldn't hold our breath on this."

Nick scratched his chin. "Wouldn't say there's no hope, but don't count on it as your only lead."

"You said 'a few things,' though," Kinsley said, wanting to hear something positive.

"Yeah, I'll also write an algorithm using the serial ID and search the internet for the number."

"If it's old, how will that help?" she asked.

"Once something is indexed by search engines on the internet, it's there forever unless you can get the search engine owner to remove it, which is usually impossible."

"But why would the number even be there?" she asked, still waiting to see how this could be a good thing.

Nick's jaw tightened as if he were getting frustrated with her. "If it was listed on eBay or other such selling sites for example, the serial number might be included in the listing."

Not quite there for her. "And that wouldn't disappear when an item is sold?"

"No. Haven't you ever searched for something online and gotten an eBay listing for an item that was no longer for sale?"

She nodded. "Yeah, I have. Frustrating when I want to buy it and it's really not for sale, but yeah, I see your point now."

Nick smiled. "So this is a possibility too. Another long shot, though."

"What about a broadcast signal?" Dev asked. "Was the drone set up to be broadcasting?"

Nick shook his head. "Wasn't built in and wasn't retrofitted with a remote ID module, so definitely flying on the downlow. Makes me mad. We just had a medical helicopter that couldn't land due to a drone flying illegally in the area. The patient died."

"That's horrible." Kinsley offered a quick prayer for the family suffering a needless loss.

"There's a reason the FAA has rules in place." Nick cleared his throat. "Time for some good news. I was able to remove the camera's memory card. It was intact, and I recovered the video."

"Not like video of our compound helps." Dev didn't bother to hide his skepticism.

Nick didn't appear to let it bother him. "There was a small snippet of an urban area recorded prior to the cabin footage. Looks like apartment buildings. I've isolated a good image to upload to the internet to search for the location, but I'm also going to send it to you to review. Maybe you'll know what the footage is of."

"Can you send it right away?" Kinsley asked.

"I'll fire it off to you as soon as we get off the phone." He leaned back and put his hands behind his head. "And on a different subject, I'll also send you the enlarged photo of the jewelry from your apartment. I wasn't able to do a lot to enhance it, but it *is* clearer and you might be able to see what you're looking for. That's all I have. Sorry I didn't have great news, but it's better than nothing."

"You're right." Kinsley smiled at him. "Thanks so much for your help, Nick."

"I'll let you know as soon as I hear anything from the manufacturer or if my algorithm turns up something actionable." He snapped forward in his seat, and the call ended.

Kinsley turned to look at Dev. "We'll just have to pray what he sends us will turn out to be helpful."

Her phone dinged a text, and the photo from Nick came through. She opened it while Dev was still standing behind her.

She looked at the screen and gasped. "It's my apartment complex."

Dev punched the back of her chair. "Look at the time and date."

She checked the photo, then flashed a look back at him. "He filmed this after the break-in."

"It's the morning you were at the apartment meeting Stewart." He clutched her chair. "If you zoom in, I'll bet you'll find our cars in the parking lot."

She didn't want to zoom, but she did, enlarging the image. Just like he'd said, their cars were in the parking lot, and the detective had just arrived.

"He could've been scared off by Stewart's arrival," Dev said.

She turned her chair to look at him, pulling his hands free from the chair. "What do you think he might've been planning to do if the detective hadn't arrived when he did?"

"I don't even want to think about it." His facial muscles tightened. "Thank God Stewart showed up."

Her phone dinged again, and the text held the photo of her jewelry that Nick had enhanced. She opened it on the screen, and the gold pendant had been enlarged. It was an oblong piece, about an inch long, with writing engraved on the side facing up.

Dev leaned over her shoulder. "Can you make out the writing?"

"No, but likely if we could, it would give away our suspect's name or maybe the name of someone close to him or he wouldn't have come back for it."

"You're probably right." He moved back to the other side of the table.

"I was hoping the picture would tell us something," she said. "But it wasn't all bad news tonight. We'll just have to pray that Nick finds something else."

"I'll let Nick know the image is of your apartment," Dev said, disappointment lingering in his gaze.

She got up to pace for a while. Not only to work out her disappointment, but she'd been sitting for far too long. Sitting. Sitting. Sitting. All she'd been able to do while she had to rely on others to figure out who was trying to kill her.

She went to the door and peeked out the tiny window. The only thing she was allowed to look out as the other curtains were pulled tight. If she stayed for any length of time, Dev would ask her to step away from the door. She remained in place long enough to see the sun drop below the horizon, but it was barely noticeable in the heavy smoke clogging the outside air.

She'd experienced bad air quality in Portland from the winds blowing in wildfire smoke, but nothing as bad as this. Poor Abby and now Hayden, standing duty on the porch. They wore a respirator, but still, it wasn't a pleasant job. She wished she could take their place, but if she could, they wouldn't need to be here. She owed so many people. Perhaps owed them her life. A debt that could never be repaid. Sure, she could try, or even pay for their services, but that wouldn't begin to cover it.

Thank you. For your protection. For sending these men and this woman. Watch over them and keep them safe.

Dev came up behind her. "You're deep in thought."

"Just thinking about the huge debt I owe all of you for making sure I'm safe."

"I hope you're not trying to figure out a way to repay everyone. As Reid said in our meeting, none of us need to be paid, so you shouldn't even be thinking about that."

"Easier said than done. I'm sure if you were in my position, you would be thinking the same thing."

"You could be right. But just know we're here for you no matter what."

"I'm very blessed by that. God smiled on me the day you came to my rescue in the parking lot."

"Not exactly what you thought that day, was it?" He grinned.

"No. No, it wasn't." She laughed. "I hope you can forgive me for being so difficult at first."

"Nothing to forgive. I'd have been the same way. I wouldn't have wanted to accept the fact that someone was shooting at me and I needed protection."

She shook her head. "Even now, I find it hard to believe.

Maybe it's because we haven't been able to narrow this down to one suspect."

"We should be able to do that if Sierra lifted fingerprints from the drone and found a match."

"But if she did, why isn't she letting us know? She said they would be done today, but the typical work day is over."

"I know she frequently works late and could still be processing things." He held up his phone. "She said she would let me know the minute she has anything."

His phone sounded a text.

He looked down at the screen. "It's Reid. He wants me to come over to his place to meet with him and Russ."

"Then you should go."

He gnawed on his cheek. "I don't want to leave you, and I certainly can't take you with me."

"Don't worry about me." She rested a hand on his arm. "With all of the suspects under surveillance now, they can't be coming for me, and I'm good with Colin in here and Hayden outside the door. Besides, you'll just be a few houses away."

"Are you sure?" He searched her eyes.

"Positive." She pushed him towards the door.

He looked back at her. "Just know I'm a phone call away, and I can be back here in a few minutes."

She nodded and smiled, but even though she was agreeing to him going, she really didn't feel comfortable with it. She didn't think anything bad was going to happen, but she'd come to depend on him. Rely on him. Want him in her life.

And not just as a protector, but as a full-time partner. Maybe while he was gone, she could stop stressing over who was trying to kill her and figure out how she could start a relationship without ruining her bond with her best friend.

18

Dev rested his hand on the doorknob and continued to look at Kinsley, whose expression was opposite of her words. "Are you sure you're okay with me going over to Reid's place? I could do a video call if you prefer."

"Go." She waved her hand.

"I'll try to make it quick. If I walk, I can take a shortcut by the lake and get there and back much faster." He checked for his sidearm, then opened the door. He peered at her to make sure her tension had seemed to disappear. She'd relaxed back in her chair and didn't look concerned, so he stepped out into the night.

He stopped on the porch next to Hayden. "Everything okay out here?"

"Nothing moving nearby but the bugs buzzing by the lights." Hayden looked bored out of his mind by the lack of excitement.

"I know you were hoping for some action, but I still need you to be alert."

"Oh, I am. Even if I don't look it."

Dev had to hope he wasn't just telling him what he wanted to hear. "I'm heading over to Reid's lodge. You have my number. Call me if anything out of the ordinary comes up. And I mean anything."

Hayden's gaze sharpened, and he gave a crisp nod, now looking like he had the situation under control. "You can count on me."

Dev liked seeing the change in the man's appearance. Feeling more confident in going, he charged down the steps, and took the path toward the lake. He didn't like leaving Kinsley in anyone else's care, but he had to take the emotions out of it, exactly as she said. Their suspects were under surveillance, and two trained protectors like Colin and Hayden were in charge of her close protection. She didn't need Dev to be present.

He kicked up speed into a jog, using his flashlight to cut through the increased smoke and to keep from tripping over any protruding tree roots. Normally the light glinted off the lake making a beautiful picture. He could easily imagine taking a moonlight boat ride with Kinsley once this was all over.

Don't get ahead of yourself. You have to find and bring in the shooter, and then talk things out with your sister. So pay attention and safely get to the lodge for Russ's update.

He made a sharp right and climbed a small hill up to the large lodge with light gleaming through the windows. Another picturesque scene that he tuned out to circle around to the front and the wide steps. He took them two at a time and pounded on the door.

Reid opened it within moments and stood back. "Russ is chomping at the bit to give us his news and get home. His baby is due soon, and he's afraid Sydney's going to go into labor."

"You could've called," Dev said as he passed by.

"I thought you'd want to hear this in person," Russ said,

standing in front of the large stone fireplace, "so you could figure out the best way to tell Kinsley."

Dev didn't like the sound of that. Not at all. He joined Russ near the dancing fire that was crackling and spewing out heat. Reid followed and perched on the arm of the sofa.

"So go ahead," Dev said. "I'm here now. What do you have to tell us?"

Russ planted a hand on the rustic wooden fireplace mantle. "I just got word on Porter Mooney. They found his partner buried in a Persian rug on his hunting property."

A murderer! Dev's heart fell to his stomach. "Seriously? So he *is* a murderer for sure."

Russ nodded. "You know Sierra recovered fibers at Mooney's home, and she's comparing the fibers recovered in the water to the rug to confirm it's a match."

"We can pretty much assume they'll match," Dev said. "But why didn't they check the property where they found the body before?"

Russ shook his head. "Mooney registered it through a shell corporation that detectives never attached to his name."

"So how did they find it then?" Reid asked.

"They got an anonymous tip. They still haven't been able to work out the caller's identity, but ground-penetrating radar located the body." He tightened his grip on the mantle. "You can thank your Veritas team friends for this one. They have GPR and their forensic anthropologist agreed to search at no cost, so PPB didn't have to wait for an assist from the state police."

"Have they acted on it?" Reid asked.

"An arrest warrant has been issued."

"Issued? Not good enough." Dev was surprised at the vehemence in his own tone. "When are they going to serve it?"

"As soon as they finish assembling their arrest team. You'll want to give whoever we have watching him a heads up." Russ's eyes narrowed. "But before you make that call, you should know, they also found a second body on the same property. A woman."

Dev's brain raced with the information, trying to process it. His thoughts came to a screeching halt. "Luongo's wife?"

Russ nodded. "The woman's clothing matched what his wife was wearing when she disappeared. The ME also confirmed that the decomposition is consistent with the time she's been missing, but the police can't act until the ME makes a positive identification."

Likely the reason Sierra hadn't gotten back to Dev when she had said she would. This murder investigation would take top priority and, in a way, helped Dev by putting two suspects behind bars where they couldn't get to Kinsley.

"So Luongo and Mooney knew each other?" Reid asked.

Russ nodded. "Looks like they were partners in the shell corporation that no one discovered. Neither of the detectives had seen them together or found any communications with each other in the phone records. They believe they had burner phones and made sure they didn't meet in public."

Dev shook his head. "What are the odds of solving two murders like this in one place?"

"It only seems high because we didn't know the men were connected," Reid said. "But now that we know the connection, the odds are probably not out of order."

"Yeah," Dev said, but he still couldn't wrap his mind around it. "And an arrest warrant for Luongo? Where do we stand on that?"

"Once they have the positive ID, they'll be bringing him in for questioning and holding him for as long as possible." Russ looked from one to the other with raised brows, as if waiting for further questions. No one spoke, and he pushed away from the fireplace. "Okay, that's it. I'm out of here. Be sure to get on the horn to our guys and tell them these men will be taken into custody soon."

Dev dug his phone from his pocket and called Gabe first. These calls weren't difficult to make. Not difficult at all. Both Gabe and Micha would likely be happy to come back home. The hard part would be telling Kinsley that one of these two murderers could be their shooter. Thankfully, by Russ requesting to meet over here instead of making a call that Kinsley could listen in to, he had given Dev the chance to think about it before he had to explain it to her.

Gabe answered at the same time Dev's phone alerted him to an incoming call from Sierra. He was tempted to take it, but he would finish up with Gabe, then call Sierra right back.

"Any action with Luongo?" Dev asked.

"Nah." Gabe didn't keep his disappointment out of his voice. "For such a notorious man, he leads a pretty boring life and looks like he's in for the night."

"He won't be for long." Dev shared the recent development.

"Whoa, seriously?" Gabe fell silent. "That's shocking news."

"It is," Dev said as his phone dinged a voicemail alert. "I need you to stay there until the police pick him up, and then you can head back here. Text me when you leave."

"Will do."

"Thanks for your help, man."

"Of course, but I have to say I was hoping to catch the guy up to no good." Gabe laughed and disconnected.

Dev wasted no time but tapped his voicemail to play Sierra's message.

No luck in lifting complete fingerprints from the drone, but the drone operator filmed himself and left the footage in the

camera like I thought he might do. His photo matched in facial
recognition. I called Russ with the details. He said he just left you
at Reid's place and wants you to meet him at your place ASAP
because he's headed there to share the info with Kinsley.

Why hadn't Nick given them that big piece of news with the information about the drone? Could be Sierra asked him not to until she could run the photo against the database. He would have to ask her when they talked.

He fired a look at Reid. "Can you call Micha? I have to go. Looks like we have a facial recognition match for the drone operator."

"To who?"

"I don't know yet. Sierra's voicemail said Russ is sharing the details with Kinsley."

Reid made shooing motions with his hands. "Then go, but call me when you know which suspect we're dealing with."

"You got it." Dev raced out into the night. He stopped on the porch to text Hayden and alert him to his and Russ's upcoming arrival so it didn't spook the guy and cause him to draw down on either of them.

He bolted down the steps and the hill. Good thing he'd walked. This was the fastest route, and he was dying to know who the photo matched.

The smoky night obscured his path and irritated his lungs as he raced for his cabin. At his full-speed press, he quickly reached the lake. Movement in the water caught his attention, but the smoke stopped him from clearly making it out. He slowed and inched closer. Something black and small moved toward the shore. Definitely not a watercraft but a human. A human in a dive suit approaching Dev.

Was it their suspect, coming to hurt Kinsley? Dev couldn't let that happen. He charged down the beach to the water. Kicked off his shoes and socks. Slipped his belt with his sidearm out of the loops, buckled it, and dropped the belt over his head.

He waded in. The biting cold water took his breath. As a former water-rescue professional with Clackamas County Sheriff's Office, he knew that going into this water without a wetsuit at this time of year could result in death in a very short period of time. He had to be careful not to submerge his full body and not stay in the water too long. But he wouldn't risk waiting for him to swim to shore. The intruder could turn and swim off faster than Dev without fins could catch him, and Dev would lose their suspect.

He panted a few times to catch his breath, then moved ahead.

The dark figure inched closer and closer, slickly gliding through the still water, leaving ripples behind. He suddenly stopped. He'd likely made out Dev's approach.

Good. Now Dev could take him down.

The black head didn't surface, leaving the slick top of his skull unmoving and just cresting the water.

Dev waded in closer, readying himself for an assault. The water gently lapped at his waist, and the cold numbed his legs.

Something whooshed through the water, aiming directly at him. A sharp barb pierced his hip. Severe pain stabbed him, radiating up his body. He fought through the pain to stay upright.

He reached down. Found a spear from a speargun piercing his hip. He let his fingers trail around to the back. The sharp spearhead had gone straight through. He knew enough first aid and anatomy to know this could've ripped through his femoral artery. He could be bleeding out. He would check, but it was too dark to see if blood filtered through the water. If he was bleeding out, he would soon lose consciousness.

Get out of the water. Now. You can't do battle with this guy until you assess your wound.

He started to back up, his bare feet sinking in the silt and slowing him down.

The spear on his hip was ripped forward. Dev stifled a shout of pain.

His assailant must have left the line attached to the spear and was jerking him into the water. Dev stood his ground, but the pain threatened to take him down. Bury him in the water.

Another jerk of the line. Another wave of excruciating agony. Injuries that contacted both muscle and bone created the worst kind of pain, and extreme anguish told him the spear put him in that category.

The assailant pulled again. The pain consumed Dev. He reached for his sidearm. The area spun around him, and he lost his balance, falling. The water slapped into his face. Cold. Numbing.

His assailant lunged out of the water. Muscular. Moving fast. He flipped Dev over. Dev saw black with the pain, and his sidearm slipped from his hand. The assailant shoved his arm under Dev's shoulder, then wrapped the line from the spear around his neck.

He tightened the hold, cutting off Dev's oxygen supply. Dev had no weapon. No defense. He clawed at the line but couldn't get his hands under the cord. A jerk of the line from the assailant, tugging on the spear froze Dev's muscles, and he couldn't continue to fight.

The area around him turned black. He was losing consciousness.

Please don't let this happen. Please don't let this guy kill me and get to Kinsley. Please protect her, Lord, please.

And with that prayer, the night went black.

19

Kinsley forgot all about the puzzle she was doing with Jada and Colin and stared open-mouthed at Russ. As matter-of-factly as reporting tomorrow's weather, he'd stepped into the dining room and announced that he knew their suspect's name.

He stopped at the table and rested his hands on his hips. "Sierra said video from the drone returned a facial recognition match."

Kinsley lurched to her feet and planted her hands on the table. "You have a name? Really? The name of the person who's been stalking and trying to kill me?"

"I do." His eyes narrowed. "Guy's name is Harry Yapp."

Colin scratched his beard. "Not one of our suspects, then."

"No." Russ studied Kinsley. "Does that name mean anything to you?"

Did it? She searched her memory. "No. Not off the top of my head anyway. It sounds familiar and is pretty distinctive. I should remember if I've crossed paths with him, but I don't think I ever did an investigation that included a guy with that name."

Russ grabbed his phone from a holder on his belt next to his sidearm. "Let me show you his mugshot. Maybe that'll ring some bells."

He swiped down the screen and held it out.

Kinsley took one look at the guy with a gleaming bald head and dark eyes and spun to Jada. "Look at this."

Jada jerked back. "You know him?"

Kinsley shrugged. "Maybe, and I think you might too."

"Me?" Eyes wide, Jada got up from the end of the table and joined Kinsley.

Jada stared at the picture, and her body stiffened. "Oh no. He's the guy who stayed at the Bluebird, and we played pranks on him when we were kids, right?"

"Yeah, it's him," Kinsley said. "And now that I think about it, I remember joking about his last name and wanting to tell him to shut his big Yapp when he insisted on having the Bluebird Cabin, and we had to hold our sleepover next door instead."

"Mind clarifying for me?" Colin asked.

"Jada and I were scheduled to have a weekend in the Bluebird Cabin," Kinsley said.

"I remember," Colin said. "It was your favorite place to stay, but it wasn't any different than the other cabins, so I don't know why."

"It was the most secluded place on the property and gave us more privacy," Jada said.

Kinsley clasped her hands together. "But then this guy shows up at the last minute, takes a drive around the campground, and then insists on having the Bluebird Cabin or he was leaving. Sandy agreed because the cabin wasn't rented for the weekend, and she needed the income. So she moved us next door instead."

"And you played pranks on him?" Colin asked.

Jada nodded. "We did a few things before Mom found

out and made us stay at the house instead of the cabin next door."

"But these were just childhood pranks," Kinsley said, thankful Sandy had gone to bed and wasn't in the room to hear this. "Certainly nothing worth shooting at us for. Especially after all these years. I mean if he wanted to get back at us, why wait so long?"

"When did he stay at your campground?"

Jada looked at Kinsley. "It was August, that much I remember because school was about to start. You were going to be a freshman that year, and I was starting seventh grade."

"So, let's see." She tapped her chin and then gave Russ a year.

Russ swiped the screen on his phone. "That makes sense then. He was arrested for burglary in September of the same year and has been in prison ever since. He was only released two weeks ago."

Colin shook his head. "Still, seems pretty farfetched that any person would wait more than ten years to get revenge for a few silly little pranks."

"Think about it, though," Jada said. "We've been considering the shooter is only after Kinsley, but maybe the shooting on Main Street wasn't a warning to Kinsley but was directed at both of us because he was out to get me, too. That would fit, right?"

"It could," Colin said. "But he might only be the drone operator and not the shooter."

"You mean we could be looking for two suspects." Kinsley didn't want to think this was actually true, but it wasn't the first time they considered this possibility.

"Either way, I'm going to head back to the office and do some research on him," Russ said. "Colin, you work your magic on the keyboard and see what you can learn, too."

Russ shoved his phone into the belt holder and gave them a long look. "Hopefully I can get someone at the prison where he was incarcerated on the phone at this time of night to give me the address he provided at discharge. If so, I can pick him up for questioning."

"You'll want to run that past Dev before you do." Colin set his jaw and held Russ's gaze.

"I can do that." Russ's amiable attitude was out of character but appreciated.

"I thought Dev would've come back with you," Colin said.

"He was making phone calls to our guys in Portland before he came back. You fill him in on this, and he'll tell you all about that when he gets back."

"Text the photo to me," Colin said.

"Will do, but I need to go. Don't let your guard down and keep your eyes open. We don't know anything about the kind of threat Yapp could pose." He looked each person in the eye, then marched out the door.

Colin turned to Kinsley. "Is there anything you remember about this guy other than he got the Bluebird Cabin?"

"He stayed for two days, and he didn't do much while he was there." She thought back to those days. "The only thing I remember him doing was scuba diving in the lake."

"He could still be a diver," Colin said. "So when Dev gets back, we should plan an additional defense against access from the lake."

Kinsley nodded and tried to come up with any other information she could share that might be helpful in finding this man. But honestly, she couldn't even wrap her head around the fact that this could be the guy who was shooting at her. A pail of water above his door and a Vaseline-greased toilet seat certainly weren't anything worth killing over. Were they?

~

The blackness receded, and Dev opened his eyes to look around. He was sitting up, leaning against a tree. Not bleeding out, thank God. The diver in the water was nowhere in sight, but his slick wetsuit and fins lay on the shore. The spear had been pulled from Dev's hip and lay nearby. The pain was more of a throbbing ache now than a sharp stabbing.

He started to get up. Pain razored into his body, but he ignored it to push with his feet. He couldn't move. His body was bound to the tree, and his wrists were tied behind him. The speargun line again. Of course his assailant would have the heaviest line used for large catches. Dev was experienced with spearguns, and this abrasion-resistant polyblend over braided line, was used for large, heavy-duty catches.

He was stuck.

Kinsley! She needed him. Needed his protection.

How long had he been unconscious? Her assailant had probably reached the cabin by now or was close to it.

No! Dev jerked hard on the line. The cord didn't give but cut into his chest, and his hip pain sent stars dancing before his eyes. He had to find a way to free himself. Or get to his phone, if it even worked after he submerged it in water.

He glanced around for anything that could help him. The spear that had pierced his hip lay discarded five feet away. He could use the sharp tip to cut through the cord at his wrists, but he had no hope of reaching it without releasing the cord around his body.

He looked up. The tree narrowed. If he was able to

shimmy up, the cords could potentially loosen, and he could duck under them.

He drew up his legs and planted his feet on the pine needles littering the ground. The pain in his hip ripped into him and those stars floated again. He thought of Kinsley and took a deep breath to ward off the pain. Then another. And another.

You can do it. Kinsley's counting on you.

He rose up. Gave a mighty shove. Ignored the increased pain. Budged the rope a fraction of an inch.

Yes! You're doing it.

Hope sprung up in his heart. He gave it another try. And then one more until he was nearly standing, and the rope had loosened. He maneuvered his shoulders around until one was free, then the other, the rope lying around his neck and dangling over his chest. He dropped down and freed his head.

He plunged to the ground, the agony nearly taking him out. But he rolled instead of letting the stabbing torture get to him until he had the sharp spear in his hands. He fumbled a few times until he finally got the spear in a position to saw at the rope.

Progress was slow. It was going to take time. Time Kinsley didn't have.

Please don't let this take too long and that the assailant hasn't managed to overpower Colin and Hayden to kill Kinsley.

20

Kinsley sat across the table from Jada, while Colin had taken his computer to his room where he could focus better on researching Yapp. Kinsley couldn't concentrate on the puzzle as they waited for Dev to return. They needed to share the information they'd learned from Russ and hear what he'd had to say at Reid's place.

Come on, Dev. Where are you?

He should be back by now, but she wasn't worried about him. The odds of him running into some kind of trouble on the secured compound were pretty low. Or at least that's what he kept telling her. Still, she wished he was there.

Fatigue settled in, and she stifled a yawn. She couldn't believe she could even be slightly tired with everything going on, but the stress was finally getting to her. She had to be alert for any danger, not yawning and closing her eyes. Splashing water on her face might help.

She stood. "I need to go to the bathroom."

Jada held up a puzzle piece. "I'll be right here when you come back, probably still trying to fit this stupid piece in somewhere."

"You could move on to another one."

"And let this one get the best of me?" She gaped at Kinsley as if she'd suggested having open heart surgery. "No way."

Kinsley laughed and strode to the bathroom connected to the room she shared with Jada in the back of the cabin, her mood a bit better after Jada's antics.

She turned on the faucet, twisted the handle to cold, and splashed her face with a shocking wake-up of water. She dried with a towel and looked at herself in the mirror. Her fear, anguish, and stress still lived in her eyes. Maybe when Dev arrived, he would have some good news to share. She needed good news for a change. If she thought about it, Russ's news was good, too. They likely had their suspect and just had to find Yapp and arrest him.

"Just." Who knows where he could be. If Ozzy had been right about prisoner behavior when they were discharged, there was no telling if Yapp was actually residing at the address he provided to the prison.

No. They would find him. They had to.

She straightened her shoulders and convinced herself to take a positive attitude, then left the room.

In the dining area, she came up short. Jada still sat at the table, but she wasn't alone. Yapp stood next to her with a pistol to her head.

"Hello, Kinsley," he said. "It's about time we talk."

"No need to use a gun," Kinsley said, sounding calmer than her quivering insides let on. "I'm glad to talk to you and force isn't necessary."

"Hah! If you were willing to talk to me, you wouldn't put all these bodyguards in the way."

"Speaking of bodyguards, what happened to them?"

"Your sidekick, Devan, is down at the lake tied to a tree." He grinned. "He found out the hard way what it feels like to have a spear from my speargun cut through a hip and then be strangled with the cord until he passed out."

"Is he okay?" Kinsley cried out, visions of Dev in need of help, maybe dying, nearly taking her down, and she had to grab onto the table.

"He'll be fine as long as you do what I tell you to do. Your buddy in the other room, too. Keep your voice down, and he won't even have to know I'm here. So far, I've overpowered your bodyguards without killing them. But you bring him out here, and he's dead. I'm too close to getting what I want to let someone interfere."

She'd thought to call out to Colin, but she wouldn't put him in danger as well. "And what about Hayden on the front porch? How did you get past him?"

"I slipped up on the side of the porch planning to incapacitate him with a well-placed bullet." He grinned, something evil and vicious. "But he thought I was Devan, allowing me to get close enough to him to take him down with a sedative before he even knew I was injecting him. He'll be out for several hours and wake up embarrassed as all get out."

She hated that he was right. That Hayden would be embarrassed to have been taken out like that. But she was sure it happened to the best of them at times. Dev included. He would feel bad, too. Was likely already feeling bad, and doing everything within his power to escape.

If he even woke up and was able to act. She had no idea how long someone might be out from an attempted strangulation. She just never had to deal with something like that, and she hoped to never experience it.

She removed her hands from the table and lifted her shoulders. "So what do you want?"

He snorted. "Like you don't know."

"I have no idea."

233

He pressed the gun harder against Jada's head, and she grimaced.

He bent low to look her in the face. "I suppose you're going to play dumb with me too."

"I won't be playing," Jada said, her voice strong, her eyes fighting back at him. "I don't have a clue what you want either."

"Then let me spell it out for both of you." He came to his full height and glared at Kinsley. "The diamonds. I want my diamonds."

"Diamonds?" She glanced at Jada to see if she had any idea what he meant.

"No clue," Jada said.

"I hid them in the base of the lamp at the Bluebird." He locked eyes with Kinsley. "The one you took for a memory."

Kinsley gasped. "How do you know that?"

"Tsk. Tsk." A snide smile crossed his mouth. "You opened your big mouth on social media. Told everyone about the special memories you have with your good friend Jada. The accompanying picture included the lamp."

"But my account is private for my friends only. So how could you even see it?"

He raised his chin. "Correction. You weren't quite careful enough. All of your posts are private. Your friends list was out there for everyone to see. It wasn't hard to impersonate one of your friends you didn't have enough contact with to realize it wasn't really your friend."

Dev had been right about her security setting. She'd changed it now, but the damage had already been done. This was all her fault. Jada had a gun to her head. Dev was tied up, perhaps unconscious, maybe dying. And Hayden was drugged. All because Kinsley didn't properly adjust her security settings.

Tears formed in her eyes, but she didn't want to cry in

front of this man. No way she wanted him to see that he had gotten to her. Once she figured out a way to safely get rid of him and call an ambulance for Dev, then she could cry and fall apart.

"All you have to do is tell me where the lamp with the diamonds is, and I'll be out of here." He challenged her with his pointed look.

"In the back bedroom. I'll go get it."

"No," he said, steel in his voice. "We'll get it together. The three of us."

He grabbed the neck of Jada's sweater and tugged her up while keeping the gun to her head. "Any funny business and I take her out."

Kinsley didn't think he was eager to kill Jada, but he seemed willing to end their lives to get his diamonds. So she led the way to the bedroom and lifted the lamp from the nightstand. She shook it but still didn't hear anything in the base.

He forced Jada to sit on a hardwood chair pushed up to a small desk in the corner and readjusted the gun. "I made sure to pack the base so it wouldn't rattle and the diamonds wouldn't be discovered before I could return to collect them. I just didn't count on the stinkin' cops finding me and not getting right back."

Kinsley looked up from the lamp. "I don't get it. Why put them in an object that easily could be discarded or moved?"

"Like I said. I planned to come right back. When I went away, I was going to send my girlfriend to get them when things cooled down and the police were no longer watching her. But no. She decided to two-time me with my best buddy, so I had to leave them and hope the lamp was still here when I got out." He smiled. "As you can see, it turned out just fine. Now pull the felt off the bottom and dump the bag on the bed."

She followed his directions, finding a black velvet pouch tucked in bubble wrap in the base. She opened the drawstring on the pouch and poured out a cascade of sparkling diamonds too numerous to count.

"Ah." He let out a long breath of satisfaction. "They're just the way I left them, and I have you to thank for that. If you hadn't taken the lamp as a souvenir, my diamonds probably would've ended up in some landfill."

"So pick them up and leave us alone."

He removed the gun from Jada's head for a second to gesture at the diamonds. "Bag them back up, then leave the bag on the bed and step away."

She sat on the bed to cup the diamonds in her hand and pour them into the bag. She had no idea of the value of this pouch of diamonds, but it had to be significant. She considered flinging them across the room so she could buy some time to pick them up, but she feared he would shoot Jada, something Kinsley wouldn't risk.

She glanced at him. "What I don't get is why you've been shooting at us? If you killed us, you would never get the diamonds."

"I never intended to kill you. Not even wing you." He narrowed his eyes. "I just wanted to scare you so when I asked for the diamonds, you knew I *would* kill to get them."

"But the opposite happened," she said. "Dev and his teammates came to my rescue and made it impossible for you to get to me."

"Impossible? I'm here right now, aren't I?" He scoffed. "But yeah, I didn't know about him and his team at the time. Still, you never got around to figuring out it was me, did you?"

"We had no reason to be looking for you. You were just some guy we played pranks on back in the day." Kinsley gritted her teeth. "But you screwed up in the end. We got your ID when you were dumb enough to leave a video of yourself on the drone's camera."

Yapp's mouth slackened. "I forgot all about that. I obviously didn't count on you getting control of the drone. Who all knows about this?"

"All of us, but who you really need to worry about is the sheriff. He knows all about you, and is getting ready to arrest you." She exaggerated, but she hoped she put fear in him so he would take off and leave them behind.

"Then we best be going. Stand up."

Kinsley raised her shoulders. "You'll get away faster without us."

"Maybe that's true, but I might get dead before that." He pointed at the diamonds. "Pack those up now! Or I start shooting."

She took her sweet time of gathering them together hoping someone would come to their aid. But no one came before she gathered all of them into the pouch and tied it tightly. She left it on the bed and walked to the other side of the room as he directed.

He tugged Jada to her feet and dragged her to the diamonds. "Put them in my cargo pocket."

She glanced at Kinsley, looking like she wanted to do something to escape. Kinsley shook her head, and Jada frowned, but grabbed the diamonds, then shoved them in his pocket. He pushed her to sit on the bed, keeping the gun at her head.

He looked up at Kinsley. "Come sit by your friend."

Kinsley gladly took a seat near her and grasped her hands.

"No time for handholding." He swiftly shifted the gun from Jada to Kinsley. "You'll be coming with me so I can make sure we get out of here without taking fire from any bodyguard."

Kinsley didn't want to go with him. She didn't want to go with him at all. But she'd much rather he took her as his hostage than Jada. She would rather give up her life than see her friend killed. Unfortunately, it might come to that, and she needed to prepare to die.

21

The spearhead broke through the cord, and Dev jerked his wrists free. His arms had been tied behind his back too long and pain radiated through his muscles, but he didn't care. He didn't care about the pain in his hip either. He was going to Kinsley's rescue at all costs.

If she was still alive. He had no idea how long he'd been unconscious. For all he knew the assailant had already gotten to her and fled the property.

Dev lurched to his feet, the smoke darker and thicker now. His phone was set to receive wildfire evacuation alerts, but he hadn't gotten one. But maybe his phone wasn't working, or one was issued while he was out of it. He patted his pocket. His phone probably wouldn't work because it was wet. No matter. It wasn't in his pocket. His assailant had to have taken it. A smart move on his part, keeping Dev from alerting anyone to the assailant's presence.

Alert or not the bad air quality said the fire was moving closer. Now, not only did he have to fear for Kinsley's life, but for everyone's lives with the fire advancing on them. He had to take action, and he had to do it quickly. But first, he needed to get his shoes so he could move even faster.

He started out at a fast clip, but his pain made him slow. Still, he fought through the pain to retrieve them from near the lake and put them on.

He turned to go.

He didn't know what he was facing. He had no weapon. He had no plan. He had no help. Would it be better to head to their armory to get a gun, maybe some NVGs, so he could surprise the guy, or would it be better to barrel ahead and make sure Kinsley wasn't in grave danger?

Protect innocent life at all costs. His mantra from his time as a deputy sounded like a warning bell in his brain. He couldn't protect her if he wasn't near her. He had to believe that she needed him right now and go to her. Believe that God would provide what he needed.

But did Dev believe that? After all, why had God allowed him to be choked nearly to death and knocked out? How could that be good in any way?

He took off for his cabin, limping from the excruciating pain, breathing deep to ignore it. He felt much like he did that day Hailey walked out and left him alone to deal with his family and friends. Hers too. Only the stakes were far higher here.

But if Dev had married Hailey, he wouldn't be free now to pursue Kinsley. So what at the time seemed devastating was a blessing in disguise. Could he believe the same thing here? That being detained by the assailant would work out for the best?

He had to. The alternative was too painful.

The cabin came into view, and he stopped to take a long look through the gritty smoke clinging to the porch. Hayden was down on the floor. Was he dead or just incapacitated? Dev had to believe he wasn't dead as the assailant didn't seem to be a killer. Or at least he didn't want to kill Dev. Just restrain him.

If Dev could get to the porch, he could get Hayden's weapon, if the attacker had left it in his holster. Dev crept forward, but his bum leg dragged, and his foot rustled fallen leaves. He had to hope he wasn't making enough noise to be heard inside the cabin.

He moved forward as fast as he could, soon reaching the porch and sneaking up on the side. To avoid being seen from within the family room, he got down on his knees and nearly screamed from the pain. He bit his lip until the pain receded, then crawled along the worn porch boards.

At the window, he peeked inside. No one visible in the family room or dining room.

His heart sank. Had the attacker taken them all hostage and driven somewhere? Or were they in a bedroom?

Bedroom. They had to be there. If not...

He had to check them out, but first grab the gun from Hayden's hip. A syringe protruded from his neck, and Dev felt for a pulse. He was alive and breathing.

Thank you!

Dev checked Hayden's cargo pocket for his phone, turned it to silent, and shoved it in his pocket, then made his way around the back of the cabin to Colin's bedroom. He peeked into the window. Colin sat on his bed with his laptop on his knees, his noise-canceling headphones on his ears.

How was Dev going to get Colin's attention without alerting the assailant if he was still in the house?

He tapped lightly on the window. No luck.

He waved his arms. No response.

He jumped up and down, frantically now, his leg threatening to buckle under him, his forehead perspiring from the pain.

Colin looked up. Blinked a few times, then set down his computer and came to open the window. "What's going on? Why the stealth arrival?"

Dev caught his breath from the pain and explained everything that had happened.

"That's a lot of blood on your pants." Colin frowned. "Are you sure you should even be on your feet?"

"I'm good." Dev worked hard to hide the strain he was feeling. "You have any idea what's going on with Kinsley?"

Colin lifted his gaze from Dev's hip. "I haven't heard a thing."

"I'm going to look in Jada and Kinsley's bedroom window. Stay here. Be right back."

Dev crept along the back of the house making sure to lift his bum leg even though the pain brought those dreaded stars back. The bedroom window had been cracked open about an inch, and he risked a glance inside. His heart nearly stopped.

Jada lay on the bed, a gag in her mouth and her arms and legs tied, fear permeating her eyes. Dev swallowed the words he wanted to shout.

The assailant, who he had to assume was the guy from the lake, had his back to Dev and pressed his gun against Kinsley's head. He was motioning toward the door to the living area. "We'll walk down the drive and out the gate to my car. It's parked on an old logging trail just across the road."

"Security cameras are going to record you," Kinsley said, sounding strong and in control.

"Then it's a good thing I took them out on my way in." He cackled.

Dev gritted his teeth, wishing the guy would turn so he could see his face and figure out which suspect had his gun at Kinsley's temple. But more importantly, whoever he was, he was going to leave and take her with him.

Dev curled his fingers into fists. Everything in him encouraged him to burst through the window and rescue her. To pull out his gun and fire a shot into the assailant's back. He wouldn't. Of course not. Killing someone was a last resort. Besides, the guy's muscles could twitch, and he could accidentally squeeze the trigger on his gun before he dropped from Dev's bullet.

He had to find a better way to save Kinsley, and he had to find it fast.

~

The last thing Kinsley wanted to do was let this man get her outside the house. Hopefully, if she stayed there, Colin would discover their situation and rescue them. But if she left the house, Jada was the only one he could discover, and by the time they caught up to Kinsley and Yapp, she might be dead.

Her heart lurched at the thought, and it kicked up speed. She had to find a way to stall. But what?

"Wait a minute," she said, an idea exploding in her brain like fireworks in a July sky. "We can't go out the gate. It's always locked, and I don't know the code to open it."

"You expect me to believe that?" He pressed the gun harder. "Stop stalling, and let's go."

"I'm not lying. I don't know the code. I've only been through it once, and I didn't see the numbers that Dev tapped into the keypad."

He studied her face. "Then let's ask your friend here. We'll go over there together."

They turned back to the bed, his gun never leaving her head.

"Do you know the code?" he asked Jada.

She nodded.

"Remove the gag," he said to Kinsley. "Once she gives us the number, retie it."

Kinsley took the beautiful scarf Jada had given her for her eighteenth birthday out of Jada's mouth.

She coughed and looked into Kinsley's eyes. "Don't try to be a hero. He means business with that gun. He's proven that."

"She's right," Yapp said. "Now tell us the gate code."

She rattled off a six-digit code. Kinsley repeated it to her to be sure she had the right number.

"Thank you, sweetie, and sorry about the gag. At least if you have to be gagged, it's with the beautiful scarf you gave me."

"It's okay. I'll be praying for you nonstop." Jada smiled, but it was weak and wobbly.

Kinsley forced a smile and picked up the scarf. She gagged her best friend and kept silently repeating the gate number so she didn't forget.

She tied the last knot.

"Let's move," Yapp said. "The longer we stay here the greater the risk of being discovered."

Exactly what she was thinking, but from a far different perspective. She could only hope when they stepped out that door that Hayden or Dev had woken up or one of their other teammates was out and about and would see Yapp take her away from the property, a gun rammed against her head.

Plan in mind, Dev raced for Colin's window, but his speed was hampered by his injury. *Buck up. You can do this. Have to do this.*

He gritted his teeth until he could clutch the windowsill to take the weight off his hip. "An assailant has Kinsley at gunpoint. He's getting ready to leave and take her with him as a hostage. Have any idea who the guy is?"

Colin shrugged. "Could be the guy Russ said matched the drone prints."

"His name?"

"Harry Yapp. He stayed in the Bluebird Cabin back in the nineties. Jada and Kinsley played a few pranks on him. That's the only relationship to them that we know about."

"Seriously?" Dev stared at his brother. "You don't think he's here to kill Kinsley and Jada because they played pranks on him when they were kids?"

Colin shook his head. "I figure he has another motive, but we won't know what until we find him. I was writing algorithms for the internet to locate information on him, and Russ is looking into him at his office." He paused. "We should call Russ."

"He would come barreling in here, lights blazing, and who knows what this guy would do to Kinsley then."

"We could ask him to run silently. He's a good cop and would do the right thing."

"Yeah, then take over and tell us to stand down. Kinsley's safety is my responsibility, and I won't back down unless I'm incapacitated." He turned to look through the smoky air that seemed to be getting even more dense and darker in color. "I need to get over the fence before he reaches it."

"What do you want me to do?" Colin asked.

"Get to a vehicle and wait until this guy exits the front gate. Give him time to cross the road to his car. It's parked on Beeker's old logging road. I'll keep an eye on him until he gets in the car. Maybe there'll be an opportunity to separate Kinsley from him. If not, you'll find me on the logging road. Untie Jada then pick me up, and we'll tail him."

Colin arched an eyebrow. "Pretty risky for him to go back to the same place he operated the drone."

"Seems like he's got nothing to lose." Dev swallowed hard, his throat dry from the smoke. "I have to go. I've got Hayden's phone. Stay in touch."

He bolted down the path in the woods leading to the fence, the thick and caustic air irritating his lungs. Then he had to slow for his hip again. No matter how much he gritted his teeth, it threatened to take him down. At least his path was a much more direct route than the driveway, and even with his bum hip, he should be able to shimmy over the fence before the assailant reached them.

God willing. With the pain nearly bringing him to a standstill, he didn't know what would happen once he got to the fence.

Don't think that way. Picture Kinsley with that gun at her head and let adrenaline take over. Give it your all. Even give up your life to save hers because it's meaningless without her.

22

Kinsley took a deep breath on the porch and coughed. An eerie yellowish-red cast lingered in the sky. It seemed like she was in one of those doomsday movies. Armageddon.

The forest fire was clearly coming closer. The logging path led in that direction. Was he really going to head into the fire? She shuddered.

"Stop stalling." Yapp jabbed the gun harder. "Keep moving, and we won't have a problem."

She held her stance. "But the fire. We can't go in that direction."

"You'll do what I say if you want to stay alive." He jerked her down the steps and onto the cobblestone walk that led to the driveway. He set off at a rapid pace, and sadly, they reached the gate before anyone came to her rescue.

"Enter that code," he demanded.

She took her time moving to the keypad and pressing the keys in the number order that Jada had shared. The gate clicked and started to swing in, the motor groaning as it pushed the wide gate open. Reid could see the gate opening if he were looking at the security program, but at this time of night, he was likely in bed and paying no attention to it.

Unless of course, after a certain time of day, it issued an alarm, waking him up.

Please let that happen.

She glanced up at the camera, eyed it, trying to beg Reid to come to her rescue. She didn't know if this was one of the cameras Yapp had taken out or not, but it didn't hurt to try something that wouldn't get her killed.

He jerked her arm and hurried across the road, then down the ditch and back up to the logging road. This wasn't the beginning of the road as there was no entrance from the main thoroughfare, but he pushed her straight ahead toward the fire.

Oh please, don't let us have an issue with the fire.

They shouldn't. At least she hoped they wouldn't. They hadn't been notified via a text message or by a law enforcement officer coming to the cabins to tell them to leave, so it couldn't have advanced close enough to require evacuation.

She tried to slow down, but Yapp grabbed her around the waist with his free arm and picked up his speed, forcing her to come along with him. She had to move quickly to keep up, but soon she saw an old rusty pickup. If they were heading toward a fire, she would much rather be riding in a newer vehicle. This one looked like the truck models she remembered in her childhood and also looked like it could fall apart at any time.

"Are you sure this truck is safe?" she asked.

"Doesn't matter. Was the only thing I could afford coming out of prison, so it'll have to do." He released his arm around her waist, leaving the gun resting against her temple, and opened a large tool storage bin in the truck bed. He pulled out a thick rope. "Hold your hands out."

She did as he asked, and he wound the rope around her wrists. He put the gun in his belt and cinched the rope hard, cutting into her skin.

Now! Run now.

She bolted away from him. She'd gone three feet, tasting her freedom. The rope jerked hard. Spinning her around. He slammed her against the side of the truck.

Pain radiated up her back, her ribs feeling like he might've broken one or more of them, and she had to fight not to cry out.

He slammed an elbow to her ribs to hold her body in place. He must've seen her reaction to hitting the truck. She didn't want to let him know he'd hurt her. To give him satisfaction. She tried to clamp down on her lips, but a cry of pain escaped before she could.

"That'll be the least of your pains if you try anything like that again." He tied the rope tighter, digging deeper into her skin.

He lifted his gun again, placing it on the other side of her head, and opened the driver's side door. With his free hand, he held the length of rope. "Get in, stay in the middle, and no funny business."

She wouldn't do anything right now, but she sure would continue to look for an opening to get away from him.

She slid under the steering wheel and across the cracked bench seat, stopping in the middle as he directed. No reason to take any chances with the gun still at her head. Even if she wanted to act, he'd given the rope very little slack, leaving her no choice but to obey him.

For now.

She expected him to climb in, instead he tied the end of the rope around his waist, then removed the gun and got behind the wheel.

Sure, she was still his prisoner, but at least she didn't have that infernal gun at her head anymore. A sense of freedom gave her hope she would find a way to escape this madman.

He cranked the engine, and it took several tries before the vehicle rumbled to life, running rough. Maybe it would break down before he could escape and someone would come to her rescue.

She glanced at the radio playing country western music. "Can we at least tune in to the local emergency channel and listen for evacuation orders?"

"Fine, but keep it low so it doesn't distract me." He shifted into gear and floored the gas pedal.

The engine coughed and caught, and the vehicle jerked forward, bumping over the rutty dirt road.

She fumbled with the radio knob until she found the emergency channel. She turned it low so it wouldn't bother him but high enough for her to still hear it. They reviewed evacuation orders starting with the adjoining county. LEVEL 2 – BE SET—BE SET TO EVACUATE AT A MOMENT'S NOTICE, WITH SIGNIFICANT DANGER IN THE AREA. Their county had just been issued the first warning. LEVEL 1 – BE READY—PREPARE TO EVACUATE AND BE AWARE OF DANGER IN THE AREA.

She hated that any emergency evacuations had been issued, but with the one for their county just having been issued, the teammates would get an alert on their phones, hopefully waking them up. Reid, being the strong leader that he was, would likely check on all of his team, discover Dev was in trouble, talk to Jada, and learn Kinsley had been abducted.

At least she prayed that was what would happen.

She bounced along with the truck, ignoring her ribs and keeping an ear out for any new alerts while continuing to search for an escape. But her attention kept going to the changing color of the sky ahead of them. With each passing mile, the color shifted from yellow to orange to red clogged with black. Despite not pulling in outside air, the inside of the truck filled with the stench of the fire, and her throat and nose hurt.

She could almost feel the flames. Imagined an agonizing death in a forest fire that burned up to two thousand degrees. Living in Oregon, where forest fires were common, the number she'd learned in high school had stuck in her head.

She glanced at her abductor. "Are you looking ahead? Can't you see that we're getting closer and closer to the fire?"

"We only have a few more miles to go, and then we'll turn off on the main road. Head in the other direction. We'll be fine."

"But you went past several turnoffs already. Why not take them?"

"That's what your bodyguards would expect me to do. They'd be thinking the same way you are that we shouldn't be getting closer to the fire. So I have to do the opposite of what they expect and throw them off our tail."

"Even if it means burning us alive?" She tried to keep her tone level, but it skyrocketed with each word.

"You're exaggerating. Now shut up so I can concentrate."

He'd no more declared that things would be fine when the engine started to catch, running rougher as if it were going to give out on them.

"Please," she said. "Don't get any closer to the fire with this mangy old truck. It sounds like it's going to die."

"I told you to shut up." He replied quickly, but he glanced at her, and the worry on his face told her what he really was thinking.

Worry on his face or not, he didn't change plans and continued in the same direction.

The truck sounded rougher and rougher with each turn of the tire. It sputtered, caught for a long moment, then sputtered again and cut out.

He coasted to a stop and turned the key. The engine whined but didn't catch. He cursed and fumbled with the knot on the rope tied to his body. He spent precious time working it until he got it loose and climbed out. "I'll check it out, but you'll come with me."

He tugged on the rope until she had no choice but to exit the vehicle. She followed him into the thick air, instantly congealing her lungs and making her cough.

It didn't seem to bother him, but based on the packs of cigarettes lying on his dashboard, maybe it didn't have as much of an effect on his lungs as hers.

He tied her up to the bumper and patted the gun in his waistband. "If you try to run, I'll shoot you in the back."

He fixed his steely gaze on her. He would fire all right, and it wouldn't take much provocation. He soon wouldn't need her anymore, and he likely planned to kill her anyway.

Dev glanced at his brother behind the wheel of his SUV. "Level 1 evacuation alert. Fires are coming closer, and they're driving right into it."

Colin's eyes narrowed. "Which means so are we."

He hated that his brother might be injured because of him. "If you want to stop and get out, I totally understand. I can go this alone, but I'm going after her no matter what."

Colin glanced at him. "I'll go with you, but we don't take any excessive risks with the fire. You and I both know the flames can change direction at the drop of a hat, and we don't want to be caught in it."

"Agreed," Dev said, but even if flames advanced too close for comfort, he would jump out of this vehicle and continue on his own into whatever he might find.

"You're sure you want to continue on this path and not take one of these side trails?" Colin asked.

"We stay the course." Dev stared out the window at the changing color of the sky. Now a reddish orange. Not good. Not good at all. "My best guess is he wants us to think he turned off, but he's continuing on because he doesn't think we would believe he would drive directly into the fire."

"Let's hope you're right."

"Even if I'm wrong, we called in his vehicle description to Russ, and his men are looking for the truck on the roads these trails feed onto."

"Good thing you saw his pickup tonight so we know he's driving the same truck as before," Colin said.

The SUV hit a rut in the road, arcing pain up Dev's side. He bit his lip until he could speak. "Having just gotten out of prison, I can't imagine he could afford even the junky truck I saw, much less a second vehicle." Visions of Kinsley terrified in Yapp's truck consumed Dev's brain. They were only minutes behind, but in a life-or-death situation, a minute made a huge difference.

Please, please! Don't let us be too late. Not by a minute. Not by a second. Not by any fraction of time. Let us arrive in the perfect time that I know You've already ordained to save Kinsley.

23

The fire was close. Coming closer.

"We have to go," Kinsley all but screamed at Yapp as an easterly wind whipped over her body, bringing heavy levels of smoke and choking off her oxygen.

He ignored her and continued to fumble under the hood, then ran to the driver's seat and turned the key. The engine groaned, but didn't catch. He tried it again. Again and again. Same results every time until it only clicked.

She raced toward him as far as her rope would allow her to move. "Please, can't you see that the fire is getting closer? That we're in significant danger here? If we leave on foot now, we have a chance to outrun the fire, but if we sit here and waste time trying to get the stupid truck running, we'll die for sure."

He looked up, panic in his eyes, his hands clasped to the wheel. He'd left the key switched on, and the radio was running. She didn't want to listen to it, but a LEVEL 2 alert had now been issued for their area. The excited announcer was saying that, with the increase in winds, things were moving so quickly they could hardly keep up with the changes in alerts. He begged everyone in the area to continue to stay tuned.

"You heard him!" she shouted to break Yapp's daze. "We have to go."

He took a quick look at her and bolted outside. Good, he'd come to his senses, would untie her, and they could leave.

He took a long look at her, then turning toward the back of his vehicle, he ran away, leaving her behind.

"Wait! Wait!" she shouted. "Untie me!"

He kept going, looking like he'd really kicked it into gear and was running at high-speed. She couldn't keep watching. She had to free herself. She charged for the bumper and clawed at the knot. The rope was tighter than she could imagine, her fingers pulling, prodding, digging. Moving it only a fraction of an inch.

She heard a yelp from Yapp, but she didn't take time to check on him. She continued to pull at the rough rope, its abrasive braid gnawing at her fingers. If she couldn't get it loosened soon, her fingertips would begin to bleed.

A section let loose. She tugged hard on it, blood now seeping onto the rope. She didn't care. She'd gotten it loose. Now to work on the second knot, which came free in her fingers far more easily. She jerked the rope from the bumper. She couldn't free her hands, so she wrapped the length of it around her body so it wouldn't trip her up.

She charged around the end of the truck and raced forward. Yapp lay in the dirt clutching his ankle.

He looked up. "I wrenched my ankle. I can't walk. You can't leave me here."

She waited for him to pull his gun on her, but saw that he'd dropped it.

She hurried to pick it up. "I can leave you behind, and I think I will."

"No, no. Please. Can't you just imagine how horrible it would be to die in the forest fire?"

"As if you cared about whether I died in one," she said. "If I died at all. In fact, you probably planned to kill me when you felt like you were free."

"I wasn't, I swear. I was going to let you go." He didn't sound very convincing.

Whether he was convincing or not, she had no intention of leaving him behind. Jesus would never leave Yapp or any person to die. He would forgive and move on.

"You'll have to get to your knees, and then I'll help you up and support you. But you'll have to put some weight on that ankle if you want to get out of here."

He gaped at her as if he didn't expect her to help him. Most people wouldn't. They would run as fast as they could away from the danger. But Christians who lived their faith weren't "most people." Even if they were in the shadow of fear like this, hopefully they would assist the other person.

She couldn't support him and control the gun, so she lifted her arm and flung it so far away that his bad ankle would prevent him from retrieving it.

"What in the world?" He rolled to his knees, moaning in pain. "What if you need that gun?"

"Why would I need a gun? You're dependent on me to get out of here, so I know you're not going to do something stupid."

He latched on to her, acting as if he were going to crawl up her body to get to his feet.

"Chill, or you'll take both of us down. Let me help you up in a civilized fashion."

He relaxed, but only a fraction.

She held out her hands. "First, you'll have to untie me."

He dug into the knot and pulled it free.

She flexed her wrists, then managed to get him to his feet and her shoulder under his arm. She started forward, and he limped alongside her, groaning nearly every time his bad ankle hit the ground. She struggled to bear up under his weight, seeming to get heavier and heavier with every step.

He glanced back. "Things are looking worse back there. We have to hurry."

"I can go faster, but can you?"

"I have to." He picked up his pace, but stopped his groaning.

They hobbled forward. She refused to look back, but the smoke got heavier, swirling thick and clogging her throat and lungs to elicit deep coughs. She pulled her shirt up over her mouth and nose. She'd always heard most people died of smoke inhalation before flames got them, and she could believe that right now.

"Do you hear that?" Yapp's excited tone broke free before he erupted in a coughing attack. "Someone's coming in a vehicle. I hear it. Tell me you do, too."

She tilted her head and listened. "I do!" Excitement took over her fear. She suspected firefighters were on their way to battle the blaze and they would help.

A black SUV crested the hill and came to a sudden stop. The vehicle rocked as the passenger door blew open. A man, tall and built, shot out and charged their way. The driver was only moments behind him.

She couldn't see through the haze to make out their identities, but they were both tall and built like Dev.

Oh, please let it be him.

The first guy limped heavily, maybe she didn't want it to be Dev after all. She didn't want him to be incapacitated, but Yapp did say he'd shot him with a speargun.

"Kinsley," the man called out as he neared.

"Dev!" she shouted. She couldn't contain her joy, even if he was injured and limping.

Please don't let it be serious.

He burst through the murky air, and she got a good look at his face.

She drank in the sight of him. "It's you. It's really you."

He picked up his speed, blood saturating his khaki pants near his hip.

"Thank God you're alive," he cried out.

"And you too." She wanted him to sweep her into his arms, but she was still holding Yapp up. She should just release him. Let him drop to the ground. He deserved that at the very least, but she wasn't vindictive.

Dev stopped and eyed Yapp. "What's going on here?"

"He ran away like a coward, leaving me behind," she said. "Then he fell and twisted his ankle. He can't walk."

"And you're helping him?" Dev's tone rose.

"It was the Christian thing to do." She smiled at the man she loved. Loved. In no uncertain terms, and once they got out of danger she intended to tell him. Because if their close call from the fire told her anything, it told her she loved him.

It still didn't free her from her promise to Jada, but she hoped they could work that out. All assuming that Dev reciprocated the feelings.

Jada! *Oh my gosh, Jada.* She'd been tied up. Kinsley had been too self-absorbed to even think to ask about her. "Please tell me Jada's okay."

"She's fine," Dev said. "We called Reid after we left the cabin and asked him to take her and Mom to his place."

Kinsley let out a long breath of air, finally feeling like this might be over.

Dev peered over her shoulder, his posture tensing. "We should go. Now! The fire seems like it's advancing fast, and we don't want to get caught in a blow-up."

She had no idea what a blow-up was, but it didn't sound good as related to fire.

"Take Yapp," Dev said to Colin, who'd stopped next to them. His anger was alive and vivid on his face as he glared at Yapp. "Try anything, and I won't be as charitable as Kinsley."

Colin grabbed Yapp around the waist and put his arm over his shoulder. Then he stepped off at a rapid pace, dragging Yapp behind him.

"Hey!" Yapp shouted. "Be careful. I'm injured."

Colin snorted and kept up his pace.

Dev swung Kinsley up in his arms, then turned to go. At his first step, she felt him stiffen. Surely his pain was too much to bear.

"I can walk," she said. "No need to make your injury worse."

"It's worth it to be holding you. When I thought I might lose you." His voice broke, and he shook his head but didn't stop moving.

He settled her in the front seat of the SUV, and he took the back where Colin had put Yapp. She wished he were sitting next to her, but she knew he had to keep an eye on Yapp. The guy was devious and couldn't be counted on not to try to escape.

Colin quickly made a three-point turn and had their vehicle heading toward the compound. He turned up the radio to the emergency station. Nothing had changed since the last time she'd heard the alerts, but their area was still under a LEVEL 2 warning.

"I see no point in hanging around the compound and waiting for a higher alert," Colin said. "We should evacuate tonight."

Kinsley was all for that, but she wasn't in charge, and she wasn't going to ask more of these men than what they didn't want for themselves.

"Agreed," Dev replied.

"Hey, Siri, call Brooklyn," Colin said.

The digital assistant made the speakerphone call to Colin's fiancée. That's the first call Kinsley would've made, too, if she were him.

"Just checking in to see if everything is okay with you and that you got the fire evacuation alert." If he hadn't been gripping the steering wheel as if his life depended on it, the strain in his voice surely made his worry for her evident.

"I'm glad you called," she said, her tone equally strained. "I wasn't sure if I should leave now or wait for the LEVEL 3 alert."

The level that freaked Kinsley out. LEVEL 3 – GO NOW! LEAVE IMMEDIATELY. EXTREME DANGER IN THE AREA.

"Tell you what," he said, this time sounding more relaxed, but the whitening of his fingers on the wheel gave him away, "we aren't going to wait for the next alert. We can pick you up on our way out of town."

She let out a relieved breath that carried over the phone. "That sounds perfect to me. I can be ready in ten minutes."

"I'm not at my cabin right now but don't be surprised if we don't get to your place for thirty minutes or so."

"I'll be waiting." She fell silent for a moment. "I love you."

"Love you too." He glanced at Kinsley, the dashboard lights revealing a sheepish look on his face.

Kinsley's heart warmed. It was so cute that the big strapping guy was shy all of a sudden because he was in love.

He turned back to the road, but tapped his phone. "Siri, call Russ."

"This better be important," Russ said. "I have my hands full with the potential evacuation."

Colin brought him up to speed. "I know you're busy, but

can you send one of your deputies to meet us at the compound and take Yapp into custody?"

"Not hardly." His tone had dropped, nearly coming out as a boom. "I'm not leaving this up to one of my men. We've been waiting to find this guy, and I'm more than happy to slap cuffs on him."

In the backseat, Yapp issued a curse under his breath. Not Kinsley. She had to resist shooting her hand up in victory and gloat. Not only was it unattractive, but it wasn't right to take joy in another person's misery, even if the person had chosen to do terrible things.

"And we'll be glad to turn him over for prosecution." Colin ended the call and looked in the rearview mirror. "After we meet Russ, we'll pick up Mom and Jada. Then swing through town for Brooklyn and leave the Level 2 area."

"Sounds like a plan," Dev replied. "But not until I know Reid doesn't need us for anything at the compound."

Kinsley looked between the brothers. "If there's anything I can do to help, just let me know."

"You don't need to do a thing except recover from this guy's manhandling." Dev sounded like he might pummel the guy sitting next to him, but he kept his focus on Kinsley. "So what was this all about anyway? I know he wasn't shooting at you because of some silly pranks you played on him when you were kids."

Kinsley turned to place her full attention on Dev and told him about the diamonds. "It's a wonder they survived all these years. Yapp put them in his cargo pocket, and they should still be there."

Dev patted Yapp's pocket, withdrew the pouch, and held it up. "And now, thanks to you, they can be returned to the jeweler where they belong." Dev smiled at her, and Yapp growled.

Both were welcome responses. She settled back in her seat to listen to the radio as they made the final drive down the trail.

They reached the main road without incident, and even with the smoke, she could make out the compound fence ahead. Kinsley had never seen a more welcome sight in her life. Okay, maybe that wasn't true. Maybe the most welcome thing of all was when Dev had emerged from the smoke to come to her rescue.

An even more welcome sight would be when she and Dev were alone, and she told him she loved him, then flung herself into his arms. Hopefully he would welcome her declaration and it wouldn't be just because everyone was safe, but because he wanted a future together.

Dev loved his sister, but he wouldn't put up with her ultimatum any longer, and he was going to tell her that the moment the opportunity presented itself. But right now, she was hugging him and had been hugging Kinsley within an inch of their lives. His mother, too.

"We really need to leave," Dev said to the group. "We can continue this love fest once we're somewhere safe."

"You mean we'll stop at the ER first." His mother jutted out a hip. "No matter what you say, you're going to get that injury checked out now."

He fully intended to have it evaluated. The spear could've damaged his muscles or nerves. But even if he didn't intend to go to the ER, her body language told him not to argue.

Still, everyone's safety had to come first, so he would compromise. "I'll go, but it'll have to wait until we're out of the evacuation area."

His mom eyed him, the same terse gaze he'd expected every time he'd done something wrong as a kid. Her look was meant to intimidate him, but at this point in his life it left him knowing how much she cared about him.

"I'll agree to that," her eyebrow rose as if her stare needed emphasis, "if you promise not to argue once we're somewhere safe and near an ER."

"I promise." He raised his first three fingers. "Scout's honor."

"Great. You'd never go back on that promise." She smiled. "With that settled, we can all quickly grab what we want to take with us."

"Make sure it's not a lot," he said, looking at Kinsley as she couldn't possibly take her entire box of memories and a suitcase with clothing. "We only have so much room in the vehicle."

They split up and Dev followed Jada and Kinsley to his bedroom where most of his things were located.

"I'll get out of your way in a flash." He went straight to the closet and retrieved his carry-on suitcase, then scanned the room to think about what he would take with him. The most important thing was to bring Kinsley, and honestly, everything else could be replaced.

Well, maybe not the picture of his dad, or the fishing reel his dad had given him. He grabbed the photo and reel from the top of his dresser. He quickly opened the suitcase and tossed in some clothing.

"My clothes can be replaced, but these things can't." Kinsley set her suitcase next to his. She opened it, and dumped all of the items from her memory box into the case. Everything minus the lamp, of course. "I can put my basic toiletries in my carry-on bag and keep it on my lap."

Dev set his suitcase on the floor. "I'll see you in the other room. Don't take too long."

"Before you go," Jada said. "I need to talk to you about something." She bit her lip. "About that dating ultimatum I gave you."

"Yeah," Dev said. "I wanted to talk to you about that, too, but we really don't have time for me to plead my case."

"It won't take long." She gave a tentative smile. "I see how the two of you look at each other, and I won't stand in your way. Just promise me if you get together, then break up and it's not an amiable split, that it won't ruin my relationship with either of you."

"I don't think breaking up is going to be a problem." Dev gave Kinsley a pointed smile. "But thanks for not holding us to the promise so we can make decisions that are best for us." He didn't want to talk about this any further with his sister, and it wasn't the time to talk to Kinsley, so he nodded at Jada's suitcase. "Get that packed and let's get going."

"Aye, aye, sir." She saluted him and laughed, the timbre lighthearted.

He rolled his eyes and gave her a gentle punch to the shoulder. He turned to look at Kinsley. "We'll talk later."

"Later," she said as if in some sort of a trance.

Maybe she was thinking about them together as a couple, something she hadn't contemplated until Jada removed her demand. He stepped out the door and did some contemplating on his own. The huge obstacle between him and Kinsley had been removed.

Well, if he didn't count his trust issue. But Kinsley wasn't at all like Hailey. She would never leave him in a lurch. She would never agree to marry him unless she planned to fulfill her commitment. If not, she would turn him down at the proposal, even if she knew her rejection would hurt him. Because she also knew the heartache he'd gone through with Hailey and understood that his proposal was the time to say no, not the day they were to be married.

At least, he had to believe that she would handle things far differently than Hailey had done. Now, he only had to figure out what he was going to say to her once they were alone.

∼

Kinsley sat with Dev in his ER room. His request for her to accompany him to the room shocked her. Leaving the others in the waiting area, he'd held her hand as they walked down the hallway to his room. He seemed sad to let go when the nurse instructed him to lie down so she could take his vitals.

She remained at his side while he met with the doctor but had to stay back when he went for a CT scan. She spent the time praying that he hadn't sustained a serious injury. He was in pain. She could see it in the strain on his face. For the trip to Portland, she'd wanted him to lie down in the backseat instead of driving. But this was Dev. The man who would go the extra mile to make sure she and his family were safe. With six people to evacuate and each with a suitcase, one vehicle wasn't enough, so they'd taken two. Colin, Brooklyn, and Sandy rode in one, and Dev, Jada, and Kinsley in the other.

They really didn't want to drive as far as Portland but had found zero hotel vacancies anywhere closer. They ended up calling on the Veritas team to put them up in condos that team members had vacated to find family homes.

"Hospitals are so good at developing patience in their patients." Dev grinned. "Seems like we've spent more time waiting than anything else."

"I'm just glad we came to Portland, where we know the hospital is top-notch and there are experts to weigh in on your injury."

He waved a hand. "I'm sure the spear didn't do any serious damage, or there would've been more blood and pain."

"You can't be sure of that. And there's got to be bacteria in the lake water which can't be good for the wound." She got up from the hard chair and stood by his bed to look him in the face. "You know it doesn't hurt to admit when something has slowed you down and you need rest."

His eyes narrowed. "I agree. But in this case, I have to fix things because I created a mess."

"You?" She stared at him. "What did you do?"

"It was my responsibility to find the person who was trying to kill you and stop him. I failed. Failed big time. On one of the most important jobs of my life."

"And now you feel guilty and think you have to make up for it."

"Something like that."

"Does that mean that because you see I have feelings for you, you asked Jada to drop her ultimatum?" She shoved her hand into her hair. "That you're going to ask me out, as a pity date?"

"What?" He shot up in his bed and winced, then shifted off his hip. "No. Not at all. I'm in love with you. I have been for years. Since you didn't see it, I guess I did a good job of hiding it. But not from Hailey. That's the real reason she wouldn't marry me. She knew I still had feelings for you."

"Oh...oh. I-I didn't know." She clutched the chain hanging around her neck—the skeleton necklace that matched Jada's skeleton.

"Well, now you know." He reached for her hand and pulled her to sit on the bed, then took both of her hands in his. "With Jada removing her ultimatum, we're free to start dating."

"Sort of, yeah."

He frowned. "What do you mean sort of? Don't you want to date? 'Cause you've been putting out vibes that say you return my feelings."

"Oh, you picked up on the right vibes, all right." She paused, uncertain about saying this for the first time. "I love you. Just as much as you love me."

He tilted his head. "So what's the problem with dating, then?"

"I live here in Portland. You live in Shadow Lake. Nearly four hours apart. What kind of dating relationship would that be?"

He frowned. "We can work that out, can't we?"

"You obviously can't leave your job, because you have to be in Shadow Lake to do it. I can do my job from anywhere, but since I have to travel so often, being close to an airport would be nice."

"I wouldn't want you to make the drive to PDX all the time. It would be unfair to ask you to do something like that, when I didn't do a thing to compromise."

"I don't know," she said, gnawing on her lip as she thought. "I do travel a lot, but maybe with the cost of living being less in Shadow Lake, I wouldn't need to have the same income and could reduce the number of jobs I accept."

"It still means you would be making all the sacrifices." He searched her gaze. "I'm not sure I like being responsible for making you change your life for me. You might come to resent me."

"I don't think that ever could happen." She made sure to give him a sincere smile. "Let's think about it, and see if we can come up with a solution."

"Sounds like a plan." He looked disappointed for sure.

So was she. After Jada removed her ultimatum, Kinsley thought she and Dev would fall into each other's arms tonight, but one more obstacle stood in their way. She could change it. Easily. Just move to Shadow Lake and change jobs. But give up a career that she had gone to school for so many years to achieve? Had worked part-time jobs to help pay for living costs? Had sacrificed her personal life and sweated over the difficult coursework?

Was she ready to let that go, to spend the rest of her life with Dev? She almost gave a sharp laugh, but held it back.

She finally had what she'd wanted for years. A life with Dev was in reach, but was the sacrifice too great? Could anything be too great to spend the rest of her life with the man she loved?

A question only she could answer, and right now, she just didn't know.

24

Dev had almost everything he could want. Charges had been brought against Mooney, Luongo, and Yapp and the three of them probably would likely never see the light of day again. And now he was free to pursue Kinsley.

He could hardly explain the sappy feelings that had taken over him. He felt like singing or humming. He felt like dancing. He felt like shouting for joy.

All due to the woman sitting across the room from him with his sister. Kinsley. He'd imagined for years what it would be like to be with her, but even his vivid imagination hadn't done the life-changing, life-fulfilling, life-altering emotions justice. He just didn't expect these feelings. He'd seen his brother and his teammates fall under the influence of a woman they loved, and he hadn't understood their behavior. He did now.

Boy, how he did.

Every movement unfolding in front of him grabbed his attention. Her joyful expression. Her hurried movements as if she couldn't contain her happiness. The way she grinned at Jada as they finally got to go through the memory box.

The fire had been contained the day after they'd fled to Portland, and they'd come home to cabins still standing. The firefighters had contained the fire two miles from home. At least home to Dev. Kinsley and he still hadn't found a way to make their separate lives come together. But for now, they decided to spend as much time together as possible and prayed that God would show them the way.

"Oh, look." Jada grabbed something small from the bed that Dev couldn't make out and bounced on the mattress while holding out the item to Kinsley. "Do you remember this? It was your thirteenth birthday party."

"Rollerama." Kinsley's mouth split in a broad smile. "How could I forget? Your mom rescued me from not having a party at all."

"Yeah, your parents didn't even remember it was your birthday. But Mom bundled us all in her minivan and took us for pizza and skating at the roller rink." Jada shot across the room to Dev and held up a ticket. "Do you remember that night?"

Did he? Of course he did. Packed into the minivan with Kinsley sitting next to him. His crush on her in full swing, and her leg touching his nearly sent his adolescent body into turmoil. Then at the rink, he had to pretend not to like her, so he ignored her, but Jada saw his desire, and that was the night she made him make the awful promise not to date Kinsley.

"You *do* remember," Jada said. "I can tell by the look in your eyes."

"Well, you should remember, too." He stared at her. "That was the night you made me promise never to date Kinsley."

Kinsley came to her feet. "It was that long ago?"

"Yeah," Jada said. "I saw him making googly eyes at you all night long, and I didn't want to lose you as a friend."

Kinsley came over to Dev and stopped in front of him. "I didn't notice you looking at me that way. All I remember is that you ignored me when I really wanted to skate with you."

"I wanted to skate with you, too, but I ignored you because that's what middle school boys do when they have a crush on a girl." He laughed. "Maybe if we would've just been honest with each other, we might have gotten together before Jada issued her decree and not lost so many years when we could've been together."

"Like I've said for the thousandth time I'm really sorry that I kept you apart." Jada's eyes got glassy like she might cry. "I wish I could change it, but I can't, so I hope you accept my apology."

"And like we said about the thousandth time," Kinsley said, "we do accept your apology, and we don't blame you. It is what it is, and we're together now, and that's all that matters." Kinsley sat sideways on Dev's lap and put her arm around his shoulders.

"Please don't tell me you're going to get all mushy on me again." Jada grimaced. "If so, I'll have to leave."

"You know," Dev said, grabbing their attention. "Do you think Rollerama is still open?"

"I have no idea," Jada said. "I haven't been out there for years.

"Well, there's one way to find out." Kinsley pulled out her phone from her back pocket. "The Google knows everything."

The three of them laughed, the way Dev hoped things would always be with the three of them.

She focused on the screen, but all he could focus on was that the woman he'd loved from afar for so many years now sat on his lap.

"Here it is. A link for the place." She tapped the screen.

"Yeah, yeah. They're still open. In fact, they're having a special fifty-year celebration on Friday night. They're calling it a Blast From the Past, and they want skaters to come dressed in sixties attire."

Jada's eyes lit up. "We should go. It would be really fun to end my time here at the rink."

"But what about the clothes?" Kinsley asked. "I don't have anything with me to wear."

"Mom's a pack rat and is bound to have something we can use." Jada rubbed her hands together. "Remember when we were kids and played dress up? She had all of those boxes of clothes from the sixties and seventies."

"But do you think she still has them?" Dev asked. "I know when she moved to the house in town, she got rid of a lot of stuff."

"She said she still had my skeleton necklace in a storage locker, so maybe she kept them there."

"She did seem pretty attached to the clothing," Kinsley said. "Remember how she warned us to be careful with it?"

Jada nodded.

Kinsley stood. "Let's get over to the cabin and ask her if she kept it. I know she can't skate, but we can invite her to come to the skating night. Colin and Brooklyn, too."

Dev hadn't been so thrilled when it was first mentioned, but now his excitement built over going back to the old roller rink. He suddenly wanted to share the night with everyone he knew. "Why don't we invite the whole team and their families? It would be a great time for Kinsley to meet everyone."

He imagined the night. The attire. *Oh, no.*

"What is *that* look for?" Jada asked.

Should he say? They'd talked about not hiding things from each other. This was minor, but... "I just thought about Barbie Maddox."

"Maddox?" Kinsley asked. "Any relation to your boss and his brothers?"

"Their mom. She still dresses like a hippie from the sixties. She's bound to have a lot of things she could share, if she's willing."

"She's a real throwback, all right." Jada rolled her eyes.

"Then let's invite her too," Kinsley said. "If she dresses like that, she must be fun."

"She is." Dev didn't know if introducing Kinsley was a good idea or not, but Barbie had a heart of gold under the wild escapades she shared. "She's always full of stories, and she'll talk your ear off if you let her."

"Then I want her to come with us even more, and we should probably make dinner arrangements too." Kinsley swiped down on her screen. "I wonder if they still do pizza, and if it's as good as I remember."

"You know what they say about you can't go home again," Dev said. "Their pizza might've been good when we were young, but now that we've experienced pizza elsewhere, it might not be so great anymore."

"Probably isn't what you'd expect," Jada said. "But it'll have the taste we remember, and even if it isn't great, it'll be another special memory."

Dev knuckled his sister's shoulder. "I never knew you were so sentimental."

She laughed. "It was hard to be girly around two brothers, so I hid that side of me. But I've released it later in life."

"They still do pizza." Kinsley's excited voice grabbed his attention. "We can get a headcount of how many people will be attending and then order the pizza in advance so it's ready when we arrive."

Dev nodded. He didn't know how a simple ticket stub turned into a Blast From the Past at their old roller rink. Something at first he thought might be kind of lame. But now? Now that it had expanded to include all the people he cared about, especially Kinsley, he was on board, and he was sure they were going to have a great evening. One for her memory box.

25

The smell of smoke still lingered in the brisk October air outside the roller rink, but the winds had blown it all out of the area. Kinsley could barely contain her excitement as she waited outside the door with Dev and Jada for the next arrival. Not only had she been able to review her memories with them, but this one had come to life.

Dev was wearing lime green pants and a matching knit shirt that had belonged to his dad. Kinsley wanted to wear a blue paisley jumpsuit with a riot of flowers covering nearly all of the fabric, but so did Jada. This was the same jumpsuit they'd argued over when they were kids, so they had played Rock, Paper, Scissors to decide. They'd used the same method last night and Jada won, so Sandy gave Kinsley an outfit of wide-legged jeans with flower patches sewn on the bells and a psychedelic blouse. A nice choice, but not the jumpsuit.

"I can't believe everyone agreed to come tonight." Jada rubbed her arms to stay warm.

"I'm excited to meet them." Kinsley didn't have to rub her arms. Anticipation kept her dancing in place as she waited for the remaining guests. Not one person had said no. A couple people even canceled plans they'd had for the evening to come to the Blast From the Past.

A large black SUV parked in the lot, and an older woman with a blond braid down her back emerged. She wore extra-wide bell-bottom jeans, an orange suede jacket with fringes, and a belt tied at her trim waist. Ryan and his wife Mia stepped out, too, so Kinsley assumed the older woman was Barbie Maddox.

Seeing all the sixties attire was equally as fun as bringing this memory to life. Mia wore hot pink stretch pants and a cropped jacket in a plaid pattern with a pink T-shirt underneath. Ryan had on a knit shirt with a collar in an aqua color and khaki pants that barely reached his shoes, revealing colorful, patterned socks.

Barbie hung a pair of roller skates tied together by the laces over her shoulder and started their way. The man accompanying her wore orange pants and a green paisley long-sleeve shirt buttoned up to the neck. Despite the fashion-forward sixties outfit, he looked pretty straight-laced, while she seemed to be a free spirit.

The older woman stopped by Dev, and a scent of honey and vanilla filled the air. "Thank you for inviting us." She turned to Kinsley and clasped her hands. "Barbie and Hank Maddox. We're delighted to meet you and welcome you to our extended family. We'll have to get together for lunch and catch up."

"I'd like that," Kinsley said, now that she knew she was going to be living in Shadow Lake.

Sandy offered to let Kinsley stay at her house in town rent-free, and with no housing to pay for, Kinsley could work part-time, and the travel wouldn't be that big of a deal. So she could definitely do a lunch with Barbie, who'd done so much to make this night special.

Kinsley squeezed Barbie's hands. "Thank you for

arranging the clothing for some of the guys. Your selections are wonderful."

"No big deal. I know the perfect retro shop in Portland, and all I needed was their sizes." Barbie studied the men. "Don't they look fab? But trust me, the best is yet to come."

She'd piqued Kinsley's interest for sure, and now she couldn't wait for the others to get there. "Pizza is served. I hope you enjoy the night."

"Are you kidding?" Ryan's eyes crinkled with humor as he circled an arm around his mother's shoulder. "This night was made for my mom."

"No truer words were ever said." Hank's lack of enthusiasm came through in his flat tone. "We'll probably be here till the place closes down."

"Now, Hank." Barbie pursed her lips lacquered in orange lipstick. "Let loose for once, and let's have a good time like we used to do before the kids and your formal accountant job."

He rubbed his neck. "I'll do my best. Just for you, my love."

"Aw." Barbie flung her arms around him. "See, this is the part of Hank nobody ever sees but me, and why we'll be together till death do us part."

Hank sputtered. "Don't want the pizza to get cold."

He removed her arms to take her hand and lead her toward the door.

Barbie looked over her shoulder. "It's good to see you, too, Jada. This guy is in a hurry to get to the pizza, and I never stand between him and food. Find us inside so I can hug your neck."

Ryan laughed. "They're a lot to get used to, but thanks for inviting them."

"And two of the sweetest people you could ever meet," Mia added. "I've known them for so many years, and not my best years. They've forgiven and forgotten all of my bad behavior in high school to include me in the family. I'll love them dearly even if our little Austin and any future children might end up wearing wide-legged jeans and tie-dye."

Ryan kissed the top of her head. "I'm glad I found a wife who appreciates them."

Mia ran a hand over her outfit. "How could you not appreciate someone who had pink stretch pants from the sixties in her closet?"

They all laughed, and Mia and Ryan stepped into the building. Not a minute passed before two more vehicles rolled into the lot.

She recognized Micha, his fiancée Ava, and Russ, but not the other two women or boy with them.

The groups merged and made their way across the parking lot, Ava and Micha hanging back. Ava wore the most interesting of outfits. She had on white go-go boots below a tiny black miniskirt, with an orange-and-black striped top boasting a heart cut-out in the middle of the chest. Micha wore brown corduroys with a green striped sweater and a corduroy newsboy hat.

The other woman wore yards of pleated fabric with a white princess neckline, like pregnant women wore in the sixties to hide their baby bumps. She had to be Sydney. Next to her, a teenager with hair dyed a wild shade of blue was wearing a modern outfit of skinny jeans and a T-shirt, and she dragged her feet as if she didn't want to be there. But the boy skipped along as if eager to get to skating. He, too, wore a basic pair of jeans but paired it with a dinosaur T-shirt.

But Russ. Russ was the real costume winner tonight. He was wearing red plaid pants with a snug mustard-colored T-shirt and zip-up ankle boots.

Russ introduced Kinsley to his son, Zach, and to Sydney, and finally to the teenager, Sydney's younger sister, Nikki.

Russ cleared his throat and folded his arms across his broad chest. "Before anyone says anything about my clothes, remember I have the power to arrest you."

The group laughed, and when it died down, Nikki stepped forward.

"No fair." She lifted her chin and aimed it at Russ. "I'll never have a chance like this again to make fun of you the way this extreme outfit deserves."

Russ knuckled the teenager's shoulder. "Sorry, kiddo. I know you're right, but cut me some slack. I only did this for your sister." He leaned closer to Nikki and cupped a hand by his mouth. "You know she's crazy hormonal, and you can't say no to her these days without putting your life on the line."

The teenager gave a solemn nod. "This baby can't come soon enough."

"Hey, now," Sydney said. "It's not like I'm not standing here. I heard everything you said."

Kinsley waited for Sydney to get mad, but she just rolled her eyes and laughed. "I know you're right, but let's not air our dirty laundry with everyone."

"Uh, Sydney." Zach looked up at her and scratched his cheek. "Are you having this pregnancy brain thing again? 'Cause we didn't bring any laundry."

The others burst out in laughter.

Zach looked from person to person, but then he shook his head. "Must be one of those things Dad says I'll understand when I'm grown up. Is Jessie here yet?"

"Already inside," Dev said, working to stem his laughter.

"Come on, kid." Sydney rested her hand on Zach's shoulder. "I'll take you to get skates, and we'll find Jessie."

Zach bolted for the door.

"Listen to Nikki," Russ called after him.

"Don't worry," Nikki said. "I'll keep an eye on him."

Russ fist bumped with Nikki, then looked at Kinsley. "He's pumped about tonight, in case you couldn't tell. Nikki not so much, but what can you expect from a seventeen-year-old who's forced to come to an oldies bash on a Friday night?"

"With her sister, no less." Sydney pointed at Russ. "I won't be skating, but I had to come along to see this guy do it. I just can't imagine him as a carefree teenager, wheeling around this rink."

"Me either," Jada said. "But Reid's telling everyone you were the best skater of the Maddox brothers."

Russ puffed up his chest. "He's right about that, but then, when you put the three of us together, I'm pretty much the best of anything."

Sydney punched his shoulder. "And modest, too."

Kinsley laughed. "When's the baby due?"

"In a week. Hopefully he won't come while Russ is wearing skates. I can just see him panic and fall. I don't need an injured father-to-be."

Russ rolled his eyes. "I didn't panic when Zach was born. I won't panic for Jacob."

"You've named him," Kinsley said.

"Out of self-defense." Sydney smiled fondly at her husband. "This one was calling him Bubba, and I was afraid it was going to stick." She laughed.

"Well, have a good time," Kinsley said. "I can't wait to see Russ on skates."

"Then you'll have a long wait." Russ narrowed his gaze. "I might've been the best of the best back in the day, but I'm smart enough to know people have cameras on their phones, and a picture of a roller skating sheriff in red plaid pants doesn't instill confidence, so it's not gonna happen."

"We'll see about that." Sydney tugged him toward the door. Russ looked over his shoulder.

"They're a hard act to follow," Ava said, "so we'll just say hello and talk to you inside."

Without a word, Micha took her hand, and they stepped toward the door.

"That Micha is really the strong, silent type, isn't he?" Kinsley asked.

"Makes him seem kind of mysterious," Jada said.

"Nah," Dev said. "He's just a regular guy who doesn't like to talk much, but when he speaks, we listen."

"Now, Sydney's the exact opposite," Kinsley said. "She's the perfect woman for Russ. She gives him as good as she gets from him."

"I couldn't agree more." Dev lifted his hand, and she slipped hers in his.

Jada shivered. "Is that everyone? I'm turning into a Popsicle and would love to get inside."

Dev snorted. "It's not that cold out here."

"Listen, buddy." Jada poked her brother in the chest. "You're talking to a transplanted California girl now. Anything below seventy is freezing."

"And here I thought you were a tough Navy sailor." Dev flashed her a wry smile, but there was humor in his eyes. "So let's see. That's Ryan and Russ and their parents, and Reid and his family got here early. So did Colin and Brooklyn. Mom's inside and Micha just arrived so that's everyone we're expecting. Time for us to go in."

"I thought you'd never suggest it." Jada bolted for the door, wobbling on her platform shoes and not looking back or waiting for them.

Dev followed, and since Kinsley was holding his hand, she had no choice but to go with him. They stepped into the dark space. The first things that hit her senses were the loud sixties music pounding over large speakers and a disco ball spinning over the circular roller rink as it radiated multi-colored sparkles throughout the space.

"This really is a blast from the past," Dev said, looking around. "Doesn't look like anything has changed except the carpet."

She looked at the black carpet with streaks of turquoise, purple, yellow, and orange running along a low, deep purple wall that surrounded the rink. The same orange tables and turquoise benches from her childhood butted up to the wall.

To her right were yellow benches with black iron legs, lockers in matching yellow, and the skate rental counter. To her left, the kitchen and snack bar took up the whole area. The air held a mixed scent of stale socks and pepperoni. Right now, the pepperoni was winning, and her stomach grumbled.

She was hungry for sure, but she would do whatever Dev wanted to do first because he was uncomfortable even thinking about getting on the skating rink. And not just from the pain in his hip, which she knew was still a problem, but from his lack of success in skating when he was younger.

She looked up at him. "Do you want to get some pizza before we skate?"

He stared out over the rink where some of their guests were skating. "I'd rather get some skating over with before everyone finishes eating and the rink is too crowded."

She hated to ask but... "Is all of this uncertainty because you weren't a very good skater?"

"Ouch." He mocked pulling a knife out of his chest. "You're not messing around, are you?"

"Hey, roller skating is serious business." She grinned. "And I should've said that in a better way. Not so blunt."

"No, you're right. I wasn't very good, and getting on that

rink is something I'll do just for you." He took her hand and led her toward the rental counter, where they each picked up a pair of worn, tan skates.

His gaze traveled to his brother, who was getting pizza. "I need to talk to Russ for a second. Be right back."

He took off and held a quick conversation, then he returned, and they sat on the bench to put on the skates. Dev eyed his suspiciously, but he didn't hesitate and slipped into them. She was proud of him for being willing to participate because she wasn't exaggerating when she said he wasn't a very good skater. She remembered him falling a lot and wanting to take his hands and help him around the rink. No matter how many times they'd come here, he'd never improved.

He stood, and his straight-legged pants got hung up at the top. He tried to pull them over, but the bottoms were too narrow to fit. "Not only will I embarrass myself when I fall, but with the color of my clothes, I'll stand out. I look like Kermit the Frog."

She resisted laughing. He was right. His knit shirt was nearly a perfect match to the lime green pants. She didn't have the same problem. Her bell-bottom jeans easily fell over the top of her skates.

She stood and took a moment to gain her balance. "It's been so long, I might take a few spills myself."

He held out his hand. "Let's do this together. One for all and all for one, I say. At least when it comes to me getting out on that rink. You don't know how many times when we came here, I wanted to ask you to help me learn to skate."

"And I wanted to help you." Kinsley shook her head. "All that time wasted, but we have to figure that God had a plan when Jada made us promise not to get together. Everything is in His timing."

"One thing's for sure," He took her other hand and faced her, "it will be all the sweeter for waiting."

"That's so true."

He lowered his head and kissed her. Not the kind of kiss filled with passion, but a sweet, soft kiss that wouldn't embarrass either one of them in public. He quickly leaned back.

She searched his face, and his love for her burned in his expression. She was tempted to throw her arms around him and kiss him soundly, but this wasn't the place or time.

"Now, about that skating," she said.

He groaned, but dropped one of her hands and started for the rink. He wobbled, even on the carpet. They reached the half-wall surrounding the rink. He let go of her hand and grabbed on to the wall as if his life depended on it.

"That's not going to help you learn to skate." She pried one of his hands free and gripped it tightly. "I'll skate backwards and hold both of your hands. Are you game for that?"

He nodded, but his expression was so pinched that guilt nearly had her stop from taking him onto the rink. But they say you have to face your fears, and there was really nothing to fear here. They could try a few laps around the rink and then get some pizza.

She took his other hand. "Let's go."

He looked her deep in the eyes. "I wasn't kidding when I told you I trust you. Completely. And that includes right now."

Love for this man nearly overwhelmed her, but she gave a sharp nod, swallowed hard to keep from tearing up, and started moving backward. He flowed along with her, wobbling a few times, but making good progress.

"See?" she said. "You're doing great. We're almost halfway around the rink and no falls."

"Can't talk," he said. "Must concentrate."

They made a complete revolution, and as they approached the middle on their second turn, he pulled back. "I need to go to the middle of the rink for a minute. Get out of the way of other skaters."

Only a handful of skaters had been on the rink with them, giving them a wide berth. She had no idea why he needed to go to the middle, but he'd faced his fears and done one and a half laps, so she wouldn't question it. She led him to the black circle painted on the wood floor.

They came to a stop, and he released one of her hands to lift his arm above his head and twirled his hand in a signal.

She glanced around to see what he was doing. "What's going on?"

"Just wait."

The music stopped, and soon the soft lyrics of "A Thousand Years" started playing. The song was popular when it was released, and she'd loved it when they played it here for slow skates for couples. Of course she hadn't been part of a couple, but she still enjoyed sitting and looking at Dev from afar, wishing she could've been skating to the song with him.

She met his gaze. "How did you know I love this song?"

"Jada told me," he said. "Plus, I wanted to skate with you back when they played it here."

"Me too." She smiled at him. "We don't have to wait anymore. We can skate to it now."

"In just a minute."

Dev waved his hand again, and Russ came racing over to him on skates. He slid to a stop as if trying to impress everyone.

"What in the world?" Kinsley said. "You said you weren't going to skate."

"Gotta help a bro out when he asks for it, even if it

means embarrassing yourself." He took Dev's hand and helped him kneel without faceplanting on his skates.

"Thanks for the assist, man," Dev said to his teammate. "I can handle it from here."

Russ raced off, and Dev reached into his pocket. His hand came out holding a black velvet box.

She gasped.

"Kinsley Pearce, I have loved you for what has felt like a thousand years, just like the song lyrics say. And I'm done waiting. I would like to spend the rest of my life with you. Till death do us part." He opened the box. "Will you marry me?"

She didn't have to think about that question. Not for one second. She held out her left hand. "Of course I will. It felt like more than a thousand years for me, and I would be most honored to be your wife."

He slipped the solitaire diamond set in shiny gold on her finger, and she lifted it up to admire it.

The Jumbotron on the side wall started flashing with the words, *She said yes!*

Their friends and family started cheering from the side-lines. She couldn't think of a better place for him to propose to her than with everyone who meant so much to her in the room. Sure, she would've liked her parents to be here, but she'd invited them, and they'd chosen not to come. Their loss.

Overwhelming happiness swept over her. She dropped to her knees and flung her arms around Dev's neck. He wobbled and tumbled from his knees to the floor, taking her with him.

"Are you okay?" He anxiously scanned her body.

"Fine. And you?"

"Fine, too." He grinned at her. "I knew I was going to end

up on the floor tonight, I just didn't think I'd take you down with me."

She stroked the side of his face. "From this day forward, we do things together, even if it's crashing on the roller rink in front of everyone."

Their friends and family started flocking onto the rink, but she didn't care. She took hold of his face and kissed him soundly. Cheers and whistles erupted from the background, but that didn't stop her from telling the man she was about to marry that she loved him completely through her kiss.

He pulled back. "Wow. Just wow."

She caressed his cheek. "Like you said, it will be all the sweeter for waiting and the waiting is over."

LOST LAKE LOCATORS SERIES
When people vanish without a trace and those who go looking for them must put their lives on the line to bring them home alive.

Book 1 – Lost Hours - March 3, 2025
Book 2 – Lost Truth - July 7, 2025
Book 3 – Lost Cause – November 3, 2025
Book 4 – Lost Lake - March 2, 2026
Book 5 – Lost Girls - July 6, 2026
Book 6 – Lost Light – November 2, 2026

For More Details Visit -
https://www.susansleeman.com/lost-lake-locators/

SHADOW LAKE SURVIVAL SERIES

When survival takes a dangerous turn and lives are on the line.

The men of Shadow Lake Survival impart survival skills and keep those in danger safe from harm. Even if it means risking their lives.

Book 1 – Shadow of Deceit
Book 2 – Shadow of Night
Book 3 – Shadow of Truth
Book 4 – Shadow of Hope – April 8, 2024
Book 5 – Shadow of Doubt – July 8, 2024
Book 6 – Shadow of Fear – November 4, 2024

For More Details Visit -
www.susansleeman.com/books/shadow-lake-survival

STEELE GUARDIAN SERIES
Intrigue. Suspense. Family.

A kidnapped baby. A jewelry heist. Amnesia. Abduction. Smuggled antiquities. And in every book, God's amazing power and love.

Book 1 – Tough as Steele
Book 2 – Nerves of Steele
Book 3 – Forged in Steele
Book 4 – Made of Steele
Book 5 – Solid as Steele
Book 6 – Edge of Steele

For More Details Visit -
www.susansleeman.com/books/steele-guardians

NIGHTHAWK SECURITY SERIES

Protecting others when unspeakable danger lurks.

A woman being stalked. A mother and child being hunted. And more. All in danger. Needing protection from the men of Nighthawk Security.

Book 1 – Night Fall
Book 2 – Night Vision
Book 3 – Night Hawk
Book 4 – Night Moves
Book 5 – Night Watch
Book 6 – Night Prey

For More Details Visit -
www.susansleeman.com/books/nighthawk-security/

THE TRUTH SEEKERS
People are rarely who they seem

A twin who didn't know she had a sister. A mother whose child isn't her own. A woman whose parents lied to her. All needing help from The Truth Seekers forensic team.

Book 1 - Dead Ringer
Book 2 - Dead Silence
Book 3 - Dead End
Book 4 - Dead Heat
Book 5 - Dead Center
Book 6 - Dead Even

For More Details Visit -
www.susansleeman.com/books/truth-seekers/

The COLD HARBOR SERIES

Meet Blackwell Tactical- former military and law enforcement heroes who will give everything to protect innocents... even their own lives.

Prequel - Cold Silence

Book 1 - Cold Terror

Book 2 - Cold Truth

Book 3 - Cold Fury

Book 4 - Cold Case

Book 5 - Cold Fear

Book 6 - Cold Pursuit

Book 7 - Cold Dawn

For More Details Visit -

www.susansleeman.com/books/cold-harbor/

ABOUT SUSAN

SUSAN SLEEMAN is a bestselling and award-winning author of more than 50 inspirational/Christian and clean read romantic suspense books. In addition to writing, Susan also hosts the website, TheSuspenseZone.com.

Susan currently lives in Oregon, but has had the pleasure of living in nine states. Her husband is a retired church music director and they have two beautiful daughters, two very special sons-in-law, and three amazing grandsons.

For more information visit:
www.susansleeman.com

9 781949 009514